THE HAUNTED CITY
COLLECTION

Published by Dark Titan Publishing. A division of Dark Titan Entertainment.

Also available in eBook format.

The Legendary Warslinger and Redemption of the Lost are available separately in hardcover, paperback, and eBook formats.

Battle For Astolat only available in eBook format exclusively.

Dark Titan Extended is a branch of Dark Titan Entertainment.

First Printing 2021

Paperback ISBN: 978-1-7363782-4-3
eBook ISBN: 978-1-7363782-5-0

darktitanentertainment.com

WORKS BY TY'RON W. C. ROBINSON II

BOOKS/SHORT STORIES

DARK TITAN UNIVERSE SAGA

MAIN SERIES

Dark Titan Knights
The Resistance Protocol
Tales of the Scattered
Tales of the Numinous
Day of Octagon
Crossbreed
Heaven's Called

Forthcoming

The Oranos Imperative
Underworld
Magicks and Mysticism
The Resistance vs. The Enforcement Order

SPIN-OFFS

In A Glass of Dawn: The Casebook of Travis Vail
Maveth: Bloodsport

Forthcoming

The Curse of The Mutant-Thing
Trail of Vengeance
War of The Thunder Gods

ONE-SHOTS

Maveth, The Death-Bringer
Mystery of The Mutant-Thing
Shade & Switchblade
Retribution of Cain
The Mythologists

COLLECTIONS

Dark Titan Omnibus: Volume 1
Dark Titan Omnibus: Volume 2
Dark Titan One-Shot Collection

THE HAUNTED CITY SAGA

The Legendary Warslinger: The Haunted City I
Battle of Astolat: A Haunted City Prequel (KOBO Exclusive)
Redemption of the Lost: The Haunted City II
Consequences of the Suffering: The Haunted City III (Forthcoming)

SYMBOLUM VENATORES

Symbolum Venatores: The Gabriel Kane Collection
Hod: A Symbolum Venatores Book
Symbolum Venatores: War of The Two Kingdoms
Symbolum Venatores: Mystery of the Magician (Forthcoming)
Symbolum Venatores: Twilight of the Gods (Forthcoming)

PRODIGIOUS WORLDS
Mark Porter of Argoron (Forthcoming)
Raiders of Vanok (Forthcoming)
Praxus of Lithonia (Forthcoming)

OTHER BOOKS
Lost in Shadows: A Novel
Lost in Shadows: Remastered
Accounts of The Dead Days
The Book of The Elect
The Extended Age Omnibus
Frightened!: The Beginning
EverWar Universe: Knights & Lords
The Horde (Forthcoming)
The Eleventh Hour: A Chevah Mythos Story (Forthcoming)

THE DARK TITAN AUDIO EXPERIENCE PODCAST
Season 1: Introductions
Season 2: In a Glass of Dawn
Season 2.5: Accounts of The Dead Days
Season 3: Battle For Astolat
Season 4: Hallow Sword: Cursed

THE HAUNTED CITY
COLLECTION

TY'RON W. C. ROBINSON II

CONTENTS

BATTLE FOR ASTOLAT

A CONFLICT OF THE HAUNTED CITY

I

The city of Astolat stood tall amongst its neighboring regions. Astolat is the city of Elaine and her father, Bernard. The city was ravaged by an army. An unseen army, who appeared from the air. The Astolat army combated the strange and ghostly force. The ghostly army overtook the soldiers, killing them within an instant. Bernard took Elaine and they both went into hiding. Having no other choice, but to escape the city as the ghostly army sacked their home and their leader appeared before them. Dressed in a dark violet cloak with his face rarely seen, although his eyes appeared to reveal themselves. The eyes looked dead, but there was another force living through them.

Residing at a secondary home, far into the wilderness, away from Astolat. Elaine writes a letter, detailing the event of Astolat's invasion and sacking by the unknown force. Bernard entered the room, seeing her writing the letter. He's intrigued.

"What are you up to, my daughter?"

"I'm sending word for help."

"Help?"

"Yes. I know of some men who can aid us in taking back Astolat."

"What kind of me are these that are capable of doing such a

matter?"

"A set-apart kind." Elaine said. "They know justice."

She finished writing the letter. Walking outside toward the pigeon cage. Placing the letter, the bird flew in the air with Elaine watching. Bernard approached Elaine from the side, also seeing the pigeon flying away.

"Hope you're right on this cause."

The pigeon flew several miles, until it reached the city of Old Jerusalem. The city was the home base to the Warslingers of the Heptad. The pigeon reached the Temple of the Heptad. Sitting outside the temple was Joshua of Ephraim. The pigeon flew to him, landing in front of him. Joshua sees the rolled letter. He grabbed the letter and the pigeon flies off, returning to Elaine. Joshua entered the temple, seeing the other Warslingers.

"Brothers, this was just delivered to us." Joshua said, handing them the letter.

Moses The Leader grabbed the letter. He opened it and read. The Warslingers stood around him, waiting for him to speak. Moses read the letter to himself and rolled it back up. Nodding, he turned to his brethren.

"It appears we have work to do. First, we make way for Old Camelot. Inform Knight Arthur Pendragon of these details. He must come along with us. For he is also our brother in this walk."

"Moses." Joshua said. "What did the letter inform?"

"It informed of some danger that has been committed. Now, it is our task to rid this malevolency from this place."

The Warslingers make ready to travel to Old Camelot, leaving Old Jerusalem on horseback. In the matter of time, Elaine awaits an answer from the Warslingers as des her father, who worries for Astolat's remains. Believing the ghostly army will turn their city into rubble and ashes.

Entering Old Camelot, Knight Arthur Pendragon was there at the gate to greet his brothers-in-arms. Standing by his sides were

Maiden Guinevere and Knight Lancelot. Moses stepped from his horse and walked towards the king of Old Camelot. Extending arms, the two hugged.

"Wasn't expecting to see you this soon." Arthur said.

"Wouldn't be here if it wasn't of importance."

"What's happened?"

"We can talk inside."

"Of course."

Walking inside the castle, they reached the Great Hall, where the Spherical Table sat. the Warslingers all sat at the table while Lancelot guarded the doors. Guinevere left their presence as they started to discuss their matters.

"Now, what's taken place?"

"We've received a letter of distress from the land of Astolat. It appears something has been ongoing in the land for a while and under our sight."

"Invasion from Old Egypt?"

"We won't know until we reach Astolat. We came because we'll need you with us."

Arthur nodded.

"I'll go along. Of course, being a Warslinger myself, it is my duty."

"Believe me, I can see you have plenty to deal with. Ruling a kingdom and being a Warslinger. Only few souls can achieve both titles and become a master at them."

"Speaking of such, how's Old Jerusalem?"

"Peaceful. *El* is there with us. Always."

Arthur nodded with a smile as they headed out of Old Camelot, traveling toward Astolat.

II

Making their entrance in Astolat, the common folk

watched in awe and fear as the Warslingers came in on their horses. They made their presence known. Moses turned to Joshua, Daniel, Henrich, and Charlton as they settled their horses near the station.

"The four of you will remain here." Moses commanded. "Keep this place guarded and the people safe."

"Where are you heading?" Charlton asked.

"Myself, Noah, and Arthur will be speaking to King Bernard at their second estate. They refuse to return here until the task is done."

Moses, Noah, and Arthur rode off, leaving the other four Warslingers to settle into the city. They looked toward one another before going separate ways throughout the city, finding a spot and keeping guard. Due to the lack of protection from the Astolatians.

"They carry no weapons." Charlton observed.

"They leave the fighting to the soldiers." Daniel replied. "They don't join in on the battles."

"But, we're supposed to protect them?"

"I know it irks you, Darrain. But, just this once, don't let it bother you."

Far from Astolat, the three Warslingers arrived at the second estate. Seeing two Astolat Knights keeping guard. They approached the door and it opened with Elaine standing in their presence. She ran out and hugged each of them with tears in her eyes. Relieved they received the letter and took the call. Bernard stepped foot outside, seeing the Warslingers. He nodded with great respect.

"It's an honor to have you here, Moses."

"We'll do anything to rid your city of the malevolency which circles it. May we come in and discuss this?"

"Of course."

They entered the home, sitting at the table near the kitchen. Elaine brought them some hot tea, due to the wintry weather occurring. Bernard sat with them while Elaine stood back.

"Tell us what's been happening."

"They appeared out of nowhere." Bernard said. "They

showed up and started ransacking the city. Killing some of the people."

"What did they look like?" Arthur asked. "Were they possible adversaries to Old Camelot?"

"No. They didn't seem to be from our world. Nor any of the Worlds."

"You're saying they possessed some mystical power?"

"They must have. To do the things they've done. Levitation, portal binding, teleportation. They had to have been very precise in their arts."

Moses nodded. He looked over to Noah, who also nodded.

'This sounds eerily familiar."

"Do tell." Arthur noted.

"Myself and Noah in the early days dealt with a small army which did such feats. This was when the Heptad was yet to be formed and the Warslingers were few in number. This was during the early stages of the Eastern World War. Those who didn't possess weapons of any kind chose magic as their arsenal. Some we trusted, turned on us, doing the same as Bernard spoke."

"So, will you help us in taking back our city?" Bernard asked.

"I must ask." Noah said. "We just came from your city and only the people are present. No signs of any threats."

"You mean they left?"

"Did they leave after the ambush?"

"Me and Elaine left before we could tell."

Moses stood up from the table. Noah and Arthur followed his movement. A Warslinger custom. Elaine walked to the table and Bernard stood up.

"We will aid you in finding the source of this mystic power. Once it is done, you may return to your city."

"Thank you." Elaine said.

"We're just doing what we must."

The Warslingers exited the home with Bernard behind them. As they sat atop their horses, Bernard approached them.

"You can stay here for the night. We have plenty of room."

"Much thanks is obliged." Moses said. "However, it is best we return to Astolat. To keep guard. We already have four Warslingers present. I will return to you once the job is done."

"I wish you the best." Elaine said.

"Take care of yourselves." Arthur said.

The Warslingers rode off.

Later in Astolat, the four Warslingers have received accommodations in the castle chambers. One to each of them. Henrich sat in his chamber, counting the hours. A knock came from the door, catching the young Warslinger's attention.

"Door's open." Henrich said.

The door opened and Charlton entered. He shut the door behind him and approached Henrich, sitting across from him at the table.

"What is it?" Henrich asked.

"You know me. You know how this all goes. What do you think's happening here?"

"Some magic wielders probably causing a ruckus. We've dealt with such before."

"Indeed." Charlton nodded. "But, have you ever considered the cost of us doing the work of another? I mean, this King Bernard has knights of his own. Why are we here doing their bidding?"

"I'm not getting what you're speaking."

Charlton sighed.

"We're supposed to protect the ones from evil. Those who can't protect themselves."

"Yes."

"This city already has protection in the form of these knights. We're not needed here. For all *El* knows, we could be needed in Old Egypt or Old Rome."

"I get your point."

"Do you? Because from what I've seen today, you've been blindly obeying every command given."

"I'm not in authority, Charlton." Henrich proclaimed. "Neither are you. We all have our place in the Heptad. In *El*."

"Yes, we do." Charlton nodded in agreement.

He stood up and walked toward the door. Henrich watched him.

"Just remember." Charlton said. "Think about why we're here and not elsewhere. They're something going on and we need to be careful."

"I'll take your word for it." Henrich replied.

Charlton left the room and Henrich laid down on the bed, falling asleep.

Later in the night, Moses, Noah, and Arthur returned to the city and entered their own chambers. All the Warslingers were asleep for the night.

<u>III</u>

The following morning, the Warslingers gathered the Astolatian Knights to the court of the castle. Moses sat before them, giving them instructions on how to prepare for the returning army and the attacks in which will be operated. As Moses continued giving the instructions, a fellow soldier bolted through the doors, his face showing minor scars compared to his damaged armor.

"They're back!" The soldier yelled before falling on the floor.

The soldiers all stood up and ran outside. Moses and the Warslingers held back as the remaining soldiers left the room. Joshua took a step forward, yet stopped by Moses.

"We need to help them."

"And we will." Moses said. "Give it a second."

"A second?"

"This army doesn't know of our presence. Therefore, we have the alterative surprise."

Moses turned to the other Warslingers and nodded.

"You know what to do. Go now."

The Warslingers went their ways outside the castle. Moses walked on and Joshua followed him. Eventually heading outside to see the battle in front of the city and on the castle grounds. They saw the army clearly. Dark armor, scaly and sharp. Their faces covered by their burnt helmets. Moses recognized such a garment.

"This isn't new." Moses said.

"What do you mean, my Leader?" Joshua asked.

"I know who's leading them. And he's close."

The Warslingers appeared from their corners around the castle, catching the army off guard. Henrich and Charlton used their arkshooters, firing rounds in the heads and chests of the mystical soldiers. The rounds from the shooters piercing through their armor like a nail through a leaf. Daniel, Noah, and Arthur swiping through the battlefield. Arthur wielding *Excalibur* while Daniel held the *Faithsword* and Noah carried the *Arkaxe*. The army was quickly being defeated with the Astolat knights cheering on the skills and fighting styles of the Heptad. Through their cheering, Moses and Joshua stepped out into the field as Henrich fired another round at the mystic soldier. The battleground set still with only the cheers of the Astolat knights. The Warslingers came over, standing next to their leader.

"This is not over." Moses uttered.

"Then, where is their leader?" Charlton asked.

"Right there." Henrich said, pointing toward the east, near the entry point of the castle grounds.

Standing before them was indeed a man, covered in scaly armor. Appeared burned, but with a violet and reddish hue. His face was with a helmet, giving him the appearance of having six eyes with a hood and cloak. The Astolat knights attempted to rush him, however, he raised his arms, lifting them off the ground and tossing them across the grounds of Astolat. He was strong in the mystic arts. Moses stepped forward.

"I know him."

"You do?" Arthur said. "How?"

"Because, he was once one of us."

"*Mosheh*." The figure spoke. "We have met once more."

"Yes, we have, Azotus Vorr."

IV

Moses and Azotus stood facing each other. Moses held his staff tightly as the sapphire began to glow.

"It has been some time." Azotus said.

"Not long enough." Moses replied. "You're the leader of this army."

"I am. They came to me after our last encounter."

"Those who sided with you became endowed with mystical abilities?"

"As did I."

Azotus held his arm out and from the thin air appeared a staff. Similar to Moses' own, yet darker, burnt, and glowing wih a violet and reddish hue of energy. The staff was endowed with the same mystical power as Azotus.

"Why don't we settle this like warriors." Azotus said.

"So be it."

The two staves collided, giving off a shockwave of energy. From there, the Warslingers aided the remaining Astolat knights against Azotus' army. The entire area of Astolat was now a battleground with Moses and Azotus standing in the middle, staves colliding and blasting energy. Henrich and Charlton stayed together, firing rounds toward the soldiers.

"What about Moses?" Charlton asked.

"He can take care of himself." Henrich replied. "We need to deal with these soldiers."

The Warslingers take the fight to the soldiers, wiping them out with some of the Astolat knights finishing them off. Moses and Azotus continued their bout, with Moses swiping the staff against Azotus' chest, knocking him across the field. Azotus arose and slammed the ground with his staff, causing a minor tremor. Stumbling Moses.

"Never did like the ground quake." Azotus said.

Azotus rushed toward Moses with staff in hand. In came closer, yet, Moses turned to him with the sapphire staff facing him. Once Azotus was in touching distance, the staff emitted a bright flash of light. The light pushed Azotus from Moses and in doing so, the soldiers of Vorr vanished due to the light.

"What kind of power is this?" Azotus questioned.

"The power you walked away from." Moses replied. "Now, go and never return."

Azotus took steps forward, trying to breach the light's power. But he could not, for the light was far stronger than the mystic power he possessed. The light did come from the staff, but its source was not in the staff nor was it the staff itself. Azotus knew this and vanished before their eyes. The Warslingers looked around and the knights appeared with them. The battle was over. Astolat had won.

Some days later, Bernard and Elaine returned to Astolat and started the reconstruction of the city. Bernard had thanked Moses and the Warslingers for their aid and effort. However, Moses did inform Bernard Azotus would not be returning to his city anymore, but he will return one day to exact payment on the lost battle. Bernard understood the Warslinger's words and chose to assist the Heptad against Vorr once the time arises. Elaine hugged Moses and thanked the Warslingers for their help. They had left the city, returning to Old Jerusalem.

On the path back, Arthur turned to Moses, thinking of Vorr and the battle. He knew the answer to his question and Moses knew it as well.

"Was he who I think he was?" Arthur said.

"He was." Moses replied. "A man once one of us. A Warslinger gone to the malevolency."

CHAPTER ONE

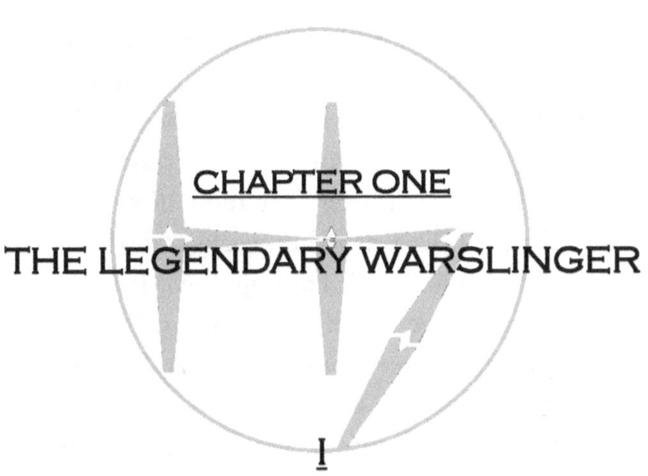

THE LEGENDARY WARSLINGER

I

"There I came and there I saw. The place where the ghouls dwelled until their own final breaths. A city that's rich with minerals and treasures of times past. Many have tried to discover the dark place, but those have all failed. The closest ones to come have only made it to the City's gates and have yet and never went through them. I figured that one day I will take up that boast and find The Haunted City myself."

Randolph Henrich—member of a group of holy warriors who combat the dark forces of the Worlds, took a stroll through the deserts of the Western World. The deserts were filled with dark sand, rarely any cactuses standing upright, most were laid down in the dirt, dehydrated by the new sun's rays. Randolph walked through the desert, kicking the dirt with the footsteps of his brown leather boots. He gazed up at the sun, placing his hand in the air to avoid the sun's rays from contacting with his eyes.

"Whatever designed you sure must be a mouthful of pain."

Henrich continued to walk, seeing what he believed to be a small town up ahead. He nodded, continuing to walk and barely able to keep standing since he hasn't taken a rest stop in hours.

"I can keep going. There's a town up ahead. I can keep going. I can keep going."

Henrich continued to walk through the heat of the middle of the day. While he kept walking, he heard a stumble from behind. Slowly turning around to see what caused the stumble. Henrich looked and seen a strander staring at him, dressed in raggedy clothing with a dirty gray duster coat and a dirty gray hat. His face looked like it hasn't been washed in weeks, mostly covered up by his facial hair and his long hair coming down from his hat. Carrying a bag that appeared to be full of many things. From a small opening, Henrich could see a bottle of water. The bag caught Henrich's eyes immediately.

"Looks like I've found myself another strander, huh?" The strander said. "Tell me what you're doing out here in the deserts of this Western World here?"

"None of your concern. Carry on about your business, strander."

"Whoa, whoa, whoa. First off, my business was to head to the town up ahead and deliver these goods here. But, now my business concerns you, strander."

"Listen, I've been through much. I suggest you go about your business."

"I don't think so, strander."

Henrich gazed toward the bag. Intrigued to know what may be sitting within it. Possible survival gear? Food? Water? Medicine? Henrich wanted to know.

"Tell me what's in the bag you're meant to deliver?"

"I'm not telling you a damn thing as to what is laying inside this bag right here. If you really want to know, you'll drag your ass onto the town and wait till I deliver it. Then, you'll see what's in this bag."

"That's not the way I see this going."

"You look like you seem to be some kind of "slinger." Hell, I doubt your one of those ancient slingers still kicking after most of them died out. Couldn't bare the heat of the sun nor the battle against the evil."

"What I am is nothing compared to what I can do to you. I

suggest you move along about your business, but if you don't go about your business keep to yourself, you'll end up in some possible trouble."

"Don't tell me what to do, boy!"

The strander put down his bag and approached Henrich with his flintlock pistol up. He placed the pistol into Henrich's chest. Laughing and smirking in Henrich's face. His breath had the stench of a corpse in the heat. His teeth were dirtier than the sands of the desert.

"Seems to me that I'm the one in charge here because I have you locked on. Dead enter in your chest, boy."

"You believe that? You believe your own foolish words of folly?"

"Folly? No. No. You're the one who's folly. Walking around this empty field of dirt with no supplies on you. Hell, I don't even see a shooter on your waist."

"I don't place a shooter on my waist."

"Humor me for this moment before I put you in the dirt, where do you keep your shooters?"

"In plain sight."

Henrich fired the revolver through his coat, the shot penetrates the chest of the strander. The strander took steps back, holding his chest as the blood began to pour out. The strander raised his pistol up to get at least one shot on Henrich. Henrich kicked the pistol out of the strander's hand and punched him in his face. The strander fell to the ground as Henrich placed his boot against his throat.

"You're bleeding, and you won't make it to town in this condition. So, this is where you'll crossover into the After-World and greet all the other bastards that have tried such a move upon me."

"Be that as it may. I sure as hell hope to see your ass there very, very soon. That way, I can beat your ass for eternity."

"Take your time and count your numbers, strander. I'll come when He says come."

Henrich looked over, seeing the strander's gear. He walked over and grabbed the bag. Searching and digging through it, finding canned food, bottled water, bullet rounds, a shotgun, another flintlock pistol, and several knifes. Henrich smirked.

"A motherlode of savers. You came prepared didn't you, strander."

"Better to be prepared than not to be prepared. Like your sorry ass. I was sent to deliver those goods to the rightful owner. From the description I read, you're not the owner."

"I'll take your bag to the town and meet with the owner myself."

"Go to Sheol, boy."

Henrich pulled out his revolver, aiming it right into the strander's forehead. The strander looked at the pistol, intrigued at its design.

"I recognize that shooter."

"You do huh?"

"Those were seen in painting with the ancient Warslingers of the past. Only they possessed such weapons. Weapons of great power."

"You know what's funny about our whole confrontation, strander?"

"What? You're one of those damn Warslinger guys?" The strander said with a laugh following. "You could never be one of them because they were all weak and now because of their weakness, they're dead."

Henrich smiled. "Yeah. You claim they're all dead. But, you've missed the point of my question. What's funny about this whole matter is you're looking at one."

Henrich fired the shot, killing the strander. Henrich grabbed the bag, ate a can of corn, he drank two flagons of water, reloaded his pistol, placed the other pistol into his left holster inside his coat, pulled out the blastshooter, loaded it up, placing it on a sling on his back. Henrich continued his walk toward the small town. He sees the town up ahead and tips his hat, walking forward.

II

Henrich walked in a mile of an inched closer to the small town. He could see the small structures that stood before him in the town and could also spot a saloon in the middle of the town, even people walking around the buildings. Henrich kept walking in the last mile before entering the town mark. The town was called Hevoc, around the town appeared to be only a small group of people who lived there. Henrich entered the town, passing its entry line as the residents turned and stared at him. The residents themselves, dressed in duster coats and hats while the women wore dresses and headscarf, stared at Henrich walking in the town toward the saloon.

"Who is this man?" a resident wondered curiously.

"Looks like one of those slingers to me."

"He can't be one of them. They're all dead and gone from this world."

"Anything is possible. He very well could be one in disguise."

Henrich approached the saloon and entered therein. The inside of the saloon was packed with men drinking and playing cards with each other. Some stood against the saloon walls and lean against them. Others sat at the saloon bar drinking. The sound of the saloon door opening gathered their attention as they turned and seen Henrich enter the place, carrying the bag with him.

"What's in the bag, strander?" said a man at the table.

"You're about to find that out." Henrich said.

Henrich walked and stood in the middle of the saloon where everyone could see him. He placed the bag down on the floor in front of him as he gazed around the saloon. Seeing the men slowly, but surely preparing themselves, reaching to their holsters.

"No need to reach for your shooters. Not just yet." said Henrich. "I am here to see the owner of this bag here. I believe that some form of a discussion could be made to what lies inside of it. Very valuable items and a good agreement between me and the owner could make this very better for all of you here."

A man walked from down the stairs of the saloon. Henrich turned and looked at him, seeing his black suit with a top hat. His moustache stood out from beside his attire. The man looked at Henrich and saw the bag on the floor in front of his feet. The man smirked.

"You're not the man that was sent to bring me that bag."

"No. I'm not. I dealt with him out in the desert fields. He wanted to do business and we did. Now, I come here to do the business that he failed to do."

The man put his hands up, shaking his head.

"You don't have to repeat what you've already said to the entire saloon here. I overheard everything from up the stairs."

"So, you know what I recommend about what's inside this bag, here?"

"I certainly do. May I have a look see?"

"Sure."

Henrich kneeled and zipped open the bag, revealing the food, water, and gear that laid inside of it. Some of the men also looked and the items peaked their interest as well.

"Sure, a lot of firepower in that there bag." said a man at the bar.

"Good you can see it."

"Now, what is the deal you're proposing to me about these items and the bag?"

"Half and half. Half the food and water stay with me. Along with half of the weapons."

"I am aware that I was supposed to gain possession of everything inside that bag for the people of Hevoc."

"Things change in this world. Either take the deal or reject it. Your decision."

The man looked out at the men and women inside the saloon. Their faces show slight concern for themselves and the man. The man turned back to Henrich and sighed.

"Well, what's your answer?"

"My answer sadly is no. I will not let you take half of everything that is inside this bag right here. The people of this town need it more than you do. See, allow me to say this to you and maybe you'll understand clearly what I am telling you. A town of people is more important to save than one man trying to save himself."

"You know how to put your words in order."

"You can say that. I mean, who else controls everything that goes on here in Hevoc. Me of course."

Henrich nodded and looked around the saloon again. Feeling the tension in the air. The man raised up his hands, looking around the saloon at the men and women inside.

"Rally up my people. We have a choice to make this day and this hour."

"You're sure you want to do this?" said Henrich.

"I have no choice, strander. It's for the people of Hevoc."

The man rallied up the men and women inside the saloon as they all begin to surround Henrich, their pistols out in the open, all pointing at Henrich. Henrich stood still, with only his eyes following the people and his arms crossed with the bag still on the floor at his feet. The man stood in front of Henrich, smiling.

"You really think we're going to let you leave after the words you've brought in here?"

"Doesn't appear that you have a choice as to who leaves or stays."

The man nodded.

"Strander. I'm going to tell you this right now and I hope to the Father Above this sinks into your cranium. You're going to die here by the people of Hevoc and after they kill you, we're going to spread out the goods in this here bag right here across the town. That way everyone will have something to continue going forward in this life."

Henrich grinned.

"For the good of the people huh. That's why you're doing all of this, right?"

"That's the purpose of this here scene."

Henrich nodded slightly. No emotion showing on his face nor in his eyes.

"Might as well get this thing started."

"You know what? You're right for a change."

The man waved his hand in the air, counting down for the people to shoot Henrich from all corners of the saloon. As the man was counting, Henrich's hands were inside his coat, locked tight onto his shooter and the flintlock. His eyes were locked on the man, still counting down.

"Seven, six five four three…" The man counted. "Two, one…"

Henrich pulled out the pistol and flintlock and fired the shot through the man's head. He fell to the ground as Henrich turned to the people and started shooting at them. Henrich's ability to shoot was very impressive that his speed was unmatched by anyone inside the saloon. The people outside of the saloon ran into their homes and nearby buildings to avoid being shot at. Henrich looked and spotted two men coming at him with machetes. Henrich nodded as he reached to his back and pulled out the shotgun, shooting the two men through their stomachs. Henrich turned and continued the shooting with his shotguns toward the ones remaining inside the saloon. Henrich stood as the last person walked in front of him, with a revolver in hand, aimed for Henrich's head.

"You're not leaving this place for all the shit that you've done!"

'I am leaving." said Henrich. "With the bag."

Henrich fired the blastshooter against the person. He grabbed the bag and walked out of the saloon, leaving it full of dead, shot up bodies.

III

Walking out of the saloon, Henrich found himself leaving, but caught the sound of a woman's screeching scream not far from the saloon. Coming close by, Henrich turned the corner, walking behind the saloon to find the woman yelling for help as she is being harassed by a group of sexual predators.

"Stop what you're doing." said Henrich.

The predators turned to Henrich, dirty as the dirt could possibly get. Their clothing worn out, tearing at the edges. Their faces are dirty as the sand, appear dehydrated as well. There were four of them and they all wanted the woman for themselves. Now, seeing Henrich gives them other opportunities.

"Look what we have here, my boys! Some strander has come into our territory."

"You know how we deal with stranders, boy? We do with them as we please."

Henrich stood still, facing the predators as they began to circle him. Measuring him from the top of his hat to the bottom of his boot. Laughing and scoffing at Henrich while showing signs of a deeper interest. One predator started licking his lips.

"You know what we should do about this strander, here?"

"What should we do?"

"After we finish with the virgin over there, we can have ourselves a strander. What do you guys think?"

"I've been wanting to get a release for weeks."

"Now, you have an opportunity my friend. Two for the taking."

"I suggest you back away from me and leave the woman alone." said Henrich.

"Or what's going to happen?"

"You heard the commotion taking place inside the saloon. What do you think will happen once that similar circumstance comes to your outside doors?"

"I think he's threatening us."

"He is. Trying to frighten us away from him and the virgin. No. It will take more than threats and trembles to move us away from what we're about to do to you and this virgin."

Henrich looked over at the woman, who's crying with tears streaming down her face. The lead predator began to unbuckle his belt, staring at Henrich. The other predators started to do the same.

"I figure we'll take you first, strander. Then, when we're finished up with you, we can enjoy this virgin over here. Corrupt her soul as they put it."

"Go ahead." Henrich said. "Make a move and you'll wish you didn't have."

"Strander still spitting out threats at us fellows. Told you it will take a lot more to frighten us to move."

Henrich blew the predator's head off with the shotgun and fired rounds at the ones remaining through the chest and heads. Their bodies fell to the ground with the echoes of the firing weapons flowing across the air. Henrich sighed as he picked up his bag from the ground and walked over toward the virgin woman. The woman showed a sign of relief as Henrich approached her and helped her up from the ground.

"Are you well?" Henrich asked.

"I will live."

"Good. That's good."

"Come on. You're coming with me."

"Why? There's nothing out there in the World for me. Nothing."

"You've never had the chance to look and see, have you?"

"I've never left this town. I was born here."

Henrich nodded.

"I can see that through your eyes. Come along with me to the outskirts and maybe you'll find a place out there that will suit you better than this lousy town."

Hesitant and fearful about her own safety, the woman followed Henrich to the exit of Hevoc and back into the desert once more, only this time, Henrich considered the woman as they entered the desert. He gave her a bottle of water from his bag. She drank the entire bottle as if she hasn't had anything to drink in days.

IV

"You never told me your name." Henrich said. "I would like to know your name."

"My name is Cara."

"Just Cara. No middle or last name to add?"

"I've only been called Cara. Nothing else besides Cara and the Virgin Woman."

"I take it, they call you virgin because you've never become one with a man. Am I right?"

"You are correct. There isn't a man around here that deems themselves to be a suitable companion to me."

"Maybe you'll find that man when you see the other places this Western World has to offer. Hell, maybe you'll travel across the Ethiopic into the Eastern World and find a suitable man of your needs there."

"You think so? You think I can find a man like that in this World?"

"I am positive that you will. Only give it some time of course."

"What of you, sir?"

"What about me?"

"You never told me your name either. I just thought that we would exchange names."

"Randolph Henrich."

Cara looked at Henrich and noticed the two pistols in his coat holster. She recognized the other one with its unique design.

"That shooter you have in your coat. I noticed the design of it. That's not one of the shooters that belonged to the Warslingers is it?"

"You know of them?"

"Everyone I believe knows of them. They protected people from the darkness of this world. A darkness that most humans have no idea even exists. I was only a little girl when I met a demon, two of the Warslingers came in and saved me from the demon. Killed it with holy bullets as they called them."

"What would you believe if I told you that not all of the Warslingers are dead. That, the few remaining are scattered across the world. Continuing their duties on their new soil grounds. Looking for a way to reunite when it's time."

"I would say I hope that they can unite and save all of us from the evil that exists out here. Be it demons, ghouls, or humans themselves. We need to be protected and I hope that the Warslingers return and prove the doubters and mockers wrong."

"They will, Cara. One day, they will."

Henrich and Cara continue to walk through the desert. Fighting against the heat of the sun's rays as clouds began to come over the desert and slowly cooling off the area. Giving Henrich and Cara some sort of comfort.

"Where did those clouds come from?" said Cara. "They just appeared out of nowhere."

"Maybe we're being watched." Henrich said with a smile.

"Perhaps we are."

Henrich continued his smile before looking toward into the desert, seeing nothing but dirt and dead cactuses. The clouds above them had cooled them off immensely. The sweat that was coming from both of their foreheads had suddenly disappeared and evaporated into the air.

"So, where would you go if you had your choice?" Henrich said.

"I do not know. There's so many places that I have yet to visit, but I'm not sure which of them would be best suited for someone like me. Where would you go, if you had the choice?"

"The Haunted City. That's where I would go."

"Why there? You know of its legends and its feats. So, why would you make the attempt to travel there? What would be there for you to receive?"

"That city has power within it that's unheard of in our World. The evidence and receiving that someone would possess while inside of the City would give them all the answers that they sought after and could even give them knowledge unknown to others in this World.”

“But, what of the one that guards the gate to the City?”

“What guardian?” Henrich said quickly. “I’ve never heard of someone guarding the entrance into the City.”

“There is a guardian at the gate to The Haunted City. People call him many names. Such as the Dark King, the Troublesome One, Lord of the Shadows. He’s truly known throughout the Worlds as the Tubal King.”

“The meaning of his name would be considered as ‘King of the Earth’. in the Old Speech.”

“They say he knows about everyone in the World. He knows about me and my past, my present, and my future. He also knows of you, Randolph. Your past, your present, and your future.”

“How can he really know?”

“Because he’s King of the Worlds. He knows all that takes place on this soil.”

“I don’t consider him as a threat to me. As anyone ever seen this Tubal King?”

“No one apparently. They say he uses his invisible power to watch over the Worlds, seeing what everyone is doing.”

“Be that as it may be, I will see to it when I come across The Haunted City that I may see this Tubal King. Hell, he can open the gate for me.”

Cara smiled with a hint of fear for Henrich’s well-being. Seeing him not tremble at the name of the Tubal King and what he can do.

“I’m sensing you’re not afraid of him.”

“Afraid?! I haven’t even met the man. I’m just now learning about him after what you’ve told me.”

“You should be afraid of him, Randolph. Be cautious for yourself and those that may travel amongst you. For they might not be aware of the Tubal King’s power as you’re now aware.”

They walked until they saw a standing sign, pointing in two different directions. They read the signs, rubbing the dirt from them to get a better look at what the arrows are pointing towards the directions. The left sign points toward 'the dark woods' while the right sign points to a place called Mega City, a large metropolitan city covered with darkness and clouds. A gothic looking place. Cara moved to the right, standing on Henrich's right side.

"You're going that way?" Henrich pointed. "To Mega City?"

"I figure I could get a better start there. I've heard about what happens to those that walk through the dark woods before and I am not about to make the same mistakes they've made by walking right up in there. So many monsters dwell within that forest I hear. Terrifying monsters."

"I understand your concern, Cara." Henrich said slightly. "Make your next step to Mega City. I will enter the dark woods and see what I can come up with on the other side."

"You've been through the forest before?"

"Darling, I've been through many places and I have seen so much in this life. Things that would make a bold man tremble in his boots."

Henrich handed Cara three flagons of water and three cans of food. He also gave her a knife and a small shooter with a few bullets. She thanked him for the supplies. Henrich began walking past the sign, going left as he watched Cara wave to him as she walked to the right.

"Take care of yourself, you hear?" Henrich said.

"I will." said Cara. "Remember what I told you about the Tubal King. He's watching us all."

"I shall keep that in mind."

Henrich nodded to Cara as they both walked their separate ways through the desert as the clouds above them began to spread out between the two. One cloud following Henrich and the other following Cara.

<u>V</u>

Henrich continued to make his walk through the desert. After several miles of traveling on foot with almost little to no supplies left inside the bag except for a couple of shooters, bullets, and knives. He continued walking and could see the dark woods in the horizon. Only several more miles were needed before he could enter the forest.

Henrich walked and walked, seemly getting tired and restless from the walking. The cloud continued to stay over him, keeping him cool from the sun and the intense heat of the desert. He drank from one of his flagons of water. He decided to take a slight break as he sat down next to a boulder and a dead cactus. He ate from another can of food thereof and finish the bottle of water.

"What will it take. What shall it take."

An hour had passed. Henrich had moved on from his resting place and continued walking forward to the forest that he could still see in the horizon in front of him. He kept walking, his pistols still loaded as he hasn't released a single shot since saving Cara from the predators in Hevoc. Cara was on Henrich's mind, thinking as to where she could be right now.

"Did she make it to Mega City safety? Has she made it to Mega City?" Henrich did not know and was well understood that whatever happened with Cara was on her hands and her decisions. Henrich walked, noticing his clothes being covered with the dirt of the desert. The dirt began to present itself onto his face. His facial hair covered with the desert dirt.

Walking, he realized someone was watching him from a distance in the desert. He could feel the presence there, behind him and on the side of him. Henrich took several looks from behind and to his sides. Seeing nothing but the clear desert around him, he continued to walk forward.

While he walked, he noticed there were skeletal remains lying around in the dirt. He looked at the bones and could tell they were not from ancient ones of the past times. He knew they were recent and very recent. Henrich slowly took his steps forward, inching closer to his pistols with his right hand almost to the handle of the pistol. He walked and instantly as if a flash of light had appeared, Henrich was surrounded by six individuals covered in black shrouds and cloaks. Their faces unseen by the hoods they wore. They didn't appear dirty from the desert, which triggered Henrich's interest in them. Where did they come from, Henrich asked himself. They were not dirty by any means. They appeared clean as if they were washed completely.

"What is this?" Henrich asked. "Who are the six of you meant to be? Druids? Don't look like a pair of hags."

"We are not druids, good sir." One answered slowly. "We are simply a means to advance your journey toward the dark woods."

"How did you know for certain that I was heading in that direction?"

"Because you're on the trail. Everyone that's been this way has always taken this trail. Nothing new over here."

Henrich chuckled. The hooded figure stood silent. Not even making a move.

"Am I supposed to find this funny?"

"This is not intended to be an act of humor, my good sir. We only want to advance your journey is all."

"If that is your main concern, move the hell out of my way would you."

"I'm afraid we cannot do that. See, we are here to advance your journey. Only, not in the way you're expecting it to go."

The hooded figure raised his right arm up toward Henrich, who's right hand is still on the pistol. The figure's skin was revealed as his arm was being raised with the sleeve pulling back with the cloak. Henrich looked at the skin and noticed it was pale. Almost as white as the clouds, bur with a hint of blue to them. The hooded figure opened his hand, showing Henrich a letter. Henrich paused for a moment, gazing at the small scroll in the hooded figure's hand.

"This letter is for you." The hooded figure said. "Once you read it, you'll understand everything that is happening here."

"Is that right."

Henrich grabbed the scroll and opened it. He read what was written upon the scroll and spotted his name being mentioned. The scroll had called him, *'Randolph Henrich of the Warslingers, the Heptad'.* He stood quiet, moving his eyes, following the hooded figures around him. He noticed on the letter as well that it called for his assassination and murder by the hands of anyone, which the one who succeeded in doing so would have to meet with someone called the Mercenary Man and would be granted a great reward.

"What is the meaning of this?"

"The meaning of the scroll is simple to understand, Randolph Henrich of the Warslingers. The Legendary Heptad. We six have come here to murder the great and legendary Warslinger."

"Where's your shooter if you've come to murder me out here in the heat of the desert?"

"We don't need a shooter nor any sort of armory to kill you."

"Then, I'm not aware as to how you're going to complete the task given to you. Hell, this looks like your last day in this World you hear."

"I hear you clearly, Warslinger. So, do my other brothers around you. We're not exactly your kind. We're something much more than human beings."

The hooded figure reached toward his hood. He slowly pulled it back, showing his face to Henrich. The other hooded ones also removed their hoods from their heads. Henrich took looks at them, spotting their eyes, they appeared dead, yet alive. Henrich also noticed their jaws, as if they had extra teeth inside of their mouths. The lead hooded figure stood in front of Henrich and smiled, showing his sharp fangs. Rotten fangs at best. Henrich knew what they were, pulling out his pistol.

"We're different." The lead hooded figure said.

"Damn vrylolakas!" Henrich said as he took fire at them.

The vampires moved around Henrich, he continued to take shots at them. One vampire ran up toward him, Henrich kicked the vampire in the face and stomp his face into the dirt. The vampires tried to latch onto Henrich, but his movements were too quickly for them to keep up, even at vampire speed. Henrich later used the shotgun, blowing the heads off the vampires. The lead vampire stood and watched his fellow brethren fight Henrich, studying his move set. Henrich grabbed one vampire and squeezed his neck, afterwards shooting him in the head with his pistol.

Only two vampires remained for Henrich to kill. The leader and his brother. The brother vampire went first at Henrich, but was unable to grab Henrich by his shoulders. Henrich kicked the brother and pulled the shotgun to his face. Henrich smiled as he blew the head completely off the brother vampire, only scraps of brain tissue remained. Henrich stood and stared at the lead vampire, who was smiling, showing off his fangs.

"I am amazed how you guys managed to come out in broad daylight." Henrich said. "I've always known the ones of many that manage to come out in the shadows of the night. What makes you guys different from the rest?"

"We submit to the Tubal King. He gave us the power to walk amongst the sunlight of the day and the moonlight of the night. He knows what we need as of what he needs. We are different as I have said to you."

"Different you are, but soon you'll all be the same as the ones I've come across before in my time. Dead and gone."

"Not until you manage to kill me as you've killed my brethren. Then your words may show some valor to them."

"What in the hell would you know about valor, creature?"

Henrich pulled out his pistol, aimed it at the vampire, reloading the gun directly in front of the vampire. The vampire stood out in the open.

"Go ahead and take the shot, Warslinger. Take it now before I bite your neck right in."

"The only thing you'll be biting this day, vrylolakas, is the bullet coming from this shooter right here and the dirt beneath our feet."

"Let's see if you're telling the absolute truth, Warslinger. Will I eat the bullet from your ancient shooter and taste the dirt beneath our feet or will I have the pleasure of tasting the flesh of the legendary Henrich and drinking the blood of a Warslinger?"

"Test me and see if which scenario will deem itself to be so in truth."

"I will do what you have said, Warslinger."

The vampire snarled and ran. Jumping up in the air, lunging itself at Henrich, who pulled the trigger back and the bullet went flying in the air. The bullet flew through the dirt filled air, inching closer to the lunging vampire and went completely straight through the vampire's mouth and exited through the back of his head. The vampire fell to the ground quickly while Henrich stood and stared at the vampire's body lying on top of the dirt.

"As I said. The bullet you'll eat as the dirt you shall."

Henrich placed the pistol back into its coat holster and looked at the scroll again. Staring at the name of the Mercenary Man. He looked forward and could see the dark woods up ahead.

"I should tend to find this Mercenary Man. See what he wants of me being blotted out from existence. Another one of many that has tried to test me in the heat of battle."

While Henrich walked away from the dead bodies of the vampires, a brown horse approached Henrich from the direction in front of him. The horse was large, greater in size than Henrich was familiar to when it comes to horses.

"Where did you come from?"

Henrich approached the horse and tamed it. Placing his bag to the side of the horse's saddle. Henrich sat atop the horse and went forward to the dark woods.

<u>VI</u>

Henrich rode atop the large brown horse that came to him toward the dark woods in the desert. While he rode through, in the near sight of his distance, Henrich spotted an abandoned gas station. He found no one around the station and decided to stop for a moment. The station had the appearance of once being active to left deserted. Age had covered even the crevice of the station. Henrich jumped off the horse and entered the station building. Inside laid nothing but dirt and dust. Spiders residing in the cracks and corners of the station. The station was hot from the sun's rays.

"Looks like we'll be staying here for the night." Henrich said to the horse.

He tied the horse to the station, giving the horse a bowl that he found from inside the station and poured water into it. The horse started to drink the water. Henrich ate another can of food, giving the horse some of the food as well. The horse stayed at the post while Henrich entered the inside of the station. He took a curtain from the windows and a small box he laid them on the ground as the sun began to set and the moon had shown herself. The air turned from a blazing heat to a chilly wind within seconds. Henrich watched the sun set and the moon rise in the sky. Henrich understood the differences between the sun and the moon. The two opposite spheres of light that sit still in the sky above him. Henrich looked around in the sky, seeing few sets of clouds.

"I doubt it will snow here. Not in this desert."

Henrich slept inside the station while the horse was tied to the post near the station's doorway entrance. Both Henrich and the horse was chilly from the cold wind through the light of the moon. A full moon. Henrich went ahead and gathered more curtains from the windows and wall to warm himself and the horse. The curtains had no effect in warming them. Neither did his coat.

"That was worth a shot at least."

Henrich later felt a small sense of heat coming from outside the station. He gazed over to the window and looked outside, seeing a cloud hovering above the station, a cloud of fire. Henrich was amazed. He looked over to the horse and it immediately went to sleep as the cloud of fire made itself known. Henrich nodded and the warmth from the cloud kept him and the horse protected from the frozen cold of the moon's light.

"Thank you." Henrich said, placing his hat over his face to sleep.

From that moment, Henrich slept the entire night and woke up the next morning from the heating rays of the sun. while getting up from the ground, Henrich could hear his horse outside kicking. Henrich ran out to see what was disturbing the horse and in the distance, Henrich spotted a large object heading toward them. The object was running and Henrich could see the tusks of whatever was coming toward them.

"A choiros. Never seen one of them this far out in the desert."

The choiros was a mutated hog with large tusks coming from its mouth and the hog was about the size of a small beetle car. The fur that laid upon the beast was dark and dirty. The stench of the creature could be smelled out from miles away. The hog snarled with rage and lust for hunger with its red reflecting eyes. Henrich pulled out his shotgun and aimed it toward the creature.

"Disgusting animal you are."

The choiros ran toward Henrich and the horse. The horse struggled to get from the post, but it wasn't afraid of the mutated hog. It wanted to attack the mutated hog itself. Henrich could feel the intensity coming from the horse and recognized its intention toward the swine ant. Henrich smiled as he untied the rope from the post.

"Go ahead and kill the creature if that's what you desire."

The horse neighed and ran after the mutated hog. Henrich followed the horse on foot with his shotgun in hand. The choiros ran toward the horse. Henrich stopped and aimed the shotgun, the horse continued running toward the mutated hog.

The hog turned from the horse and went straight after Henrich.

The closer the hog came, Henrich started firing shots from the shotgun. The rounds hitting the hog in the sides and legs, but the creature continued to run after him. Henrich sighed while firing countless shots at the hog. The hog screeched as it ran into Henrich with its tusks, cutting his left leg. Henrich grunted when he fell to the ground from the choiros' ram. The hog snarled at Henrich, its eyes showing a look of intense hunger. The hog ran again toward a down and injured Henrich, but this time the horse of Henrich jumped into the way, between Henrich and the choiros.

"What do you know." Henrich said.

The hog snarled at the horse as it ran toward the horse with its tusks in front. The horse jumped over the hog's head. Turning around from behind it and ramming it into the ground. The hog laid on the ground as the horse began to stomp on its body. Henrich looked in awe at what he was witnessing. The horse kicked the hog in its head, the blood form the creature started to pour out from its body, coloring the dirt of the desert darker. Henrich stood up, holding his left leg.

"Seize yourself."

The horse stopped stomping on the hog and walked away from the creature. The hog squealed from the pain as Henrich approached its beaten body. The hog's eyes turned to Henrich and the hog desperately tried to stand up to kill Henrich. Sighing from the pain in his leg, Henrich placed the blastshooter onto the head of the hog.

"Unclean beast." Henrich muttered as he shot the choiros.

Henrich returned to the station alongside the horse. There, Henrich took some rags that were inside his coat pocket and used them to wrap up the cut on his leg from the hog's tusks ramming. Henrich looked at the horse and it didn't have as much as a scratch or injury upon it. Henrich nodded with a slight smirk. The horse neighed at him.

"I hear you."

Henrich gathered his gear and got atop the horse. Looking out forward toward the dark woods. He rode along in the heat of the desert, leaving the station abounded once more and the corpse of the choiros for the hovering vultures to feast upon.

VII

Riding out in the heat of the desert and the dark woods not far in the distance from his current location, Henrich rode along the trail that continued to follow. While on the trail, Henrich stopped to rest himself and the horse. While they rested, Henrich pulled out the scroll he received from the hooded vampire. He read the scroll again, memorizing every word that was written onto the scroll.

"I, the Mercenary Man, hereby call for the assassination and murder of the one, Randolph Henrich of the Warslingers, the Heptad of the Holy Knights. The one who succeeds in doing this quest will be confronted by myself and the Tubal King to receive a great reward unheard of in this World."

Henrich smirked, rolling up the scroll and placing it within his coat. He nodded in silence, only hearing the wind of the desert blow past him and the sounds of the scowls in the air.

"It's me they want, I see. They will receive me, that they want. In the due time."

CHAPTER TWO

A FRIEND COMETH

I

Henrich continued his journey toward the dark woods of the desert. The sun still shining down upon the land and the heat continued to be extraordinary. While Henrich continued his journey down the trail lines, he noticed a small and steady outlander post. Intrigued by its landmark and position so outside of urban and civilized locations, Henrich decided to look around the post. He circled the post atop the horse, the post only looked to be similar like a subway station. Henrich spotted the doors to the post were unlocked from a small crack in the door.

"What do you know."

Henrich removed himself from the horse and approached the door. He went to open it slightly after taking a small, but steady peek through the post's dirty windows. Smeared up with dirt from the desert and old drops of rainfall from past nights. Henrich went to open the door and from the other side came a young man, whom burst through the doors as if he was thrown out of the post. Henrich didn't startle at the young man's appearance from the doors, though he did take several steps back toward the horse.

"Who are you?" Henrich said.

"I… I am… Cody Landon."

"What were you doing inside this old post here?"

"I was looking for resources to carry on my journey back home.

I couldn't find any in there before I was ambushed."

"Ambushed by what exactly?"

"Those beasts. They're vicious creatures."

"What kind of beasts?"

The doors bolted open, shoving Henrich and Landon back into the dirt. While Henrich stood up, he could see three wild beasts come from the post doors. One looked like a bull, but with the legs of a lion. The second appeared to be a wolf, but had the wings of a hawk and the talons of an eagle. The third and last beast was a horse, but with the legs of a spider. Randolph stood in front of them, facing them with his shooters in hand, blastshooter on his back ready to be of use at any moment. Landon sat on the ground, scared and intimidated of the beasts and Henrich.

"Get up, boy."

"I can't fight them."

"Why is that?"

"I don't have any weapons on me."

"You mean to tell me you brought yourself out here in this wild desert and you don't even have a shooter on you? Much less a blade upon your belt?"

"I was taught that using weapons was wrong."

"Who in the hell taught you such folly?"

"My parents, sir."

"Your parents were damn fools. They practically sent you to your own death."

Henrich took one of the shooters from his holster and tossed it to Landon. He caught it and stared for a moment, not sure what to do with the weapon. Scared and confused at his current place in the moment of life and death.

"Use the shooter on the beasts, boy!"

Henrich started shooting at the three wild beasts, which were running toward them at a faster speed than what they knew beasts could run. Landon stood up from the ground, shaking in fear, the sweat covering his face and his palms slipping away from the shooter. Henrich looked at him for a moment and kicked him in his side.

"Why are you just standing there like a shivering statue?!"

"I'm scared."

"Gird up your loins and help me kill these beasts!"

Henrich fired up his shooters. The bullets of the shooter helped slow down the beasts for seconds, until they regained their regular speed. He reached to his back, pulling up the blastshooter as he started blasting the beasts with the blastshooter. The spider legs of the horse beasts were being blown off its body, screeching in the pain of losing its legs. Landon slowly pulled the trigger, firing the shooter toward the wolf beast, shooting it in its left eye. Henrich nodded.

"There you go, boy. Keep going!"

The bull-lion came at Henrich with hits horns, but Henrich's horse rammed into the bull-lion's side, knocking it over onto the ground. Henrich ran over toward the beasts and blasted the creature's head right through with the blastshooter. The blast frightened Landon and shook him up. Henrich looked over toward Landon, seeing him shaking. Henrich shook his head in shame for the young boy.

"You need to grow yourself a pair, son."

"I'm just afraid. I've never encountered things like this before."

"You are now. So, get used to it. Two more beasts left to kill, and you'll be on your way."

Henrich fired the blastshooter at the Wolf-Hawk, seeing it can only see out of one eye thanks to the shot from Landon. The Horse-Spider tried crawling quickly toward Landon. Landon backed away from the Horse-Spider, Henrich fired a shot at the Wolf-Hawk and kicked the Horse-Spider over, blasting it in its head with his blastshooter.

"Use the damn shooter, then they'll stop trying to kill you."

Henrich stared at the Wolf-Hawk, he smiled as he walked toward the wild beasts. His horse walked behind him as well toward the beast. Landon only started at Henrich and his horse, unable to make up what's he witnessed so far after meeting the man. Landon nodded to himself and follow behind Henrich.

"The last one, huh." Henrich said to the Wolf-Hawk.

The Wolf-Hawk howled at Henrich. Its teeth sharp and the growling was deep. The Wolf-Hawk's remaining eye was locked on Henrich and staring at his neck. Henrich held the blastshooter facing the Wolf-Hawk as it could barely move from the previous shots it's taken.

"What are you going to do now." said Henrich.

"Are you going to kill it, sir?" Landon said.

Henrich turned to Landon and looked at the Wolf-Hawk. Henrich nodded and handed the blastshooter toward Landon. Uncertain as of how to use a blastshooter, Landon stared at Henrich with uncertainty in his eyes. Henrich could see it, but it didn't faze him to take the blastshooter back from him. He only pressed it closer to Landon much more.

"Use this blastshooter and kill this fowl beast where it will remain. In the dirt of the desert."

"I don't know how to use one of these, sir."

"Learn. You have right now to do it."

Henrich stared at Landon as he aimed the blastshooter toward the Wolf-Hawk, which snarled at him with saliva coming from its mouth.

"This kind of beast shouldn't even be in existence. But, with all this World has been through over the course of the eons, things alter themselves and become even more corrupt than they were before."

"I'm not fully comprehending what you're telling me."

"Shoot the damn creature. Right now. Kill it before I allow it to kill you."

"You wouldn't allow it to kill me while you're standing right here."

"Boy, you don't know who I am and what I've been through in this life. I will leave you here to die by this beast's hands if you do not kill it right here. Do you understand what I am telling you?"

"I am."

"Then take your shot. Kill it now."

Landon pressed the blastshooter closer to the Wolf-Hawk, which made the attempt to rise and snatch the hand off Landon, Henrich kicked the beast back to the ground, snatched the blastshooter from Landon and finished off the Wolf-Hawk by shooting its head completely off its shoulders. The echo of the shot went through the air, sounding off after Henrich placed the blastshooter back to his back.

"I'm sorry." Landon said. "I'm just afraid. I've never seen things like this before."

"You better learn, and you better learn fast. Because in this World, this Western World, there are only those that survive and those that die."

Henrich took the shooter back from Landon, placing it into its coat holster. He opened the post doors and scanned the interior, seeing nothing living inside. Only seeing a bag, he knew it belonged to Landon.

"Go get your stuff, boy."

"Yes sir."

"I'm giving you a choice to make right now. Either you can come along with me until you've found yourself a safe place to reside or you can go on your own path and try to find a place yourself with no skills of defense against a World of monsters and disasters waiting to consume you."

Landon stared. Quiet to Henrich and to himself.

"Make a choice now. Before I end up far out of your reach."

Henrich got himself atop his horse and rode away back on the trail to the dark woods. Landon stood by himself, quiet, looking at the dead bodies of the three wild beasts. He sighed and re-entered the post, grabbing the bag of his possessions that he had, exiting the post, Landon ran as fast as he could after Henrich, following him down the trail to the dark woods of the desert.

Landon ran quickly after Henrich, who rode atop his horse down the trail to the dark woods. Henrich looked back as he could hear Landon's pacing footsteps approaching him.

"I'm coming with you, sir." Landon said.

"At least you've made yourself a choice. I hope you're ready for the things you're about to witness. Maybe with me, you'll get some proper training and become a skillful warrior."

"Like one of those Warslingers."

"What makes you say that?"

"Because they're an inspiration to me. The way they protected people from dark matters in this World. Those things are unheard of today and possibly can never be replicated. If it's possible to do so."

"So, you know of them and what their purpose is in the World?"

"I've read so many scrolls and tablets that speak of their presence and their accomplishments. I even know their names."

"Do you now?"

"I certainly do."

"Why don't you share them with me. Enlighten me on them if you could."

"Their names were Charlton Darrain of the Ark, Knight Arthur Pendragon, Joshua of Ephraim, Moses the Leader, Daniel of Judah, Noah of Lamech, and Randolph Henrich. They are the *Warslingers of the Heptad*. Protected us from great evils. They were called holy warriors by many who witnessed their strength and courage. Their faith also prevailed in perilous times."

"I take it you've done some studying in your alone time. Before you decided to roam this dead desert."

"I did a lot of studying. I needed to know the history of the lands and how these Worlds were formed."

"So, are you from this Western World or the Eastern World?"

"Neither. I come from the Northern World."

"The Northern World? I thought that land was desolate with ice. No living person could sustain such frigid weather."

"I lived in an area that we could keep the surroundings warm from the frozen rainfalls and strong winds that could freeze objects within reach."

"How did you survive the snow bears or frost lions?"

"We did what we could. Some of us died fighting against them. Others froze to death hiding from them."

"It must've been hard for you to live in such circumstances. Fighting for your life day and night. Trying to survive not only against the beasts of the cold, but the cold itself. The Northern World is unstable in all of its ways."

"I was the only one who apparently had common sense and I left the Northern World to come down to the Western World. Hoping to find something worthwhile to live for."

"You will have to look harder and fight as hard if you're searching for something to live for that's considered worthwhile."

"If I may ask you, why are you out here by yourself? What are you searching for?"

"Me. I'm searching for a place that many consider a legend. A folklore tale told to us as children to make us dream of bigger possibilities to live for."

"What kind of place?"

"It's called The Haunted City. A place where the ghouls reside and die. In their ways. Hell, I even hear the place can give those who enter its gates eternal life and will grant entrance to other worlds that exist within our universe."

"Sounds like a scary place to visit."

"I wouldn't call the place scary as far as fear is concerned. I would say, it's a place that many seek after and die not finding. I intend on becoming the one who finds the City and lives afterwards. That is my current mission and goal in this World."

"So, The Haunted City is somewhere here in the Western World?"

"No. The City itself dwells in a place called the Outer-World."

"I've never heard of an Outer-World."

"Because its kept secret by those who know of its location. Keeps the petty people and strangers from reaching its gates. Basically, saving their lives in the process."

"But, how do you know of all these things? You seem to me like an old regular guy."

"I'm not just some regular guy, boy. I'm part of something much more than the average life of Man."

"How would that be? I'm just curious."

Henrich sighed and pulled out his shooter and tossed it to Landon, who caught the shooter with little ease.

"Be careful with it. Look at the handle of the shooter. Tell me what you recognize."

"I don't know what I'm supposed to look at. it's a unique design for a shooter handle."

"Look closer. The symbolism of the handle. The colors of the handle. You should know this. You've studied as you said."

"I'm looking at it closely."

Landon's eyes stayed at the designs chiseled into the shooter handle. He gazed his eyes to the symbols, analyzing them to his memory. He could spot a small menorah in the middle of the design, surrounded by swords and a crown. He knew what the emblem meant and looked at Henrich with awe.

"You're one of them, aren't you? You're one of the Warslingers?!"

"I am one of them. Yes."

"Which one are you?!"

"Randolph Henrich. The Legendary Warslinger."

Landon held the shooter tightly with his emotions running wild. He rubbed his head and eyes, even pinched himself to see if all he heard and witnessed were true. Henrich stared at him, seeing Landon trying to consume himself of the shock of meeting and talking with a Warslinger.

"You'll get used to it. It happens to many people when they

find things like this out."

Henrich handed the shooter back to Henrich, placing it into his coat holster. Landon slowly breathe his way back to regular status, putting his emotions down and cooling off himself.

"So, what happened with the other Warslingers?"

"We were scattered abroad. To find each other near the end of these Worlds."

"Why were all of you scattered? What did you do?"

"We lost a battle."

"Wait, you guys lost a battle?! Against who?!"

"The Evil One. We had a betrayer in the Heptad."

"No way."

"Yes. To this day, I hope to find him and make him pay for all the misery he has created for us all."

"Which one was it?"

"I won't tell you."

"Why not?"

"Because if I did, it would change your mind on the entire Hectad and how we handled things in the past."

"I'll find out, won't I? Or will you just go ahead tell me outright who betrayed you?"

"Possibly, both will come to your mind. Until then, don't give it any focus at all. It'll cause you to slip and fall."

Landon nodded as he walked behind Henrich's horse down the trail paths. Henrich gave Landon a bottle of water to drink during his walk behind him.

"I hope you're prepared for what we're about to come to once we get there."

"What's at the end of this trail?"

"The dark woods of this wild desert."

"Hold on a second. A forest in the middle of a desert? This desert?!"

"Yeah. Things are different around here than what they're told about to people."

"What's inside the dark woods?"

"Answers and unnatural creatures. Possibly people of Man as well. Traveling about on their own little journeys out here."

"What's on the other side of the dark woods?"

"A closer gateway to the Outer-World. Which means closer to The Haunted City. Makes complete sense to me to travel therein."

"Will I need to use your shooter again when we're inside the woods?"

"More than likely. Yes, you will. Hope you're set your mind on fighting instead of running."

III

Walking through the desert, Henrich caught the scent of water and flowers. Around him was nothing but dirt and stench air. Landon looked out in the distance in front of them. He looked at the ground, seeing something dark around the dirt of the desert. Landon ran toward it, causing Henrich to kick his horse to run after Landon.

"Slow down, boy!"

Landon ran fast after what he was looking at while Henrich's horse immediately caught a second wind, running through the desert behind Landon. Henrich shook his head, while he kept his eyes locked on the running Landon.

"What is he running after?"

Landon ran and ran, pacing his footsteps in the dirt of the desert. He stopped for a moment, catching his breath. As he looked up, he noticed a series of plains covering the desert grounds in front of him. Green grass across the entire desert. Landon looked back at Henrich, who was right behind him.

"Well, what do you know." said Henrich. "Plains out here."

"I thought something like this would be impossible." Landon said. "Who actually planted these plains out in the middle of the desert?"

"No one planted them. They were grown here due to the dark

woods. Its power must've spread across this region. Maybe it still is spreading and hasn't grown out in other parts of the desert yet."

"We should check to see if there's any fruit or vegetables grown in them."

"I don't think we should, boy. No one knows what could be living inside these plains. You see how high the grass reaches. No telling what's around them or what could be growing inside of them."

"We should check you know."

"Boy, you need to listen to me."

Henrich looked at the tall grass, the scent of the grass blown across his nose from a gust of wind. He took in the scent of the tall grass. Landon continued to run through the plains, searching for fruits or vegetables to take with him to eat.

"I haven't found anything yet." said Landon. "What's on your end?"

"Grass. Tall, green grass."

Landon giggled. Henrich shook his head as he padded the horse's head. While looking through the grass, Landon stumbled upon a young girl, dressed in a pink skirt and a white blouse, she was dirty, and her hair was light-brown, lighter than the dirt of the desert. She appeared petite, as if she hasn't eaten in days or weeks. She was crouched down in the grass. He paused for a moment, trying to conjure up words to say to her. The young girl just sat there, seemly crying to herself.

"Ma'am, are you well?" Landon said. "It's ok."

Henrich didn't hear nor see Landon anywhere near him through the grass. Henrich looked in every direction.

"Cody, where the hell are you?"

Getting no response, Henrich rode through the tall grass, cutting it down with his machete. His horse pacing through the grass as if it was the same as the desert. Moving quickly and swiping as fast as he could through the grass, Henrich doesn't see Landon around his location.

"Where in the hell are you, boy?"

Landon stared at the young girl and crouched down toward her, looking at her face and rubbing the tears from her eyes. The young girl turned to him and stared for a bit, deciphering who Landon could be and why would he be out in the plains of the tall grass. She smiled, and Landon smiled.

"What's your name?"

"My name is Lamia."

"Well, nice to meet you, Lamia. I can take you to safety. Me and a friend are out here on a trail. You can come with us."

"Really? Thank you."

Landon helped Lamia stand up and from the grass came Henrich, bolting through with his machete.

"Henrich, good you could come over here." Landon said. "Meet Lamia."

Lamia waved at Henrich. He only stared.

"Lamia?"

"That's what she told me."

The horse paused itself. Henrich looked at Landon and stared at the young girl. Henrich noticed something strange with the young girl's eyes. Her pupils were like that of a lizard. Henrich recognized what creature possessed such eyes. He pulled out his blastshooter and fired toward her. She jumped out of the way, behind Landon.

"Boy, move!"

"But, she's just a young girl. She's lost out here."

"She's not some ordinary girl, boy."

Lamia shoved Landon to the ground of the plains. She growled at Henrich with her eyes glowing toward him. Her fingernails turn into sharp claws and her teeth sharpened up to that of a wolf. Lamia removed her skirt, revealing her lower body to be that of a serpent. Landon stared at her with fear, crawling away from her and getting behind Henrich and the horse.

"I told you not to go roaming around!"

"I'm sorry I didn't listen."

"Screwing around with a damn Lamia, while looking for some

apples and tomatoes."

"She said that was her name."

"She told you the truth about that. But, you have no idea what a Lamia is do you?"

"I've never heard of one."

Henrich stared at Landon before facing Lamia with his blastshooter. He aimed the blastshooter at Lamia.

"Well, boy. Now you know."

Henrich fired the blastshooter as the Lamia dodged the round, roaming through the tall grass. Unable to be seen by Henrich or Landon. They stayed close together, circling their surroundings as they could hear the Lamia slithering through the grass around them.

"Watch your sights. She can appear anywhere."

"I'm sorry. I didn't know."

"You can do your apologizing another time. Right now, put your mind to focus on killing this creature."

The Lamia burst through the grass, swiping Henrich off his horse with her tail. Landon ran through the grass and the Lamia followed. Henrich stood up and could see the trail that Landon took. He jumped back onto his horse and followed Landon's trail. The horse plowing through the tall grass, following Landon's trail. Henrich could hear Landon hollering for help further up.

"Go faster, my boy!"

The horse ran faster as the Lamia's screech was hear from nearby, almost close to Landon's screams.

"I'm coming for you, boy!" Henrich yelled. "Hold yourself together!"

Henrich rode through the tall grass, the screeching of the Lamia continued to roll through the air along with Landon's cries for help. The screeches and screams were growing louder as Henrich came closer to their location. The horse burst through the grass and into an open field, Henrich looked over and seen Landon atop a tree as the Lamia tried to pull the tree down with her tail. Henrich jumped off the horse and walked toward the Lamia with his blastshooter and machete.

"Sex demon!" Henrich yelled. "Face me and leave the boy alone!"

The Lamia turned to Henrich and slithered her way to him. Landon looked as he slowly made his way down from the tree to the ground. The Lamia sat in the face of Henrich, who showed no ounce of fear in his expression nor in his eyes. He stared into the Lamia's own green, reptilian eyes.

"You believe that I fear you? I don't have any fear of your kind. There are things in the Worlds that I've faced that would make you shed your own hide to get away."

The Lamia screeched in Henrich's face. Yellow saliva and green mucus poured out from the Lamia's mouth. The smell covered Henrich's face and the air around him. Henrich nodded and wiped the liquid fluids from his face with a rag from his coat pocket. Placing the rag against the grass, rubbing it down to remove the saliva and mucus from it. He faced the Lamia with a smile.

"Catch."

Henrich threw the rag into the Lamia's face and as she wiped the used rag from her face to the grass, Henrich swiped at her with his machete, cutting her head clean off her body. The head rolled across the grass and stopped at the tree, where Landon was standing. Her body collapsed by its own weight to the ground.

"There." Henrich said. "That is done."

Landon walked from the head of the Lamia, its eyes still moving and her mouth opening and closing from the nerves. He walked to Henrich who pulled out a lighter and burned the Lamia's body and head to ashes. Henrich turned to Landon and slapped him across his face. Landon fell to his knees from the impact of the slap.

"The next time you refuse to heed my words, I'll put a round in you myself."

"I... I understand." Landon said slowly. "I just wanted to know what was in the plains."

"You found out didn't you. You discovered a shadow creature

waiting for her next meal. Luckily, I was here to save your scrawny ass from getting killed. Again."

"I just need a weapon of my own."

"I gave you a damn weapon and you refuse to kill. Your parents screwed that nonsense into your head. Causing you to stumble."

Landon stood up, rubbing his face from the slap. Henrich stared at him and suddenly looked beyond Landon. Landon turned around to see what Henrich was staring at and behind him was straight plains of grass. Their entire surrounds covered with grass and trees and bushes. There were even birds and insects flying around the area. Henrich looked back and looked forward.

"You see what I'm seeing, sir?" Landon said.

"I am." Henrich replied "There's no more desert."

IV

Henrich and Landon look out at the open plains around them, fields of tall grass are also present around them in different corners of the fields. Landon was astounded by the sight of butterflies and bumblebees.

"Do you see all of this?" Landon asked.

"I do. Something strange is happening here."

"What makes you say that?"

"We were just in the middle of the desert and now after killing a Lamia through some tall grass, we find ourselves in an open field with trees and living insects."

"Maybe it was a portal transference."

"There was no portal. I would've known it to be because it would've made itself known to us. Portals don't just open and close to their will. Hell, they have no will of their own."

"I thought portals come and go as they pleased."

"Where did you hear that from?"

"Some old friends up in the Northern World. Portals would appear up there nearly every day. In random locations. We never figured out where the portals led to."

"Luckily you didn't take the chance of seeing it. Could've killed yourself by transporting to a world you have no idea even exist."

"I've studied up on the possible theory of a multi-verse."

"You're saying you believe there's more than the universe that we're already in?"

"It was only a theory that I read up on. Could be a possibility."

"We'll get to that once we come across it. Besides, you're not even ready for something like that to appear on your doorpost. If you can't handle the creatures in these Worlds, how will you handle yourself against more powerful creatures that may dwell in other universes. The strength they could possess and the power that might harness."

They walked through the open field, butterflies and bees flying across from them. The birds were chirping to each other in the trees. Henrich gazed up at the trees as his horse neighed at the small critters running through the field. Landon looked up ahead and seen trees covered with fruit.

"There's fruit!" Landon said running to the fruit trees.

Landon approached the trees, seeing the trees to be covered with apples, peaches, pears, strawberries, and cherries. Henrich went over to the trees as the horse pulled an apple from the tree, eating it. Henrich smirked, he reached over and pulled off a strawberry and ate it.

"It's been a long time since I've tasted strawberries."

Landon stuffed his mouth with strawberries and started grabbing apples and eating them. Henrich stopped him from stuffing his mouth completely.

"Why don't you place some of those fruits in your bag, huh. Safekeeping."

"Oh, yeah. You're right, sir."

Landon grabbed as many apples, peaches, pears, strawberries, and cherries as he could gather and placed them inside his bag. Henrich grabbed some of the apples and peaches, putting them in his bag and the strawberries in a small pouch attached to the interior of his coat.

"Did you gather enough?" Henrich asked.

"I gathered enough so we won't starve on our journey to the dark woods."

"Speaking of the dark woods." Henrich said looking outward from the plains.

Far out from the plains stood the dark woods, Randolph and Landon stared at its dark trees and eerie appearance. Landon ate an apple and looked at the dark woods.

"What do you think lives in there, really? More creatures?"

"No telling what lies in there, boy. We'll come to that conclusion once we're inside its settings."

They walked away from the fruit trees and continued moving on forward, toward the dark woods. Other animals approached. Raccoons, hares, foxes, and among other animals that walked through the plains. The horse neighed at them to move from their trail, the animals moved with no exception, startling Landon as he looked at Henrich's horse.

"Where did you find that horse?"

"I didn't find the horse. The horse found me after I had to slay six Vrylolakas in my presence.

"Those things are out here too?!"

"Yeah. You're afraid of them or something?"

"I hear they drink blood from the people of Man. I also hear they can see in the dark and are afraid of the sun's rays."

"They are. But, the ones I ran into were not harmed by the sun's rays. They were protected with some stronger power. A power that block the sun's rays from harming them. Though, the barrier wasn't strong enough to keep me from killing them where they stood."

"The power that protected them from the sun's rays must have been a powerful force of power."

"It is a powerful force from a powerful figure."

"You know who it is or what the power could come from?"

"I may have an idea as to who possess that dark power to

protect those blood-suckers from committing their own suicidal deaths."

While they were walking, Henrich started to hear critters running through the tall grass that stood next to them. Landon finished eating his apple when he started to hear the scurrying sounds coming from the grass.

"You here that?" Henrich referenced.

"Maybe it's one of those animals from the field. Could've gotten itself lost in the grass."

The scurrying continued with little faints of laughter following. Henrich knows the laughter and reached down for his shooters. Landon noticed Henrich going for his shooter and looked around, stopping in his tracks.

"Keep walking, boy." Henrich said. "I can deal with them on my own."

"Are you sure about that?"

"What can you do about them? Really?"

From the tall grass, out runs four demons. The demons stood in front of Henrich and Landon, in their way of the trail to the dark woods. Henrich nodded as he pulled out his shooters toward the demons. Landon stood still with the remains of the apple in his hand.

"What are you going to do, sir?"

"I have a way of doing this. Won't take long."

The demons stood and laughed at Henrich and Landon. The demons were dark red, covered with black lines across their slim bodies. Their claws and nails were sharp as blades and dark as the night sky. Their eyes glazed red, like a burning fire. Their scent was that of sulfur and brimstone. Looking at the demons would possibly cause someone to lose their mind and go insane, but Henrich and Landon didn't turn insane.

"Keep yourself still, boy." Henrich said. "Before they come for you first."

The demons laugh and snarl at them. The sulfur in the air causes Landon to lose his grasp on what's going on. Becoming

unconscious and losing sight. Henrich looked at him and tossed
him a rag, where Landon placed the rag against his face, covering
himself from the scent of the sulfur.

"Throw your apple remains at them."

"What? Why? What good will that do?"

"Throw it at them now."

"All right, sir."

Landon tossed the apple remains toward the demons, they
jumped up and stared at the remains. They picked it up and sniffed
it, shaking their heads with disgust. The demons formed a single-
file line facing Henrich. He chuckled under his breath as he pulled
the triggers of his shooters, blasting straight through the demons'
chest and heads each, killing them with one shot from both his
shooters.

"Holy." Landon said. "How did you--"

"I have my ways of doing things, boy." Henrich said. "Best you
watch me, so you can learn and do it yourself."

Henrich placed the shooters back into the holsters and
continued moving forward the trail with Landon following him.

V

Walking through the open fields and surpassing the tall grass of
the fields, Henrich spots a small community nearby. Landon sees
people standing outside in a hoard. He pointed toward the mass of
people.

"You see all those people?"

"I do. Something must be taking place over there."

They proceeded to enter the small community. Henrich left his
horse at the gated entrance and upon passing the gate's sign, they
notice it's actually a very small town with close people. They see
homes and community buildings around the area. In the distance
by some of the homes, Henrich could spot children playing in the
yard with one another and the parents sitting on the porches of the

homes, talking and laughing. The people were dressed in what looked like 18th century to 19th century clothing. The homes and buildings around them looked to fit in with those two centuries.

"What kind of place is this?" Henrich said.

"Looks like a good place to stay."

"We'll have to see if that's the truth, don't we." said Henrich. "Let's go over there to where all the people are gathered. Maybe we can find something out about this place from them."

"All right."

They walked toward the gathering of the townspeople and immediately, Henrich noticed a structure, made of a large and wide wooden square platform and on top of it sat three guillotines, ready to be of use. He also spotted three men standing up on the side of the guillotines, wearing all black with scarlet lining and purple interior shirts. The men looked middle-aged and were known for their purpose.

"What is going on here?" Landon said.

"There's a judgment taking place. Someone is about to be judged according to these judges' rules and laws."

"I wonder what their laws are that would have them chop off people's heads. Must be something major I would guess."

"Only one way to find out. We'll need to get a little closer to the scene."

They walked up behind the townspeople as they witnessed the judges bring three men up to the guillotines and lay their heads down, preparing them for their final moments of living. One of the judges stood out in front of the crowd.

"I hereby, bring to you and to our faithful town of Savel, that we at this very moment, sentence these three men sitting on their knees before you, to their death."

The crowd cheered on for the deaths of the three men. Henrich and Landon stood in the back and were quiet the entire time. Only watching the executions take place right before their very eyes. The people were militant in their speech and in their actions, throwing vegetables at the three men and calling them out of their names.

"KILL THEM NOW!!!" The crowd screamed with boldness. "CHOP OFF THEIR DAMNED HEADS! SEND THEM TO THE FIRES BELOW!!!"

The judge signaled the guillotines as they fell and chopped off the heads of the three men. The crowd cheered the deaths of the men and ran over in hordes to their heads, which were laying on the ground. The crowd gathered the heads and committed heinous acts to them. Some kissed the heads, other proceeded to place the heads toward their genitals and behinds in gesturing movements. The judges threw the bodies down toward the crowd, which they began to tear the clothes apart from the bodies, leaving them naked in their presence. They proceed to have sexual intercourse with the dead bodies along with urinating on them bodies.

"What the hell is all of this?!" Henrich said.

"I don't know." said Landon. "But I feel we need to leave this place right now."

"The spirit of Old Sodom dwells over this town. I can sense it in my spirit."

"What is Old Sodom?"

"You have much to learn, boy. Now isn't the time for the teaching."

One of the judges looked and pointed at Henrich and Landon. He looked at them with confusion, moving his head over to the other judges that were sitting next to him.

"Have you seen those two here before?"

"No. I have not."

"They must be outsiders. Probably here to ruin our laws in this place."

"Maybe you're right. Let's make an example out of them shall we."

The judges stood up and gathered the crowd's attention with clapping and whistling. The judges smiled at the crowd, who's faces were filled with unclean lust and desires.

"It seems we have two visitors who have come to the town of Savel."

The crowd turned and looked at Henrich and Landon. Licking their lips and chanting for their executions. They stood their guard, backing away from the crowd. Some of the crowd members were lusting for Henrich and Landon. Calling for them to strip down in front of them so they could fulfill their desires.

"Tell me, what are your names and your business here in our town."

"I am Cody Landon." said Landon with his voice trembling. "This is my friend here, Mr. Henrich."

"Henrich?" The Judge said. "I only know of one Henrich and he died years ago in a great battle. Tell me, you cannot be the one I'm speaking of."

"I am more than what you deem to know based on appearances, filth."

"You dare call me filth, peasant?! You're in my town! You're surrounded by my homes and my people! Do you know what I can do to the two of you right now if I demanded it?"

"I know what you could do? You'll attempt to execute us, so your disgusting people could sodomize our dead bodies."

"The crowd does what they please with the remains of those that have died by our guillotines. Nothing I can do about that."

"There's plenty you could do about them and the actions they have committed this day before you."

"You talk as if you're an ancient man. You look like a present man, but with the tongue of an ancient. That isn't exactly possible around these parts."

"You're still looking based on physical appearances and yet, you have no idea of what's to come of you and your town full of uncleanness."

"Enough!" The Judge said. "I am growing tired of your backtalk, outsider."

The Judge sat in his chair and looked at the other two judges. Each of them nodded their heads and looked down at the crowd. Pointing to Henrich and Landon with a smile on their faces. Large smiles with their teeth shining against the sun. their teeth dirty, almost rotten completely.

"Bring the two of them up here for their executions! Let them taste the sharpness of our guillotines!"

The crowd cheered and yelled as they ran toward Henrich and Landon. Grabbing their clothes and pulling them. Some of the crowd placed their hands in the interior of their shirts and pants.

"Get off me!" Landon yelled. "Get off!"

"I WANT THE YOUNGER ONE!" A man in the crowd yelled. "LEAVE HIM TO ME!!!"

"NO! I WANT HIM AND HIS OLDER FRIEND" Yelled a woman in the crowd. "WE CAN HAVE SO MUCH FUN WITH THEM!!!"

"You people are about to take in your last breaths." Henrich said. "Hope you're ready for the next World."

"YOU TWO ARE ABOUT TO DIE!!! HOW DO YOU FEEL ABOUT THAT?!!!"

Henrich pulled out his shooter and shot two of the crowd members in the head, causing the crowd to stop in their tracks and the judges to be afraid. Henrich tossed the other shooter to Landon, who smiled.

"You know what to do now."

"I do." Landon said.

Both began firing at the crowd, whom tried to outrun the gunshots. Henrich fired one and blasted him in the head. Henrich ran toward a few of the crowd members, spearing them to the ground and shooting them to their deaths. The judges were appalled, seeing their townspeople being shot and killed by Henrich and Landon in their presence.

"Those outsiders are killing our people!"

"What should we do about them?!"

"Let's deal with them ourselves."

After firing upon firing bullets, Henrich and Landon killed everyone that stood in the crowd. All that remained were the three judges. Henrich placed the shooter back into its holster and walked up the steps atop the large structure toward the judges. The judges started backing away from Henrich as he threw them against the post of the guillotines. Each of the judges are sitting down with the guillotines above their heads.

"You can't do this to us!" The Judge said. "This is our town! Who will take charge of it if we were to die?!"

"You can leave that to the remaining townspeople that have some form of sense."

Henrich prepared the guillotines to fall upon the judges' necks. The lead Jude looked back at Henrich. Shaking his head in anger and despair.

"Tell me before you end my life, who are you really?"

"I am Randolph Henrich of the Warslingers of the Heptad."

"The Heptad. No."

Henrich pulled the lever, the guillotines fall and kill the three judges. Landon walked over toward him, looking at the dead bodies of the judges. He handed the shooter back to Henrich. Randolph looked at it and gave it back to Landon.

"You did good right there."

"Really?"

"Yeah. For right now, you can hold on to that shooter."

"I don't know how to thank you."

"You don't have to. Not now anyway."

They looked around the town of Savel. Seeing only the children running around with their parents at the homes. They left the town, returning on their trail to the dark woods.

"You think there are other places like this out there?" Landon said.

"There are many in various fields. There are many."

VI

Walking down the trail to the dark woods, Henrich and Landon decided to move forward and simply focus on the dark woods. After several miles of traveling from the wild desert to the tall grass fields to the small town of Savel, they finally make it to the entrance of the dark woods.

"This is it." Henrich said.

"We made it." Landon replied. "Do we just walk on in there?"

"It appears that is our only option."

They approached the tree field entrance of the dark woods and from out of the ground, rose up a dark cloud of smoke. The cloud was incredibly dark that Henrich and Landon were unable to see through it, nor could they even walk past it, sucking the air from the lungs when making the attempt to surpass the smoke.

"What kind of smoke is this?!" Landon said.

"I do not know." said Henrich. "But, I know it's made of magic. A shadowic magic."

They took steps back from the smoke with Henrich's horse neighing as it backed away from the smoke. Henrich noticed the horse was sensing something from the other side of the smoke and when he took a closer look at the smoke, trying to see through it, Henrich discovered three figures were standing on the other side of the smoke.

"Landon, we have company before us."

"What do you mean? Where are they?"

"Standing on the other side of the smoke cloud. They appear to be of small stature. But, from what the horse is sensing, and I can sense it too, their shadowic creatures."

Henrich pulled out the shooter and fired shots through the smoke, making the attempt to kill the three shadowic creatures standing on the other side. The bullets vanished inside the smoke, with no sound of impact following. Henrich held the shooter steady, still aimed at the smoke where he could still see the three figures.

"Why don't you lay down this smoke cloud here and face us like the creatures you are."

The smoke withered away with a gust of wind that appeared from out of nowhere. Henrich looked and found himself and Landon staring at the three figures. The three figures looked and smiled at them both.

"What do you know." Henrich said.

"What are they, sir?" said Landon. "I've never encountered women like this before. Ever."

"That's because you wouldn't find them outside of their comfort zones. The two on the sides are called Mares and the one in the middle is known throughout the Eastern World as the Cailleach."

The three women laughed at Henrich and Landon. The women on the sides appeared old in age, but nightmarish in their eyes and aura. The one in the middle stood with a staff and looked like a huge, hideous old woman. Her long white hair stood out from underneath her black and gray hood connected to her robe. The Cailleach's face appeared as a dark blue and she also wore a plaid.

"It appears that we have visitors, my ladies." The Cailleach said. "How should we make them feel comfortable?"

"Let us pass and enter the dark woods behind you." Henrich said. "That's why we're here standing in front of you anyhow."

"My dear man, why would we ever allow such a thing? You believe that you can proceed on your little journey to The Haunted City isn't it?"

Henrich stared at the Cailleach with a mere shock going across his face. Landon shivered slowly, while keeping his hand toward the shooter on his belt.

"How do you know about that?" Henrich said. "How do you know who I am?"

"We know many things, Warslinger of the *Heptad*." A Mare said.

"We know so many things." The other Mare said with a laugh.

"I am surprised that your horse caught our scent."

"This horse is nothing that you already know of in the Worlds around us."

"I can sincerely agree with you on that statement."

"Sir, what should we get ready to do?"

"Nothing yet, boy. Nothing just yet. But, we are getting past them and entering that forest there. That I can promise the both of us and these hags."

The Cailleach clapped and stomped her staff into the trail way. Smiling as the two Mares laughed, clapping their hands in excitement.

"What are you preparing to do?" Henrich said. "State your point of blocking our way inside?"

"We have a proposal for the two of you." The Cailleach said.

"What do you mean?" said Landon.

"I'm listening." Henrich said.

"If you can solve our little puzzles of threes here before you, we will grant you entrance to the dark woods behind us. If you fail to solve the puzzles of the threes, you will give us your souls."

"I'm not liking this, sir." Landon said.

"What are your puzzles of threes?" Henrich said. "Enlighten me."

The Cailleach swiped her staff in front of them and slammed it to the ground again. She stared at Henrich, who kept his hand on the shooter and finger laid tight to the trigger.

"The threes are here before you. Determine what they are and what they mean to your futures to come."

"The hell are you talking of, hag?" Henrich said.

From the sky above them, snow began to fall. Landon looked around, seeing the fields covered with snow as the entire landscape is turning a pale white. The Cailleach stood in front them along with the two Mares.

"Solve your first puzzle, scowlers." The Cailleach said. "Solve this one and the second will present itself to you."

From the Cailleach's plaid dropped rocks that started to cause a small earthquake. The land shook as the snow began to fall heavier and thunder followed. Henrich looked around as Landon tried to cover his face from the snow falling toward his eyes.

"What is happening around us, sir?!" said Landon.

"We're experiencing a shadowic snowstorm accompanied by a tremor."

Henrich continued to look at the heavy snow and the feeling of the earthquake. He gazed over at the Cailleach, who stood there, non-affected by the snow nor the earthquake.

"The puzzle is inside the weather she has formed." Henrich said. "But, what is it?"

Henrich looked around the land, jumped off his horse and started moving around in the snow-covered grounds. Landon followed him and copied what Henrich was doing, but uncertain of it at the same time.

"What are you looking for, sir?"

"The answer to her puzzle. Maybe it's buried beneath the snow she has created."

Landon looked around and stared at the Cailleach, looking at her staring down at Henrich, holding the staff down to the ground with the other Mares laughing on the event.

"Maybe it has something to do with her place of origin."

"She is from the Eastern World after all. Let's give that a chance."

The Cailleach stared at them, her patience warring out from their searching through the thundersnow storm.

"What is taking them so long, Madam?" One Mare said.

"They have no idea what to do." The Cailleach said. "They have failed the first puzzle."

While searching, Henrich stopped and looked at Landon with a confidence, possibly knowing the answer to the first puzzle.

"Sir, what is it?"

"I know what the answer is."

"You do?"

"I believe so."

Henrich stood up and looked at the Cailleach. He nodded toward her. She stared at Henrich.

"Have you discovered what is it to solve this first puzzle?"

"This weather is based off Beira, the Queen of Winter. She had the abilities to do great feats across the lands of the Eastern World. The snowstorm, the earthquake, the thunder, and the rocks that came from beneath your plaid. Those are all signs of Beira. Which implies to me that Beira is the answer to your first puzzle."

"You have done well." The Cailleach said. "I am impressed."

She raised up her staff and the snow stopped falling and the earthquake steeled down. The snow melted from the sun's rays. Landon went ahead and stopped searching through the snow-covered grounds, turning his eyes to the Cailleach, who is staring at Henrich.

"Why did you stop the storm?" Henrich said.

"Because, you speck of dirt surpassed the first puzzle, I am prepared to give to you the second puzzle. This one shouldn't be much of a troubling task since you've managed to surpass the first one."

She slammed her staff to the ground again, only this time, snow didn't fall from the sky. Henrich and Landon looked around and the sky immediately brightened, and the air turned a slight cold. The air was deeply cold that it formed small speckles of ice in the air around them. Henrich looked over at the field and noticed the grass nor the trees were frozen solid from the air.

"The trees." Henrich said. "They're not frozen."

"How could that be, sir." said Landon. "This air around us to freeze almost anything solid and the sky is so bright that it should provide some form of warmth."

The Warslinger raised his hand up toward the sky. He took another look at the trees and the grass. He nodded.

"That must be it."

"What must be it?"

Henrich looked at the Cailleach and stared into her eyes. She looked at him as if she was looking for the answer.

"Do you have what will solve this puzzle?"

"Yeah. I do."

"Speak of it, Warslinger."

"Samhain and Bealltainn. Samhain, the first day of Winter. Bealltainn, the first day of Summer."

The Cailleach stared at Henrich. She shook her head slightly.

The Mares were in awe of Henrich's answer that they looked over to the Cailleach, waiting for a response. The Cailleach stomped her staff to the ground, returning the air and the sky back to its original state.

"You are indeed correct, Warslinger."

Henrich nodded. Landon stood impressed at the Warslinger's knowledge. The Mares were upset that they slightly turned their backs to Henrich and Landon. The Cailleach screeched at them to turn themselves back around.

"You have been doing well." The Cailleach said. "Are you ready for the third and final puzzle of the threes?"

"We are." Henrich said. "Bring the puzzle to us."

The Cailleach stomped the staff and within the fields formed a lake, which Henrich and Landon approached. As they approached the lake, Henrich noticed it started to grow out in feet, then miles.

"What is this?" Henrich said.

"It's a lake, sir. Water freely flowing that way."

"I can see that. But, its enlarging itself. Growing in length."

Laying on the ground in front of Henrich is a dirty gray and black plaid. The plaid is a great plaid. He picked up the plaid and analyzed it. Landon walked over to see the plaid. Unfamiliar at its purpose of lying next to the water.

"Why is this out here, sir?"

"Maybe it has something to do with this lake here. I should say gulf. It's grown out even larger than I thought."

The Cailleach watched them very closely with the plaid in Henrich's hands.

"Let's see if they know of this one." The Cailleach said. "Let us see."

Henrich took the plaid and looked around it. Landon touched the plaid and thought to himself a possible solution, which was to bury the plaid in the dirt next to the gulf. Henrich declined, stating there's something more to the plaid than just burying it next to the water.

"There's something else that we're supposed to do with this

plaid, and I am certain it involves the water in some capacity."

"How about laying the plaid down into the water and letting it flow away. Like the past flowing away to give room to the future."

"Maybe. But, I doubt that's the purpose of the plaid and gulf."

Henrich looked around at the gulf and the dirt surrounding it. He found a small rock and kneeled to grab it. He took the rock and the plaid toward the water. He entered the water and started scrubbing the plaid with the rock. Landon didn't know what to make of the scene.

"Why are you washing the plaid, sir?"

"Trust me on this, boy. I know what I'm doing."

Henrich continue to wash the plaid with the water of the gulf and scrubbed it with the rock. The Cailleach watched him washing the plaid. She slightly smiled as she stared at him. The two Mares stood in silence. Not understanding what was taking place.

"He knows of his Worlds." The Cailleach said. "This man knows a lot of things."

After scrubbing the plaid, Henrich dipped it underneath the water and held it there for a few seconds and scrubbed a second time. He dipped it underwater again and pulled it back up. Scrubbing a third time and placing it underwater again. The wind started to pick up around them and it started to chill down. Landon held himself tightly to keep himself warm from the cold air.

"Why is it getting cold again?"

"Because of this." Henrich said, pulling the plaid out from underneath the water.

The plaid was a solid white, pure white as snow. The Cailleach gasped at what she had seen. The ground around them was covered in snow. Henrich took the plaid and approached the Cailleach with it. He handed it to her and she held it in her hands. She looked at Henrich.

"Do you have what will solve the third and final puzzle?"

"I do. The Gulf of Korryvreckan. The place where you would bring your great plaid to wash it for three days to where the season of Winter would make itself known to you and the gust of winds would pick up."

The Cailleach nodded and slammed the staff to the ground, the great white plaid and the snow vanished in thin air. Henrich looked around as his horse walked up to him. Landon stood by the hose as they faced the Cailleach and the Mares.

"You have finished the puzzles of the threes, Warslinger and partner." The Cailleach said. "I congratulate you on your victory. You have much knowledge."

"I've been around for a very long time."

"I can sense it in your aura."

"We have completed your puzzles." Henrich said. "Now, may you let us pass and enter the dark woods?"

The Cailleach nodded and moved herself over to the side. Henrich went atop the horse as Landon stood by. They walked past the Cailleach and Mares, making their way inside the dark woods. The Cailleach stopped Henrich, calling him out. He turned around to face her, staring into her eyes as she glared into his. The Mares had vanished into a small puff of black smoke.

"Don't mind them." The Cailleach said. "They know of what their purpose is around here."

"Why did you call me out?" Henrich said. "What else do you have to say to me?"

"You have much knowledge in your memory. You are a Warslinger of the *Heptad*. But, you are not the only living one in the Worlds."

Henrich looked at The Cailleach. Landon turned around and watched the two speak to one other.

"What do you mean I'm not the only living one in the Worlds? You're telling me that the others are still walking among the Worlds this day?"

"They are in various parts of the Worlds. They are not together yet. It seemed that you were all scattered apart."

"Yeah. I already know that. I was there when it happened."

"That's not what I'm getting to."

"Then, what are you getting to? You should at least just let it out of your mouth and spare yourself the trouble of staring at me."

"You will all meet each other soon. Very soon. You'll all meet at one location in the Eastern World."

"What location in the Eastern World? Tell me."

"You will all gather together at the remains of an ancient kingdom that belonged to a king that was also a Warslinger. You know who I am speaking of, don't you?"

Henrich nodded, "I know exactly whom you're talking about."

"That is all I must tell you, Randolph Henrich of the Warslingers of the Heptad."

Henrich nodded and rode away into the dark woods with Landon following him on the side. The Cailleach started at them as she waved her hand in the air and beat her staff to the ground again, creating the thick black smoke. She walked into the smoke, vanishing.

"We shall meet again, Warslinger of the Heptad."

Henrich could hear her last words before she vanished into the smoke. He turned his head back, seeing only the black smoke. He stared for a moment.

"Maybe we will." Henrich said.

Landon looked ahead into the dark woods, seeing nothing but the darkened trees and the dark green leaves around them. The bushes within the dark woods were a dark green and the darkness of night could fit in with them and appear to be just of the same color. He looked at Henrich, who was moving past him.

"Are you ready for what's inside here, boy?" Henrich said.

"I don't have much of a choice do I."

Henrich smiled at Landon while gazing inside the dark woods, hearing hardly nothing but the sounds of insects and forest animals.

"Not really."

CHAPTER THREE

SHADOWS OF THE WILDERNESS

I

Entering the dark woods, Randolph Henrich and Cody Landon slowly made their way through a filled pathway covered in limbs and bushes. Henrich chopped down the limbs with his machete. Landon bypassed the falling limbs, shoving himself away from the bushes filled with small insects. Landon looked at the flying insects, seeing their glowing colors across their small hollow bodies.

"What kind of insects are these?"

"Those would be called the *shroudoks*. They're shadow insects. They reside wherever little light can be present."

"Really? So, light can kill them?"

"Bright light. The heat of the light, such as the sun would be even too intense for those small critters. That's why they hide out in darker areas. Such as this forest."

They continued through the dark woods, seeing and hearing more insects crawling and flying around them. From mutated butterflies with a dark hue of blue across their wings to cockroaches almost the size of small dogs running through the bushes.

While they moved through the trail, created by previous others who have entered the dark woods, Henrich began to feel a slight disoriented. Landon noticed Henrich slightly tilting his head over his left shoulder, before catching it himself.

"Sir, are you alright?"

"I'm fine, boy." Henrich said. "It's the ghouls who are in here.

They're attempting to attack with my immune system."

"Wait a second. They can do that? I've never known any kind of ghoul that could bother someone's immune system by doing nothing."

"These are a different kind of ghoul, boy. Remember, we're in their territory now. Their power is increased abundantly without the sun's rays beaming down on here brightly."

"That's something."

"You think it is. Wait until you see them in their nightmarish forms. They'll come flying toward you like a bat out of its resting place."

From the trees, bolted down a ghoul, glowing a bluish white and its eyes and mouth in complete darkness. Screeching out toward Henrich. Landon looked at the ghoul with fear in his eyes as he went to pull out the shooter. As he raised it up, the ghoul was shot and evaporated in his sight from Henrich's shooter.

"Don't worry, boy." said Henrich. "I know how to deal with these shadowic beings. Not my first time coming through a place like this."

From the shadows of the forest rained down more ghouls, all in various shades of colors. Dark blue, gray, dark violet, and white. Screeching and screaming at Henrich and Landon. They move quickly through the woods, following the trail in front of them. Landon looked back and seen the ghouls coming after them through the trees. He started shooting at them, evaporating a few of them in the process. Henrich looked back and started firing his shooter toward them.

"Keep your shooter aimed on them at all cost!"

"I will do my best, sir."

Henrich's horse rode his way through the tree limbs, crashing them down. Landon ducked from the falling limbs as the ghouls went right through them. Landon continued to shoot them. Henrich reloaded his shooter and continued firing at them. They hear scurrying coming from the bushes in front of them. Henrich looked and spotted a set of red eyes gazing at him from within the bushes. A low growl was also heard by both Henrich and Landon.

"What was that, sir?"

"There's demons here as well." Henrich said. "I'll be damned this day has become a whole lot messier than before."

From the bushes, bolted out the demons. The demons appeared to be from the same species as the demons from the tall grass. Except these were much smaller and could move at a much faster pace. Henrich's horse ran through the demons as Henrich fired at them and Landon kept the remaining ghouls at bay.

"I'm almost finished up with the ghouls." Landon said.

"Keep at them, boy!" said Henrich. "I'll handle the demons. They won't be much of a problem."

Henrich pulled out the blastshooter, firing at the demons, who scurrying around the trees and the bushes. Swinging on the limbs to sneak up on Henrich. Landon turned around and shot one of the demons off the limbs, its body fell to the ground, burning up the grass beneath it.

"I appreciate that."

"It's my job, sir." Landon said with a nod.

Henrich continued to fire at the remaining demons while Landon handled the final two ghouls hovering and circling him. Henrich jumped off the horse and walked up to the demons, shooting them one by one.

"How many times do I have to deal with your kind." Henrich said. "How many times."

The ghouls circled Landon. He nodded and tossed a blade at one and shot the shooter toward the other. The blade distracted the ghoul, but the bullet evaporated the other one. The last ghoul looked and stared at Landon with hatred piecing from its eyes and the horror could be heard from within its screeching cry. Henrich fired up the blastshooter's shots, killing the demons that were around them. He looked back, seeing Landon pull the trigger, evaporating the last ghoul.

"Seems you've improved somewhat." Henrich said. "About damn time."

"We're currently inside a dark forest with shadow creatures around us at every corner. I have no choice but to improve my fighting skills."

"I can understand that. Anyhow, it's a good thing to see how you're holding up with that shooter. Maybe in time, you'll get to have this blastshooter for yourself."

"One day. Maybe."

"Let's keep moving along, boy. Find out way through this darkness."

They moved through the woods, not confronting nor being stopped by any other shadow creatures that are lurking around within the dark woods. Throwing Henrich and Landon off for not seeing any of them, they continued to move forward. Several minutes later, they found themselves exiting the woods and entering a land surrounded by dark green grass, rugged mountains, and ridges. Henrich looked out and the land was large and massive. No end could be seen of the land by the naked eye.

"What is this place? I thought we were just inside the forest." Landon said.

"We were. This place is something else."

"Like what?"

Henrich looked around and spotted a macabre alter sitting in the forefront of the land. They went toward it and upon getting closer, the horse neighed itself suddenly, stopping its feet in its tracks. Landon stopped immediately while Henrich looked around the altar.

"What's wrong with the horse, sir?"

"He knows something we don't. I know of this place. I've seen it before in the visions of the day and the dreams of the night."

"Well, what is this place?"

"We're in the Valley of Death."

II

Looking out at the Valley of Death, Henrich and Landon noticed more forests were covering the trail that they were following previously. Landon nodded and looked back at the dark woods. He looked forward at the other forests that surrounded the valley.

"I see there's more than one dark forest."

"Appears there is. We need to be careful going further into this place. Many have died here."

Henrich and the horse moved on from the altar, continuing to move forward with Landon following them. He looked around, seeing the sun's rays slightly beam down from the gray clouds above them. The air appeared a mixture of warmth and freezing. The sound of the wind could be heard if listened to very carefully.

"How many have died exactly?"

"Too many to number."

"Oh. So, what was that altar all about? Was it some shrine to a god or someone's burial grounds?"

"It was a shrine dedicated to a powerful god."

"Which god? I'm just curious to know since we're walking down this path where this god apparently resides."

"A pagan deity. A powerful one at best."

"I would guess those ghouls and demons back there were maybe its soldiers in the woods. You know, patrolling the place. Maybe those women at the entrance were like this god's gatekeepers."

"Those hags were only there to frightened those that approached the entrance and to have them fail the puzzles of threes to diminish their self-confidence and shatter their faith. Those ghouls and demons back there, were just there. We trespassed on their territory. Death is their sweet savior. They desire it."

"They desire it?"

"Just as those of Man would beg for food when his stomach began to quake on him. Same factor to the shadow creatures when it comes to death. Death is their food and substance of which they sustain on. Without death, the demons, the ghosts, the ghouls, and whatever else lies out here in these forests within this valley, would cease to exist throughout all the Worlds."

"I take it that's why the Worlds needed men like you. You know, Warslingers."

"I would take that as a small form of a compliment. Yes, we did save many from treacherous times and malevolent forces. Though, at times there were benevolent forces that turned tragic and considered the malevolency to be more seductive than remaining in their benevolent state."

"You mean to tell me that there were some that betrayed the good of these Worlds?"

"It was one of our own. A Warslinger. Couldn't take the battle much further and saw a way out of this life. By doing so, he committed us to failure as we lost the battle and we were scattered across the Worlds in a instant. I have yet to see one of my brethren since that day."

"All because he was seduced by the malevolent force of power."

"Do not underestimate the power of the malevolency. It can even change the purest man into the deadliest man. The seduction that power possesses, it can alter any man, woman, child, beast, creature, angel, demon, possibly gods. I'm not sure on that matter. But, I have seen it with my own eyes before and I know that power continues to ruin the lives of many this day."

"Do you have any idea as to where the malevolence power source may be kept?"

"It's held at the gate to the city. The Haunted City."

"That's why you're going there isn't it. To reverse the wrongs of the past and what that power has done to the ones it has affected."

"That's not why I'm going to The Haunted City. I have my own reasons for taking this daring task. Many before tried to talk me out of it. I told them that the City itself has power of its own. A power much stronger than the malevolency and the benevolency."

"If we make it through all that we might have to face on this trail way, we'll get to see this Haunted City that you're talking about?"

"We will be there. Staring at its glorious feats. Its buildings made of materials not known of the Worlds. Created and designed by an entity not of these Worlds. That City will be the place where all the answers will be revealed to anyone who dares to enter it."

"Here's hope to reaching the City in one piece."

"I wouldn't say one piece. I would speculate, few to many pieces. A lot of men have died on this journey. I intend to survive."

"The way you are, sir, I believe you will."

Henrich nodded.

'I'll see that it happens."

While moving along, from the ground arose three ghouls, like the ones from within the first dark woods. Henrich sighed as Landon pulled out his shooter.

"There's more of them." Landon said.

"Just deal with them as you dealt with the first ones." said Henrich. "They'll be out of our way soon enough."

Landon fired shots at the ghouls while Henrich loaded up the blastshooter. After loading it, a pair of ghosts came down from the gray clouds toward them. Henrich looked up, seeing the ghosts, appearing as white and gray mists with disfigured faces. He raised the blastshooter toward the two ghosts.

"Mist Ones out here as well." said Henrich. "Amazing."

Shooting the two ghosts with the blastshooter, evaporating them from eyesight. Landon eliminated the ghouls, but he noticed more coming from the dark woods in front of their trail. Henrich also spotted several more ghosts coming down from the clouds and even a few arose up from the ground.

"Appears we've stumbled ourselves to a spirit smorgasbord."

"It appears that way, sir."

Henrich and Landon continue shooting the ghouls and ghosts while making their move toward the second dark woods. Firing shot after shot, evaporating the ghosts and eliminating the ghouls. They moved with a quicker pace toward the dark woods and as soon as they made themselves near its entrance, the remaining ghouls and ghosts had vanished into the thin air, some levitating themselves up into the clouds.

"I'll be damned." Henrich said. "They left."

"Maybe they're afraid of what could be living inside this second pair of woods."

"If that is the truth, then we have much more trouble on our hands, boy."

Henrich and Landon began slowly making their way into the second set of dark woods within the Valley of Death.

III

Entering the second set of dark woods, Henrich and Landon noticed something strange about its interior. They could smell a deep stench within the woods, the smell of decay and death. It withered throughout the woods. The trees and bushes appeared to be slowly dying and the ground was covered in waste from the animals and creatures that dwell within the woods. Landon watched his steps while walking through the woods.

"This land, its covered in filth." Landon said. "It smells like corpses."

"It smells like shit." Henrich said. "You can go ahead and say it. You know it to be true."

"Ok, it does smell like shit. But, more of a corpse stench if you ask me."

"I get where you're coming from with this. No doubt there are bodies lying beneath our feet."

"Humans or animals?"

"Both. Generations of Man have come and died here."

"I wouldn't think there would be any ghosts, ghouls, or demons in this kind of woods. No matter if it's dark."

"Only way to find out is to make it through this place. Though, I am sure that we'll run into something. Its second nature for us now."

The ground began to tremble, slightly. The horse stopped walking, Landon looked around the trees and Henrich kept his head down, moving his eyes, scouting their surroundings.

"Is this a tremor?"

"Feels like one." Henrich said. "Yet, not one of earthly origin."

"What do you mean, sir?"

"It's being caused by something beneath the ground. Its rising up slowly. Whatever it may be."

The ground started to crack, breaking apart beneath their feet. The bushes and trees rose up from the ground, their roots showing up from beneath them, flying into the air. Henrich and Landon watched on and from the holes in the ground, jumped out small creatures. They looked to be demons, but also appeared to be dwarves, elves, some looked like goblins.

"What are they?"

"Something strange. We'll have to take them out anyhow."

Henrich fired his shooters at the running creatures. Landon fired shots with him toward the small creatures that were running in packs. The packs were rabid, going in many directions in front of Henrich and Landon. Both continued to shoot at the creatures. Their small stature was somewhat a threat as a few would duck down within the horde of creatures to be unseen by Henrich and Landon.

"How many of them do you think there are?" Landon asked

"By the end of this, it won't matter." Henrich said. "So, keep your shooting going."

They continued firing the shots toward the horde of creatures. Unsure of the bullets hitting the creatures, Henrich shrugged his shoulders as he reached for his blastshooter and began blasting the horde entirely. The horde suddenly ran from them like fleeing birds, though Henrich had most of them down and dead. The horde had been killed off except for a certain few that managed to escape the blast fire of Henrich. He turned to Landon, who only looked around at the dead bodies.

"Don't have pity on them, boy. They were already dead."

They continued to walk through the woods of the Valley of Death. Noticing the light of the sun was beginning to set, Henrich and Landon made a stop by a nearby tree. The tree was a tall one, where if it were to rain, the tree would be able to block the falling water from above them, to keep them dry. The cold wind blew past them as the moon arose into the sky, revealing herself once more.

"Give it a few hours and we'll be back on our feet onto the trail." said Henrich. "You understand me?"

"I understand you, sir."

Landon laid down next to the tree, going to sleep. While Henrich took watch over the campsite, he noticed the bushes in front of him to rattle. Hesitantly reaching for his shooter, from the rattling bushes came out a dog, not an ordinary dog, but a phantom dog. The dog had black fur and its eyes were red and as bright as the moon's own light. Henrich stared at the phantom dog, not making any sudden movements. He could recognize the dog had a solid body, but its body was see-through. A white mist had surrounded the dog and smoke exited from its mouth. The dog took a series of scouting around the bushes and woods, searching and turned its head and spotted Henrich, the dog stared back at him. Growling underneath its breath. The two kept their eyes locked onto each other tightly. Henrich nodded at the dog and the dog nodded back before walking away into the woods.

"Didn't expect that." Henrich said as he laid his head down to sleep, placing his hat over his eyes.

The phantom dog had walked into the bushes, which were covered in darkness and the bushes didn't make any sound as the dog walked through them. As if the dog itself had vanished into the air while walking into the dark cloaked bushes.

IV

Awaking from their sleep, Henrich and Landon continued their journey through the woods, shoving bushes and small trees out of their way. Henrich, riding atop his horse, could sense a presence deep within the woods. While making their way, Henrich could see a structure nearby, built in the middle of the woods.

"We have something ahead of us." Henrich said. "It looks big."

"What does it look like, sir?" Landon said. "Is it something that could probably assist us in our journey?"

Henrich took a closer look as the made their approach toward the structure. The large structure was large and almost towered over the trees of the woods. The outer scale of the structure appeared to be made of a solid glass with a neon texture to it. Yet, upon Henrich and Landon fully making their approach toward the structure, they happen to find out it wasn't glass that covered the outer area of the structure, but a mineral unknown to many humans. A mineral that was once used in a great war. Henrich knows of the mineral as he glances down at his shooter.

"What is it, sir?"

"I recognize this material that covers this structure. It is an ancient mineral. I've seen it during my times with the Heptad. We learned of its origin and its desire. This structure is built for a purpose and it doesn't hold something good within. This mineral was designed to keep evil from escaping their prisons."

"So, there could be something locked within the walls of this place?"

"There is something locked within. Because this isn't some ordinary prison facility in the middle of the woods."

Henrich took his hand and wiped the wall of the structure. Looking within and happens to see a set of stairs within. Though, there is more than one set of starts. Nearly over a dozen to be exact. Henrich turned to Landon and kept his eyes locked onto him.

"This is a labyrinth, boy."

"A labyrinth? So, there's something very large that is trapped within its walls?"

"Not trapped. Imprisoned for a purpose. I have heard of the tales of what lies within a labyrinth and if those tales are in fact true, we have a bigger issue facing us."

They walked through the labyrinth, trying to find their way towards the end. While they went through the labyrinth, the ground began to rumble. Landon didn't know what to make of it, but Henrich knew what was the cause of the rumbling. As it began to increase, Henrich prepared himself with his hand to his side.

"What's going on?" Landon asked.

"It's on our path."

"Our path?"

As the rumbling increased, Henrich looked behind himself and Landon to see the cause of the rumblings. Landon turned slowly and witnessed what Henrich was looking at.

"What is that?!" Landon asked, pointing toward what they're seeing.

"It's known across the Worlds as the Minotaur." Henrich answered.

The Minotaur stood on the other end of the puzzled walls, facing Henrich and Landon. The Minotaur was tall, almost over twelve feet in height. Its physique was peaked beyond human possibilities. Smoke derived from its nostrils as it stared at Henrich and Landon with its red pupil eyes.

"What should we do?!" Landon said.

"We make a way out of this place."

Henrich and Landon made a run for it and the Minotaur roared, chasing them down. The three of them ran through the labyrinth, Henrich and Landon made it their goal to find the way out while the Minotaur sought them out for slaughter and claiming them as food. While running, Henrich looked back, seeing the Minotaur chasing them. Henrich raised up his shooter and started firing at the creature.

"Is it dead yet?!" Landon yelled.

"Not now." Henrich said.

Henrich continued to shoot at the Minotaur, but the shooter wasn't having any effect on the creature. Henrich looked around at the strange interiors on the walls and knew there was something more that had to take place between them and the creature to escape the labyrinth.

"Boy." Henrich said. "Stop running."

"What do you mean stop running?!" Landon yelled. "That thing wants to kill us both!"

Henrich stood boldly before the Minotaur. Landon couldn't understand why Henrich would tell him to stop or why Henrich even stopped running himself. Henrich approached the Minotaur and faced the creature. The Minotaur glared into Henrich's eyes before letting out a loud roar in his face, blowing his hair.

"What are you doing?"

"This labyrinth isn't like the other labyrinths I've come across in my day."

"Well, what's so different about this one?"

"Usually, in labyrinths, we would have to find our way out of here. But, this one. The Minotaur is our way out."

Landon shook his head. The information given to him by Henrich isn't sinking it fully just yet. But, Landon knows he can trust Henrich about any circumstance.

"So… how are you going to get the Minotaur to lead us out of this place?"

"Very simple."

Henrich reached to his back, raising up his blade. The Minotaur pounced around on the ground, prepared for a fight. Landon still couldn't understand what the two of them were doing. Only that they were faced off against each other in what appears to become a fight.

"If I can kill this creature, it will lead us out of this labyrinth."

"I'm not understanding how that's going to work."

"You'll see."

Henrich and the Minotaur faced off against each other in a fight. Landon stood back and watched the battle. Henrich went for several swipes of the blade, cutting the Minotaur's rough skin. The Minotaur grabbed Henrich and slammed him into the wall, later shoving him through the wall. The Minotaur prepared to ram through Henrich and the wall and Henrich knew this was his opportunity. The Minotaur roared and ran toward Henrich, the creature came closer as Henrich took his blade and jammed it into the creature's throat. The Minotaur slowed down and fell to the ground. The Minotaur is dead.

"Wait, that's it?" Landon asked.

"Yeah. It is."

"But, I thought it would take more to stop a monster like that."

'It would've. But, our circumstances don't call for it."

From the Minotaur's body arose a bluish-white fog, presumably the spirit of the Minotaur. The spirit moves across the air, going down the labyrinth. Henrich and Landon chase the spirit and as they chased the entity, it led them right toward the exit. Now on the other side of the Valley of Death. Landon shook his head.

"I guess that's how it works."

"It's not as simple as people would perceive it to be, boy.

<u>V</u>

Henrich and Landon exited the labyrinth and continued to make their way through the other side of the Valley of Death. Not knowing who or what they may come up against on the other side. Although, they could tell the air was slightly different and it wasn't as dreary as the previous side. In a sense, they could breathe comfortably on the other side of the valley.

"Aren't you getting a funny feeling?" Landon asked.

"What kind of feeling are you talking about?" Henrich said. "Are you speaking of this clean feeling on this side?"

"Yes. The air is just… fresh. Like if we're on the right path or something. I don't fully understand it all. But, I can sense that we're heading down a better path than what we went through before."

"We'll see about all of that when we get closer to the exit, boy."

"I hope we will."

They continued to move through the wilderness, knowing that

it is completely different than the previous side of the Valley. So far, they have yet to come up against any creatures before from the other side. It calmed down Landon, he feels comfortable on this side. Though, Henrich is slightly concerned. For he knew of a place such as this with this amount of silence is something to keep a guard on.

"Something's not right around here." Henrich said with a stern look.

"What do you mean? Its peaceful on this side. We haven't run into any of those shadowic creatures or some giant half-man half-bull monster. Plus, we haven't entered another one of those labyrinths. So, what's the issue, sir?"

"Something is watching us. I can feel it."

"Are you sure?'

"I am positive about it, boy." Henrich said. "Make sure your shooter is prepared for firing."

Landon took a glare down to his side, where his shooter was placed. He checked it for ammo and there was ammo. Landon felt confident that nothing would go wrong on this side of the wilderness. Yet, Henrich was certain that something was keeping an eye on them and he knew it was only a matter of time before it showed itself to them.

"We haven't seen anything yet." Landon said. "Maybe it's just the surroundings. You know, how they look slightly like the previous side."

"That's not it, boy." Henrich said. "There's something going on here."

"I'm not getting it."

"Because you're not trained up to a level to comprehend it."

The horse turned another angle, getting both Henrich and Landon's attention. The horse could sense something was lurking in the trees.

"What's wrong with your horse?"

"Nothing's wrong. He's sensing what I'm sensing."

"Which is?"

From the nearby trees, fell long, thick branches. They moved with slow pace and from atop the branches are two women, they are naked. But, they're glowing a neon blue and their hair is glowing white as snow. Henrich looked at the women and he knew what they were. Landon was unsure as to what the women could be.

"The hell is going on?" Henrich said.

"I was about to ask you, they look like women. But, women I've never seen before. Ever."

"We are glad to see two men in our area." One of the women said. "For it has been a very long time since we've seen a man."

"Enough of this talk. I know what you are." Henrich said. "Tell me how two succubi found their way inside the Valley of Death?"

"You don't know do you?" The other succubus said with her soft voice.

"What should I know?"

"You should know that not all things are easy to understand. We've been within these trees for centuries. Looking for any man that would give us what we desire."

"Desire?" Landon asked curiously. "Like what?"

"We cannot feed off each other for the rest of the days ahead. We need others to give us the energy we seek."

"I'm not understand what they're talking about. Henrich, sir, if you may, please tell me what they're going on about?"

"They want us to have intercourse with them."

"Pardon me for a moment. You just said intercourse."

"You heard me, boy." Henrich said, looking at Landon. "They feed off sexual energy. You should've done more homework on other things that live in the Worlds rather than just the Warslingers."

"If you want to pass through this section of the wilderness, you must come into us and give us the desire that we seek."

"This stuff is crazy." Landon said. "Just crazy."

"Give me a minute here, boy." Henrich said. "Let me think on this."

The two succubi were awaiting their answers. Henrich knew the women were pleasant to look upon and their glow only enhanced their beauty and their sexual attraction. Landon was attracted to them, but was unsure of going through with the procedure.

"So, what will it be, men? Will you go into us and give us the energy we seek to desire?"

Landon shook his head. No answer could come from his mouth. For if he were to agree, he wouldn't know what to do during the procedure. For if he were to disagree, he feared what the power of the succubus could do to him. Immediately as Landon was about to speak, Henrich shut him down and faced the two women.

"I'll do it. Both of you."

"Have you lost your mind, sir?" Landon asked loudly. "How can you do two of them at the same time?"

"I didn't say at the same time, boy."

"Do you women agree to my answer?"

"We certainly do."

The two women grabbed a hold of Henrich's arms and brought him into their tree. Landon stood next to the horse and waited until Henrich came out of the tree. Landon shook his head and seen the horse doing the same. Landon nodded.

"I see you agree with what I had asked."

In the tree, Henrich went in unto the first succubus and she drained as much of his sexual energy as she could. After Henrich was finished with her, he went into the second succubus and she received a portion of his energy. Henrich continued to pleasure the two succubi as Landon waited for him. Henrich slightly enjoyed them and continued to please them even more, until Landon could hear their screams coming from the tree.

"The hell is going on in there!" Landon said.

Some few minutes after, Henrich was finished with the succubus and they were filled with energy as they began to kiss and suck on each other. Henrich looked at them and seen their actions.

The succubus turned to him with a smile on their faces.

"We have to thank you for this energy. It gives us the strength to pleasure each other even more than we hoped to imagine."

Henrich smirked for a moment, he was about to tell the succubus something. Something that they weren't even aware of during the intercourses.

"The intercourses had their good shares. But, did the two of you know what would become of you both after I laid with you?"

"What do you mean?"

"What are you getting at, Man?"

"You are now my wives and now I must give you a bill of divorcement. In a different way."

Henrich pulled out his shooters and fired them into the heads of the succubus. Killing them both as their bodies fell atop each other. Their glow disappeared and the blood from their heads created a small pond for their bodies to lie in. Henrich nodded and returned to the ground. Landon looked ahead and seen Henrich approaching. Henrich came down from the tree and Landon looked back at the tree for the succubus.

"What happened to the women? I heard you guys screaming, then later I heard gunshots."

"We can move past this area, boy." Henrich said. "So, let's keep moving."

Henrich continued moving forward. Landon nodded and followed Henrich along through the remainder of the wilderness.

<u>VI</u>

"So, what really happened with those women back there?"

"I did what I had to do for us to continue further through this place."

"Did you really have intercourse with them? With both?"

Henrich sighed as he turned to face Landon. He knew the young man was curious about what had just happened. Henrich believed the boy to not have the understanding as of all that took place. He could see the innocence in Landon's eyes. Henrich's age and his experience was known throughout the research of Landon's study. But, Landon didn't know all there is to know about Henrich.

"All that you need to know is that I handled the matter."

"But, that's not really an answer, sir."

"If I were to give you all the details, you might think twice when you see a woman that you may desire."

"But, I'm not understanding, sir."

"Someday you will understand what I'm telling you and you will thank yourself for hearing it clearly."

"I guess I will."

Henrich and Landon continued moving through the Valley of Death. On their walk, they catch the jittering sounds of something running through the wilderness nearby. Both of whom are intrigued by the footsteps that are echoing throughout the valley. Henrich is unsure as to who or what it could be, though Landon is not as fearful of the footstep as he would believe himself to be.

"You think someone else is in here with us, maybe?" Landon asked.

"Could be the case. Although, I prefer that we be cautious about it."

Moving on through the valley, slowing listening to the footsteps, a young woman appeared before them, running into Henrich. She fell to the ground and slowly raised up her head, seeing Henrich and Landon. Both were unfamiliar with the young woman, as she was dressed in clothing that didn't fit in the Worlds that the two of them have come to know. The young woman moved her long blonde hair from her face as she stared at them. Henrich could sense that she didn't know why she was in the wilderness.

"Who are you?" Henrich asked. "Why are you roaming on about in these woods?"

"My name is Beth Grasslands and I don't know exactly how I

got here."

"Then, where did you come from?" Landon asked.

"I'm from Washington D.C."

Henrich's expression seemed unusual, for himself and for Landon. Landon was even confused by Beth's answer as he and Henrich knew something about D.C. that Beth wasn't known to. She continued looking around the wilderness, standing still somewhat, gazing at Henrich and Landon. Seeing them carrying weapons and dressed in strange apparel.

"What do you mean Washington D.C.?" Landon asked. "I don't understand what you mean by that."

"That's where I'm from. I live in D.C."

"That cannot be possible, young lady." Henrich said. "Not to my understanding."

"Well, what do you mean by that?"

"Because Washington D.C. doesn't exist anymore. It was destroyed in a nuclear attack by enemies during the War of the West."

"Destroyed? War of the West? I'm not understanding what you're telling me. I was just in D.C. a few seconds ago."

"How so?" Landon asked. "Could you give us some details as to where you were last located?"

"I was in the middle of a paranormal investigation with my teammates and I took a turn down a corridor and suddenly I ended up here. In this forest. I've been looking for a way out ever since and that's when I ran into the two of you."

"Paranormal investigation?" Landon said confusingly. "What is that?"

"That's when you hunt spirits of the dead." Henrich said. "I've heard of such practices before in my youth."

Beth shook her head, trying to take in the information told by Henrich. She believed that she was dreaming, but everything around her was just too real. She later thought it was all a hallucination, though the surroundings are confirming it to be one. She decided to get as much information as she possibly could to find her way back home.

"Who are you two?"

"Well, my name is Cody Landon and this is-"

"Randolph Henrich."

"He's a Warslinger."

"What is a Warslinger?" Beth asked, looking at Landon strangely.

Beth twisted her face at Landon. She didn't know what a Warslinger was. It took Landon a few seconds to realize that for himself. Henrich could tell Beth was not from their World or any of the Worlds they're familiar with. Henrich knew he had to explain as much detail as he could to Beth, otherwise she would just go crazy within the wilderness.

"A Warslinger is one of a knightly group. I am a Warslinger of the Heptad. One of the Seven."

"So, where are the other six members of this 'Heptad'?"

"They're scattered abroad. I have yet to encounter any of them for some time now. Though, we will all meet each other again."

"If I may ask you both, where are you headed?"

"We're heading towards the exit of this place." Henrich said.

"Yeah. We're going to find The Haunted City."

"The what now?"

"The-," Landon said. "Never mind me."

"If you don't mind, you should come along with us. Until you find your way back home."

"I was going to ask that, but since you've already invited me. I will take it."

"That is good to hear. Because I fear for you of what you may not know of this World or the other Worlds."

"What do you mean by other Worlds?"

"You'll soon find that out."

<u>VII</u>

After Beth decided to tag along with Henrich and Landon through the wilderness of the Valley of Death, they seemed to come upon a set of trees, though these trees are peculiar to the rest. They are bulkier and are covered in much greener. They appear to be built up of more grass than bark. Henrich approached one of the trees and placed his hand upon it. Feeling it.

"What's going on?" Beth asked.

"I don't know. He's checking the tree apparently." Landon said. "They do look strange."

"I've never seen trees like this before.

"That's why I suggested you travel with us. You almost came into this area on your own."

Henrich rubbed the tree and could feel the grass and could also feel something flowing through the trees. Like a streaming river. Henrich couldn't see any water, but he could see a greenish milky substance buried within the grass covered areas. A low-pitched moan had sounded from the tree.

"These trees aren't trees."

The tree began to burst and move. Arms grew from its sides and legs grew out from beneath. Henrich stepped back as the tree increased in height and a face was slowly forming from the spot where Henrich had previously placed his hand. The arms were made of what appeared to be strong grass mixed with bark as did its legs appear the same.

"What is that?" Beth asked with fear.

"A walking tree?" Landon said.

"No. it's a Green Man. One of many in this area."

From the Green Man's face grew out a beard, made of the grass. The remainder of its body was surrounded and covered in a composition of foliage, oak leaves, and small branches that were twisted up in the Green Man's grassy hair.

"Why have you trespassed this place?" The Green Man asked. Authority spoken through his deep-pitched voice. "Why have you come into this place uninvited?"

"We come to leave this place." Henrich said. "We are only on our way out of here. That is all."

"You come to escape, yet you entered into its doors. How wise are you to believe your own words? Your words speak of escape, but I sense an entry you have done."

"We just want to leave." Landon said hesitantly. "That's all we ask of you, tree-man."

Beth measured the Green Man. She was astounded, though with a sense of fear that had slowly grabbed her. Henrich looked at her for a moment and could see she was intrigued by the Green Man and how Landon had feared for his life as he tried to stand as far back from the Green Man as he could.

"How can a tree move around and talk?" Beth wondered. "What kind of forest is this?"

"One of another World." Henrich said. "There are other places just as strange to you that you have not seen."

"Tell me your names." The Green Man commanded. "First and last."

"Cody Landon, good tree-man, sir."

"Beth Grasslands."

"Randolph Henrich."

The Green Man paused and looked closer at Henrich. The name struck him, and it struck him strongly. The Green Man could recognize Henrich's attire and he could also see the shooters on his sides.

"You're one of them."

"I didn't know that your kind knew about Warslingers."

"For a time, we did. But, that was ages ago when you and your brethren walked this World together as a unit. Before the fall. Before the separation."

"So, that's it?" Landon asked. "We can get pass now since you know of the Warslingers?"

"I will allow you to pass. For you show no signs of evil."

"We appreciate it." Beth said.

"But, I must warn you. When you reach near the exit of this valley, you must watch out for the nature and shadowic creatures and scavenge these portions of the valley and you must also watch your surroundings for The Mercenary Man and his fire shots that fly across the skies and zoom through the air."

"The Mercenary Man?" Henrich said. "He came through here?"

"Very recently, he did. From what I could sense from his presence, he is waiting for you."

Henrich nodded. "It was an honor to speak to you, Green Man."

"More of an honor to converse with a Warslinger of the Heptad."

The Green Man moved aside and allowed them to continue further in the wilderness. He gave them the warnings that they would need to escape the valley in one piece.

<u>VIII</u>

Walking on through the wilderness, Henrich gazed up into the air, looking toward the sky through the surrounding trees and he could tell that the sun was about to set. He thought to himself that if he kept moving continually, he would be out of the Valley of Death and closer to finding The Haunted City. The more they walked and the less disturbances that came to them, Henrich was slightly relieved, but concerned. Since there could be something following them and could attack them at any moment. He kept in his mind what the Green Man had told him. To watch out for the fire shots of The Mercenary Man and the Scavengers that are abroad.

"How far do we have before we reach the exit?" Landon asked.

"Not that far. We have just a little bit more moving to do."

"So, what's on the other side of this forest?" Beth asked. "Is there a town of some kind. Like a rest stop?"

"Truthfully, I do not know what lies on the other side of this

wilderness. I only know that the trail we are on leads to The
Haunted City. Which is my primary mission."

"The Haunted City?"

"It is a place unlike any other place in the Worlds. For the City
has the power to grant anything of Man's desires. Only if he sees fit
to use them in their proper order according to the rules of the
Worlds."

"So, what are you seeking there?"

"Truth. Some seek immortality, others seek wealth and fame.
But I, I seek truth."

While they walked, Landon noticed something glowing on the
ground in front of their path. He took a closer look and seen a dark
rugged pot. It sat in the middle of the trail as if it was placed there,
but left alone for some period. The pot was almost like a vase, but
smaller and within the pot was gold. A collection of gold coins. The
coins' glow had mesmerized Landon. Henrich and Beth seen
Landon's attraction to the gold.

"What are you up to, boy?"

"It's gold, sir." Landon said with a stutter in his voice. He was
drawn to the gold like an insect to a blinding light.

"Best you leave it be." Beth said. "Were not sure who left it
there. Maybe they're on their way back to retrieve it."

"How could they be? You don't just leave a pot of gold lying
around in the middle of a forest. That's idiocy."

Landon kneeled in front of the pot and raised his hand,
reaching toward the gold. Henrich's horse began to act uneasy as it
started to kick its legs around. Henrich looked over to Landon and
immediately could tell that something wasn't right with the pot of
gold.

"Boy, move!" Henrich yelled.

From two of the trees that stood on the sides of the pot, came
down a large net and from underneath the dirt of the trail rose up a
large net. The two nets intertwined with each other grabbed

Landon and Henrich ran toward him. While Henrich ran, Beth attempted to help him, but the net also snatched them and raised them up into the air, where they sat. Henrich's horse had ran off due to the snapping sound of the falling and rising nets.

"What is your damn problem!" Henrich yelled.

"I… I didn't know that it was all a trap."

"You didn't think to wonder about that before you tried to touch the gold."

"So, what set up the trap?" Beth asked.

From one of the small bushes arose a man, short in stature, appears almost like dwarf, but dressed in green with golden buckles on his shoes and wearing a high-crowned hat. The man laughed at them, looking up to them from the ground. The man stood next to the pot of gold and took the pot, placing it underneath one of the bushes nearby.

"The hell is that?" Landon said.

"He's a leprechaun, boy." Henrich said. "Nothing to be afraid of."

"Leprechauns are real?" Beth asked. "I thought them to be only folklore story figures."

"In these Worlds, your folklore figures are real as the air you breathe."

The Leprechaun continued to laugh and giggle from the ground.

"It appears that one of you managed to steal my gold." The Leprechaun said. "Now, which of you was it?"

Landon looked at Henrich and Beth. He pointed to himself and pointed to the Leprechaun. Henrich and Beth only stared at him as they know it was his fault for their current situation.

"Do I really have to tell him."

"Tell him, boy. Or else you'll have to deal with much worse."

Landon shivered as he gazed down at the Leprechaun. The Leprechaun waived his hand to Landon, who also waived back.

"Um, good Leprechaun sir." Landon said. "It was me. I tried to steal your pot of gold."

"And could you tell me why?"

"Because it was just sitting there. Alone on the trail. It was bound to be taken by someone."

"How do you know that? How would you know that?"

"I don't know the answers."

"Yet, you continue to speak to me. Thief is what you are."

"Leprechaun." Henrich said. "Would you care to release us from this trap of yours?"

"Why would I do that? You look fine from down here."

"I beg to differ. For I do not appear to be fine up here, and I would rather like to be back on the ground."

The Leprechaun laughed again. From his side, he pulled out a staff. The Leprechaun reached up and waved the staff in the air beneath them and from them came falling down their weapons. Their weapons fell through the nets as if they were liquid, but yet they were still solid. Henrich was upset even more so, now that his weapons were in the hands of the Leprechaun.

"You little runt." Henrich said. "Let us go."

"I'm afraid I cannot do that just yet, good man. For there is much more for the three of you to do."

"What are we going to do?" Landon said.

"Do either of you have a knife on you?" Beth asked.

"I believe I do." Henrich said, slowly reaching into his boot for the small knife.

The Leprechaun danced around on the ground, coveting their weapons and rubbing them against his face. The sight disgusted Henrich. Landon was still afraid, and Beth was unsure as to what World she has now found herself living in.

"We want our weapons back you know." Landon said. "What do we have to do to get them?"

"What you must do is simple, my good boy. You must capture me in the maze of the bushes. When you do that, you will have your weapons back and you may continue on further out of this forest."

The Leprechaun picked up their weapons and tossed them into

the maze of bushes, where they would be difficult to find without the Leprechaun's assistance. Seeing that site enraged Henrich a tad bit. He wasn't interested in playing some game with a leprechaun.

"How would we find you when we're still stuck up here?" Henrich said. "Isn't it unfair."

"Isn't everything unfair."

Henrich pulled out his knife and started cutting through the net. The Leprechaun noticed and started to have a panic attack. Pacing back and forth on the ground beneath them.

"No. No. No." The Leprechaun said angrily. "You're cheating!"

"Not exactly." Landon said.

"You're making a mockery of my game!"

Henrich cut through the net and the tree of them fell to the ground. The Leprechaun started backing up as Henrich looked toward him. The Leprechaun ran for his life into the bushes and Henrich followed him. Landon helped Beth up off the ground and she admonished him for doing so.

"Are you alright?" Landon asked.

"I'm fine."

Beth looked around for Henrich and the Leprechaun, but didn't see them as she turned to Landon, seeing on the two of them in the location.

"Where did Henrich go?" Beth asked.

"He went after the Leprechaun."

"Well, shouldn't we be following them."

Beth walked off, following the sounds of the Leprechaun's screaming and Henrich's yelling. Landon followed her as she followed the sounds. Henrich looked around the bushes for the Leprechaun, but couldn't find him. Henrich stared kicking the bushes to see if the Leprechaun could be hiding within them. His anger was slowly kindling, but his focus was still on his mission.

"You're wasting our time, dwarf." Henrich said. "Show yourself and give me my weapons back."

"I don't think so." The Leprechaun said from afar off. "It's not fair for the game."

"I don't give a damn about our mystery game. Give me back what belongs to me."

"Just rude you are."

"Don't play around with me any further. For your own good and for the sake of your own life."

Henrich continued moving and found himself standing in front of six small bushes. All covered with leaves and entangled with branches underneath. Henrich looked around the area and could see the Leprechauns footprints in the dirt, which disappear at the six bushes.

"If this is how you want to play your game." Henrich said, pulling out a small shooter from his back. "Then, this is how I'll play along."

Henrich fired a shot at the first bush. The shot rattled through the air and caused fear to consume the Leprechaun. In the distance behind Henrich, Landon and Beth heard the shot and they ran toward the area. Henrich fired a second shot at the second bush. Yet, no sign of the Leprechaun, though, Henrich knew he was there. Somewhere.

"You're about to exit this life if you don't show yourself." Henrich said. "I know you're in there."

Henrich fired a third shot at the third bush. Within the bushes, the Leprechaun rattled and Henrich could see the bushes rattling. The Leprechaun panted for his breath. Fear had indeed consumed him.

"Come out of there."

In the bushes, the Leprechaun looked at the weapons and closely noticed one of the shooters. He recognized it and knew it belonged to a Warslinger. The Leprechaun thought for a moment and a fourth shot fired through the fourth bush, grazing the Leprechaun's hat. Henrich fired a fifth shot at the fifth bush, where the bullet flew past the Leprechaun's chest. The Leprechaun came to the realization that Henrich was indeed a Warslinger.

Henrich aimed closely at the sixth bush, where the Leprechaun was hiding. He focused the shooter onto the bush. The shooter was ready to fire. Landon and Beth came from behind Henrich and stood by him.

"This is the last warning." Henrich said. "Come out of there or die in there. Your choice."

The Leprechaun bolted out of the sixth bush with his hands up in the air. Henrich knew that the fear has taken over him. The Leprechaun had given up and waved his hands in the air, while dropping his staff.

"Alright, alright!' The Leprechaun said. "You win the game."

"Now, give us our weapons."

The Leprechaun picked up his staff and waved it around the bushes and from out of the bushes arose their weapons. Henrich grabbed his shooters and machete. Landon also retrieved his shooter. The Leprechaun walked over to Henrich slowly.

"You're one of them."

"I am."

The Leprechaun nodded. A smile appeared on his face.

"All going well."

"What's going well?" Landon said. "What do you mean by that?"

The Leprechaun walked away from the area, allowing them to continue further. The Leprechaun stopped and turned to Henrich only. He winked at Henrich.

"In time, you'll learn why these matters are happening. In time."

The Leprechaun vanished into the air with a puff of smoke. Henrich's horse had also made its return and Henrich was relieved at the sight of it. Landon still wanted to know what the Leprechaun had meant with his words, Beth was in questioning of all she has recently seen.

"What did he mean by that, sir?" Landon asked.

"Guess we'll find out once we're out of this place."

IX

Almost nearing the exit of the Valley of Death, Henrich, Landon, and Beth grow tired from the walking that they have done and the chasing they've done after the Leprechaun and now it is almost sunset, and they have yet to reach the exit. Henrich kept his eyes on the sun, seeing its preparation to set. The wind blew across them and Henrich could sense the energy of the moon slowly rising in the horizon. He knew full well that they could not continue moving through the wilderness during the night, for they would be sure to get lost and perhaps lose their minds. It's an effect of the wilderness. The shadows of it can do harmful things to the minds of Man.

Walking still, from the trees come down three fairies. The fairies appeared out of nowhere and were almost a light to their path in the forest. The fairies' bodies glow a golden hue along with a bluish touch to them. Their wings were silver and glittered through the light. Their light even touched the trees and gave them light within the wilderness. Henrich was somewhat uneasy seeing the fairies as they appeared from out of nowhere.

"Why are you three walking about in the wilderness?" One fairy said. "Don't you see the sun is preparing to set and the moon is preparing to rise."

"We can see that, fairy." Henrich said. "Why have you appeared before us? Does it concern more troubles that we may find in this valley?"

"No troubles you will receive from us, sir." The Second Fairy said. "We are only the light of the wilderness. Here to give to you a pathway toward the exit."

"How far is the exit?" Landon asked. "If I may wonder."

"The exit is not far. If you continue on foot for a matter of an hour, you will come to the exit. But, the night is almost here, and it is not good for those such as yourself to walk through this forest during the night."

"The darkness lurks at night." The first Fairy said. "It consumes those who move around in its dwelling place. It doesn't take it nicely."

"So, how are you three moving on around?" Beth asked. "How can you move through the darkness during the night?"

"We are made of light. Light that is rarely seen in these parts. But, there is something much more going on here."

"Like what?"

The first Fairy flew toward Beth. The fairy measured her from the head to the feet. The fairy glared into Beth's eyes and could instantly see where she was from and where she would be going. As if the Fairy herself possessed psychic abilities to tell he past and future of a person's life. Though, this Fairy possessed a power as such, but maybe more than expected. Beth stayed calm and still as the Fairy measured her. Henrich knew what the Fairy was doing and as for Landon, he couldn't think of anything that would make sense about the Fairy's actions.

"Why is she doing that to her, sir?" Landon asked.

"She's searching her spirit."

"How so?"

"Some fairies possess that kind of power. Others don't."

The Fairy backed away from Beth and seen the sadness in her heart. The sadness of her previous life was being buried within her spirit. The Fairy nodded to Beth with compassion in her own heart.

"I know you missed them and they miss you as well."

"I know." Beth said, tearing up a bit.

"There may be a way for you to return to your home world. But, it may come with a price."

"What are you talking about, fairy?" Henrich asked. "How can she return back to her world?"

"She will have to travel to The Haunted City. There, she can return to her home world safely and without harm."

Beth turned to Henrich and he looked at her. He thought to himself the possibilities that The Haunted City might give to her and to himself. It is his mission to reach the City, but what he may have to face between now and then is something of mystery not only to Landon and Beth, but to himself. He looked at the Fairies and could sense that they knew who he was and that he was heading to The Haunted City himself. Their energies are strange to Henrich as he's never seen Fairies such as these in his lifetime across any of the Worlds.

"We will not hold the three of you up any longer." The first Fairy said. "You may pass. But, I will suggest that you make your rest here for the night and in the morning of dawn, you may reach the exit."

Henrich nodded. "That we will do."

Henrich and Landon walked away from the Fairies. Beth followed them, but she turned back to the Fairy that spoke to her and the Fairy could see that she was saddened by the truth of her spirit, but also intrigued about going to The Haunted City to return to her own world. The Fairy nodded with a smile and waved to her.

"Go." The Fairy said. "Go with him and you will find your way back home."

"Thank you." Beth said.

"Go." The Fairy replied.

Beth caught up with Henrich and Landon as they walked near the exit. In the distance, Henrich could see the exit of the valley. The sun's light shined on the grounds and in an instant, the sun's light started to dim. The air slowly became cool. Henrich looked up past the trees and could see the shifting in the air between the sun and the moon.

"We make rest here for the night."

The three of them made their stop at the particular spot within the wilderness, a few feet from the exit and as they made their rest, the sky was darkened, and the sun was gone. Only the moon and the stars covered the sky and shined their light onto the ground. The moon's light was bright, but it wasn't bright enough to enter completely into the wilderness. Henrich looked over to Landon and

Beth and they were both asleep. As was the horse. Henrich laid back against a tree and fell asleep.

In the dream Henrich had, was of a distant memory of times past. A time where the Warslingers of the Heptad roamed the Worlds and the Worlds knew them to exist among them. In the dream of Henrich, The Warslingers were facing off against a foe that appeared to hold magic in their hands. The battle amongst them took place at a castle. A castle that belonged to one of the Warslingers. Within the castle walls, Henrich fired at the foe with his shooters. Though, the foe was powerful enough to turn the bullets into dust.

"He's too strong." Henrich said to the other Warslingers.

"How can he be." said Warslinger, Joshua of Ephraim. "We can take down this mage."

While facing the mage, the castle walls begun to quake and Henrich knew something was wrong. The entire kingdom was being overthrown by a power much greater than the mage. The Warslingers made a run for it, knowing they couldn't stay at the castle, for it was being destroyed and crumbling from within. As the Warslingers run into the nearby woods, one of the Warslinger, Knight Arthur Pendragon turned back and looked at the castle, which was his and the kingdom which also belonged to him. By the castle doors, he could see a woman, a pale woman, dressed in black and violet, cheering on with soldiers of her own. Arthur knew the woman and he knew her too well. Henrich approached Arthur, seeing him spiritually destroyed as he kingdom was taken from him.

"We have to go, brother." Henrich said. "We can return another day to face them."

"But, my kingdom." Knight Arthur said. "My home. It's gone."

"You will reclaim it. In time."

Arthur turned to Henrich and nodded. He followed him and the other Warslingers into the wilderness, away from the pale woman's soldiers as she became the new ruler of the kingdom. The Queen of the Castle she became.

X

The sun arises in the morning and through it Henrich awakened. He prepared himself and the horse for the exit of the forest. Landon and Beth also awoke and prepared themselves. Landon approached Henrich and looked over, seeing the exit in front of them, just a few feet away.

"We're almost out of this place." Landon said. "I'm sort of thrilled about it."

"I can understand your energy." Henrich said. "Though, it is best that we be cautious as to what sits on the other side of that exit."

They gathered their gear and left for the exit. As they came closer to the exit of the wilderness, the sun's light grew brighter in front of them. Signaling a change was to come once they exited the forest.

After moving on and coming closer to the exit, the sun's light touched them individually and through that they made their exit out of the Valley of Death and its wilderness. The three of them were relieved of finally being out of the long forest. Landon was ecstatic, and Beth was calm. Henrich looked around and could see plains of green grass and rugged mountains all around. The sky was clear as the sun shined from it. In the distance, he could see what appeared to be a town of some kind. Unsure of it, he thinks about going there to see if he can gather more equipment and food.

"What do we do now?" Landon asked.

"We make way for that town up ahead." Henrich said. "It appears to be one."

Henrich turned and noticed Beth looking around at the plains and the mountains. She was in awe of its beauty and she's never seen a place like it before. She looked at Henrich as she pointed around the plains and the mountains. He knew she had never seen anything like it nor experience such a place before.

"Best you take in as much as you can." Henrich said.

"It's beautiful. I've never been in a place like this. I've never seen a place like this before."

"Don't they have plains and mountains in your world?" Landon asked.

"They do. But, not like these. These are strangely different and more colorful than the ones back on my world."

Henrich showed a faint smile to Beth. Seeing her come to grips with the World she finds herself living in. From the sky sounded a cawing sound. Henrich looked up and a bird flew past their heads. Only this bird appeared differently as it looked like a vulture, but had three legs instead of two. Henrich knows about birds of that nature and their presence isn't something to be glad over. The three-legged bird's appearance signaled trouble. A dark trouble.

From the exit of the forest appeared a silhouette of a man. He spoke clearly as Henrich turned to face him. Landon and Beth also seen the man. He was tall, almost to the height of Henrich. He was lean, but physically fit. He wore what seemed to be armor, torn and cracked armor, made of some clad material, possibly from the rocks of the mountains, though they were painted black. His eyes were a pale blue and his facial hair proved him to be at a certain age. The man applauded with he set his sights on Henrich.

"This is beautiful." The man said. "I knew you would make it out of there."

"Who are you?" Henrich asked.

"You mean you don't recognize my apparel? I think you should."

Henrich looked at the man's apparel and the Man laughed at him. Henrich's mind raced as to who could wear that type of apparel. Many faces came to his mind, but neither of them fit. He later thought of what was written on the scroll and what the Green

Man had warned him about. Henrich raised up his shooter to the Man. He now knows who he is.

"You're him." Henrich said. "You're the Mercenary Man."

"Guilty."

"Wait, this is The Mercenary Man?" Landon said. "He's the guy?"

"Yeah, young man. I am that guy. But, I'm not here for you or that beautiful young woman there. I'm here for this guy and he knows why."

"So, the scroll. What was written on it was true. A bounty was placed on my head. For your Tubal King."

"You need to speak better when mentioning his name, Warslinger. The Tubal King knows who you are and has been watching you ever since you came into this life. He knows your strengths and your weaknesses. He knows the location of your brethren and their current actions."

"Can't be possible. How can one man have his eyes over all the Worlds and over everyone?"

"Because the Tubal King isn't a man. He isn't made of the same flesh and blood that you and I are made of. The Tubal King is different. He is an entity. Born in the times of the Ancients. He gained his power through deception and evil. Through that he was able to conquer The Haunted City, where he now rules over and once he enters the City, he will acquire the power to have full dominion over all the Worlds. The ones that we know and the ones that we don't know."

Henrich kept his shooter aimed at The Mercenary Man. Who only laughed at him continually. Landon and Beth were uncomfortable in his sights as he would gaze at them sinisterly and would wink at Beth, gawking at her at times and making mentions toward her breasts and legs.

"All I will tell you and all that you should know is I will kill you." Henrich said. "And after I kill you, I will reach The Haunted City and I will kill this Tubal King of yours."

The Mercenary Man clapped his hands and scoffed at

Henrich's words. He knew that Henrich had no comprehension nor understanding of The Tubal King's power. But, The Mercenary Man took Henrich's words closely, as he knows he would make the attempt to turn them into reality.

"Well then. You have your chance to kill me now, Warslinger." The Mercenary Man said scoffing. "Do it and you can reach the City and try your best to kill The Tubal King."

Henrich fired the shooter at The Mercenary Man. But, he dodged the shot and took off running. Henrich ran after him in anger while Landon and Beth made their attempt to catch up with the two men. The Mercenary Man ran into the plains, where he continued to laugh at Henrich. Henrich followed him and took another shot, this time shooting him in his right leg. The Mercenary Man fell to the ground as Henrich approached him. The Mercenary Man did not move. Not even a flinch.

"The hell is this?" Henrich said, looking at The Mercenary Man's body.

Henrich kneeled and turned his body around, face up and what Henrich saw he couldn't believe. The Mercenary Man has completely transformed into another person. When Henrich looked the Man in the face, his eyes opened, they were not human. The Man's eyes were black, and his pupils were a dark red. The Man stared to laugh as Henrich stepped back from him. The Man arose from the ground and stood face to face with Henrich. Landon and Beth stayed far back from them, seeing that The Mercenary Man has transformed into someone else. The Man appeared ageless, yet old as he was no longer dressed in the same apparel, only this time he wore a black and red cloak, with a hood that covered his head and his hands were glowing with a powerful that only fit those of evil.

"Who are you?" Henrich asked.

"I am the Malevolency Embodied." The Man said. "I am all that is evil in the Worlds. I am a force to be reckoned with."

"Give me a name."

"The Ancients knew me as the Antichrist, but you may get to

know me by the name of Judas Arkdragon."

"So, you're the Mercenary Man?"

"I'm just a pawn for The Tubal King. I am here to tell you that he knows your intentions and he's not pleased with them. He wants you to cease your mission and return to your home."

"I have no home and I will not cease because of his words."

"That is fair. Anyhow, in time, I will be seeing you, your brethren, and your partners again very soon."

Henrich fired another shot, but the shot flew through Judas' body as he evaporated into a thick blanket of smoke and disappeared. Landon and Beth approached Henrich, confused as to what they've just seen. Henrich looked around and instantly, from some source, he could recognize their current location. He walked about, looking around at the plains and mountains once more and looked out further toward what appeared to be the small town. Landon approached him, trying to stop Henrich from walking constantly about.

"Sir, what's going on?"

"Things have changed for the us, boy. Things have changed."

"What do you mean by that?" Beth asked. "What has changed for us?"

Henrich looked around and focused his attention on Landon and Beth. He knew what to tell them, only if they could take it in. He looked back around the surroundings and he knew where they were. Somewhere unpleasant.

"This place. I know it now. It is trouble."

"What is this place?'

"The Land of the Survivors. Where those who scavenge survive and those who do not perish."

Henrich looked out toward the small town. He now knew it was filled with Scavengers. It is a place that many seek not to enter. A place that is deemed for only those of the strong to truly survive. Henrich's knowledge of the location came from something, but he isn't sure where it came from. Only that it appeared in his mind and now he must use it to move on further in his mission. He turned to Landon and Beth as his horse stayed to his side.

"So, what should we do before we enter that town?" Landon asked.

"Be careful and keep to yourself." Henrich said. "Unless you want to be taken capture by the Scavengers."

"Before we enter, who are these Scavengers?" asked Beth. "I'm just wandering."

"They are a group of uncaring generations of Man. They seek what they want, and they take it from anyone who possesses it. They are dangerous people and they do not care for the young, the old, the widow, or the stranger. They only want what they desire and will do anything to get it."

"So, what will they take from us if they could?"

"Just as much as anything they want. From our weapons to ourselves for their own use and for their own pleasure. I will say that you must guard yourself while we're here. Don't make any kind of mistakes or signs of mistakes, for they will notice, and they will not hesitate to approach you."

Landon nodded. "I understand, sir. I understand."

"I understand as well." Beth said. "I will make sure to keep cautious."

Henrich nodded. He could see they were serious, but, they were afraid. Afraid of what could happen once they reach the town. Henrich looked out and he stared at the town.

"Watch yourselves. The Scavengers are abroad."

CHAPTER FOUR

SCAVENGERS ABOUND

I

Looking ahead toward the small town and knowing the location of which they stand in, Henrich prepared his mind as he, Landon, and Beth began to move toward the small town. For within that small town may very well be people of a good countenance and of a good heart. But, most of them around the area are known as the Scavengers and are not to be taken as a light-hearted gesture of words. While coming toward the small town, the face of Judas Arkdragon was seared into Henrich's mind. He tried to remember any memories that could give him some past insight on the mystical strander, but there was nothing in his mind that matched the strange energy and malevolency that was embodied in Arkdragon.

"What is our main goal in this area, sir?" Landon asked.

"We get the supplies we need, and we keep moving forward." Henrich said. "We will not stop until we've reached The Haunted City. Until then, we must guard ourselves and stand firm in the face of adversity. And a lot of adversity we are going to surely face."

Nearing the small town, the sounds of people echoed out of the town. Some of conversation and some laughter. It sounded like a place where people were good to one another. A possible place where those of evil may not dwell. Henrich tried to keep an open mind concerning the sounds he was hearing from the town, but, knew in his spirit that there was something more going on than what was seen with the naked eye.

"Those people in the town." Beth said. "It sounds as if they're not in any harm whatsoever."

"The sounds can be of deceit, young lady." Henrich said. "Although, I do have a hope that we come across some people of a good heart and mind."

They walked into the small town and there are people walking about its pathways. The people are dressed in what appeared to be casual clothing, but mostly dirty and torn in places. The people themselves appeared to be those of a quiet nature and a good heart. Henrich knew that appearances are deceiving as he continued to walk through the town's pathways as he looked ahead and seen a convenience store. Landon waved to the people with a smile on his face. Beth only nodded to them, keeping herself guarded from their possible actions. Whether their actions become verbal or physical.

"We make our way toward the store." Henrich said. "Grab some supplies and we keep moving."

"Gotcha."

"I understand." Beth said. "So, what kind of supplies will we be getting?"

"Food, water, and perhaps other things that will suit our needs of the journey ahead."

"Like ammo, right?" Landon asked. "I'm sure after all the shootouts that we've been through over these past moments, we certainty need more ammo for our shooters. I know I do."

"If we find some ammo, boy, we'll get the ammo."

"Good. Good. Because I'm sure with all of what's going on with the Mercenary Man turning into some strange man and possibly dealing with these Scavengers that lurk around here, we'll definitely need some more ammo for our shooters."

"I know that." Henrich said. "Just make sure you keep your eyes open for any signs that relate to the Scavengers."

"Umm. What are the signs of the Scavengers?"

"Fear. Dread. Terror." Henrich said, looking at Landon and

Beth. "Those are the signs of the Scavengers. When you sense them, you'll know they're nearby."

"Sure." Beth said. "I got it."

"Same here. I just wonder when they'll show up is all."

Henrich tied his horse to the post in front of the convenience store. The horse stayed calm as they entered the store. The horse was protected by a force, though not many knew what kind of force it could be. Within the store, Henrich saw food, water, and other supplies suited for their needs. Landon went to grab the food, Beth went for the water, and Henrich walked toward the back counter, where the weapons and ammo were being kept. Henrich looked at the weapons clerk and pointed toward the ammunition boxes on the back shelf.

"Give me four of those." Henrich told the clerk.

"And what will you do with them?" The Clerk asked, handing Henrich the four boxes of ammunition.

"Why would you need to know about my business with them?"

"Because it is a new standard. The people of this town usually fear those who's agendas are not known to others. Secrets get these people killed and they are always killed by the Scavengers."

"So, the Scavengers have been around here."

"Yes, they have. They come and go as they please. When they come, they make an entrance for themselves and bring a posse of sorts. They come with bags, demanding that we give them our food, our water, and our weapons. They only leave when we don't have enough to meet their demands and they give us some time to reacquire what they've taken from us."

"So, you send people to their location to steal back your stuff?"

"No. We have an agreement with one of the cities nearby this region. They deliver the stuff here and we keep it here until the Scavengers make their return for it."

Henrich nodded as he placed the ammo boxes in his bag. He looked around the interior of the store, seeing only the people of the town and Landon and Beth gathering the food and water. Henrich turned to the Clerk and came in closer to him.

"When was the last time the Scavengers came here?"

"About three weeks ago."

"What is their standard waiting period?"

"Two to three weeks at best."

Henrich cocked his head as he took out one of the ammo boxes along with his shooter and began loading up the weapon. The clerk didn't know what to make of Henrich's actions, although he could sense something strange and old with Henrich, as if he's been through similar events before and he has. The clerk noticed the shooter that Henrich was loading and he could tell it was from another place.

"That shooter you have there. Where did you get it from?"

"I didn't get it from anywhere." Henrich said. "It was given to me for my sole purpose."

"But, only those ancient Warslingers carried such a weapon. It is said their shooters are made from the gold of the Outer-World."

"You're about right. They are made in the Outer-World, but are only made for those who are within the purpose."

"So, are you one of them? A Warslinger?"

Henrich stared at the clerk as he waited for an answer. Most likely an answer that would probably terrify him or give him some level of hope in the town. Seeing a Warslinger in their town would possibly enlighten the people. But, would also draw fear unto them. For they know of the legends that speak of the Warslingers and what they stood and fought for in their time.

"Make the decision for yourself." Henrich said. "You should be able to come to some conclusion."

Landon and Beth approached Henrich, showing him the food and water they've gathered. Henrich was impressed and he handed them one of the ammo boxes and Landon grabbed the box and loaded his shooter. The Clerk looked at Landon, seeing him holding the shooter.

"Isn't he a little young to be carrying open of those?"

"When you're out there, you always need some form of protection on you. He prefers a shooter."

"It's my standard now. I guess."

The sound of a loud continuous roar entered from the outside. The sound was distant form the town, but grew larger and louder. Henrich looked out toward the windows and doors. He noticed the people of the town were immediately entrenched in fear. Landon and Beth didn't know what was happening and Henrich turned to the clerk, who also appeared to be in fear.

"What's happening right now?" Henrich asked.

"They're coming." The Clerk said jolting. The Scavengers are coming."

Henrich placed his hands on his shooters as he could see what appeared to be dirt bikes riding into the front of the store. Landon looked at the bikes and was drawn to them.

"What are those?" Landon asked.

"They look like dirt bikes." Beth said. "We have them back on my world."

"Over here they're called dirt-speeders."

"I want one of those."

Two dirt-speeders were parked in front of the store as the two men who rode on them entered. The two men appeared dirty. Their clothing was dirty from sand and soil. Their countenance wasn't a pleasant sight and their energy was of evil. They looked around the store at the people, smiling at them with their rotten teeth.

"Don't be afraid of us, people!" One had said. "We're only here on our average trips."

"We're here for our stuff that you owed us weeks back and we've come to collect it."

The Scavengers started walking toward the back of the store, where the weapons Clerk stood. While they approached him, they seen Henrich, Landon, and Beth also standing in the back. Amazed at them, the two Scavengers have never seen them before in the area and it makes them feel comfortable to see what they would call new people.

"My, my. This is something to behold right about now. You

folks aren't from around here are you?"

"No." Henrich said. "We're not."

"This is good. This is really good, and you want to know why it's really good that you're not from here?"

"Tell us why."

"Really simple. You're all stranders in this town and as you might not be aware of. We run this town as well as this land."

"I can tell who you two are. You're both Scavengers."

"So, you've heard of us, huh."

"I know of your people and what you do for yourselves."

The Scavengers appalled Henrich for his knowledge of the Scavenger. They gave him a small, but good form of respect. Both Scavengers turned to Landon and Beth. Seeing them, two young people. A quality fit for the Scavengers.

"This young man and woman with you?"

"They are."

"My, I've never know of the times where young men and women are taken by an older mysterious-looking man. What say of this journey of yours?"

"It is classified."

"Classified you say? Really? How can it be classified? I'm sure it is of good importance."

"It is certainly of good importance." Henrich said.

"Then you don't mind telling us what it is."

"I'm afraid I will not tell you what it is. It is none of your concern, boys."

"You don't get it, old man. You're in our town! You're in our land! You answer to us whatever questions we ask of you. You will answer us, and we will always get the truth out of you. By whatever means."

The Scavengers glared their eyes past Henrich toward the clerk. The smiled at him as he slightly waved his hand. Still in fear of them and in fear of his life. The Scavengers walked past Henrich and toward the counter.

"Do you have it ready?"

"Yes. Your stuff is prepared and ready." The clerk said with a trembling voice. "In the back. Take it."

The Scavengers clapped as they jumped over the counter and shoved the Clerk into the shelves. They grabbed two boxes, both were the size of a shoe box and in them contained food, water, and weapons such as small shooters and knives with ammunition boxes. The Scavengers had what they've come for and were prepared to leave the store with their hands full. They jumped back over the counter, grabbing their boxes and they walked away. One of them made the intention to stop and gazed back toward Beth. He measured Beth's body and he desired to have her. He approached Beth with a smile. An uneasy smile at best.

"You don't need to be hanging around these two assholes." The Scavenger gestured with a grin. "Come with me and I will show you a life worth living. A life of pleasure and a life of fun."

"I don't think I can do that." Beth said. "It's not who I am."

The Scavengers shook his head. Slightly disappointed.

"Don't be afraid of me. I know of some female friends of mine that would love to be around you and they can show you things that I can't. Things that would bring not only pleasure to themselves, but pleasure to you as well. What say you to that?"

Beth shook her head, disagreeing with the Scavenger. The other Scavenger came back around to his partner, seeing him trying to bring Beth back with them.

"What are you doing?"

"What does it look like I'm doing. I want to bring this girl back with us. She can be of use. Just look at her."

"We don't have the time for this. We only came here to get what we needed."

"Brother, she is what we need. How many of today's women would suit most of us in a daily basis. Not a one of them. But, this young woman could. She has the energy and the figure for it."

"Let's go."

"Do what your partner says." Henrich said.

"Don't talk to me. You keep your mouth shut."

The Scavengers reached into his pocket and pulled out a knife. He reached the knife to Beth's throat. Henrich was ready to fire at any moment and so was Landon. The other Scavenger stood back, with his hand on his own shooter. A shooter smaller than what Henrich and Landon have. Beth stood still as the Scavenger laughed with the knife in his hand.

"Oh, what the hell." said The Scavenger. "I guess I'm going to have to take you with me by force."

The Scavenger snatched Beth by the arm and instantly within a mere second, Henrich raised up his shooter and fired it. The bullet flew through the Scavenger's forehead as he dropped the knife and fell onto the ground. The other Scavenger jumped when seeing his partner dead on the ground. He looked up at Henrich, who kept the shooter aimed toward him. The Scavengers shook his head in anger and in rage as he raised up his shooter.

"You bastard!" The Scavenger yelled.

Landon noticed the Scavenger raising up his shooter and he took the shot, killing the second Scavengers. The two Scavengers are dead, and the entire store is in shock and awe. Seeing two Scavengers killed in their presence brought a sense of a possible hope and a possible fear as to what the other Scavengers will do to them. Henrich grabbed the box of which the Scavenger held and returned it to the Clerk.

"I don't understand." The Clerk said. "Why did you kill them?"

"Because I had no other option." Henrich said. "Keep the boxes."

"What do we do now?" Landon asked.

"We keep moving."

Landon left for the outside as Henrich approached Beth, who was slightly in fear of her life. Henrich knew that she would have to get used to the new World she finds herself in. He understands her fear and he knows in time it will pass by.

"Don't worry about it." Henrich said. "There more in these Worlds that can do far worse than what he could've done."

They exited the store and Henrich went atop the horse as did Beth. They left the store and continued moving further down the pathways. While going down the pathways, they find themselves being followed by what appeared to be more dirt-speeders. Meaning more Scavengers. Henrich turned his head around and seen them.

"Landon, we have trouble."

Landon turned to see the Scavengers chasing after them. Yelling out negative words to them and threatening them in many ways possible. Landon prepared himself to shoot them if they came closer as his hand was placed on his shooter. Henrich was the same, prepared to fire if necessary. Within minutes, a few of the Scavengers came closer to them and they started shooting them. Their dirt-speeders crashed into the mountains nearby and other flipped across the plains, setting the grass on fire.

"What do we do now, sir?!" Landon yelled.

"We take out as many of them as we can!"

Henrich and Landon continued their firing toward the Scavenges. Taking out many as they could reach according to the shooters' aiming. One Scavenger rode his dirt-speeder onto the right side of the horse. Henrich spotted him and shot him in the head. He reached over and handed Beth one of his shooters. She turned to him and gazed at the shooter.

"You use it when necessary." Henrich said.

"I will."

Moving further down the pathways, they still had to shoot own the oncoming Scavengers. It appeared to be when more we killed, more appeared and they appeared in masses with their dirt-speeders. They could not be stopped, nor could they slow themselves down if they could. The Scavengers eventually caught up to them and one took a lasso from the side of the speeder and snatched both Henrich and Beth from the horse. The horse stopped as they fell onto the ground where the Scavengers surrounded them. Landon was tackled to the ground by two Scavenger men, who laughed at him.

"He tried to shoot us! Can you believe that kind of shit!"

"I can now. Seeing he has a shooter on him and a good looking one at best."

Henrich looked around for his horse and the horse was gone. Out of the sights of the Scavengers. Henrich smiled for a moment.

"Good job." Henrich said.

He turned to see him, Landon, and Beth were surrounded by Scavengers. All of whom ranged from different ages and nationalities. They all appeared to be dirty and they carried with them an energy of fear. Henrich could see why the people of the town feared them. They feared them because of their number. Henrich, Landon, and Beth were rounded up and tied up by the Scavengers. As they prepared to leave the site, one of the Scavengers approached Henrich and stared him in the face with a smile.

"You aren't from around here."

"I am not."

The Scavenger nodded as he tapped Henrich's hat with his finger.

"Very well. Let's bring these people back to our camp. We have others who would like to see them."

The Scavengers rallied them up and brought them along, returning to their campsite. A campsite where only the Scavengers resided, and wickedness flourished.

II

Being captured by the Scavengers, they sit on three separate dirt-speeders, driven by one Scavenger each as they make their way to their campsite somewhere in the outskirts of the small town. The campsite of the Scavengers is only several miles away from the small town and is not a faraway area to find. Although, most of the campsite is hidden behind sets of trees from a nearby forest. Inching closer toward their campground, Henrich took looks at the surroundings, marking locations for himself to keep in memory. He made sure he knew where the Scavengers were going in their own direction. He was able to mentally measure the amount between the small town and the Scavengers' current pathway.

"What are they going to do to us?" asked Landon.

"Don't speak." The Scavenger said. "Otherwise, they'll fill your mouth up with something to keep it shut."

Landon looked at Henrich, who could tell that he was somewhat shaken up by the recent events, but he held his own. Not giving into the fear that he is feeling moving around him. But, Landon held on to confidence and patience. Henrich nodded toward him and looked at Beth, who stayed quiet during the entire way to the campsite. Henrich understood why she was silent. The dirt-speeders started to slow down and Henrich could see their campsite right in front of them.

The Scavengers entered their campsite, surrounded with even more Scavengers than Henrich, Landon, or Beth could count on their own. The campsite appeared to be covered with tents, trailers, and even some used abandoned vehicles. The Scavengers are sitting by sets of fires as they see the Three on the back of the speeders. They are intrigued, and they arose from their current sitting spot to approach them. They looked at them and some smiled with ideas and others looked with disgust as to why they would bring other people to the site.

"Who are they?" One Scavenger asked.

"They are our guests for this day. Just be patient with them and you'll see why we've brought them back with us."

The Scavengers exited their speeders, some grabbed the Three, bringing them over to a table next to a wooden pole. On the wooden pole was a light, used for the night when light would be needed. While being escorted to the table, Henrich looked and seen a pit not too far from the campsite. He wondered why they would have a pit and from the pit he could see smoke emitting from it, as if there was something within the pit burning.

"Sit yourselves down." The Scavenger said, placing Henrich, Landon, and Beth at the table.

The Scavengers leave them at the table, their hands still tied together as they looked at the Scavengers gathering together, cheering and hugging as if they haven't seen each other in ages, but, they've only seen each other last for a period of hours. Through their own actions, Henrich could tell they were of one mind and of one accord. He respected that, but, he remembered with contention between the two Scavengers that he and Landon killed back at the store. Therefore, Henrich knew that within the Scavengers, there were a few that could destroy the entire clan.

The Scavengers sat together, a few feet from Henrich, Landon, and Beth. They talked with each other and started looking around for the two Scavengers that went to the store to pick up the supplies. But, as Henrich knew, there weren't present, and neither would they be coming back. One of the Scavengers looked at Henrich and walked toward him. The Scavenger stood in front of Henrich at the table, towering over him as Henrich sat in the seat.

"What do you want?" Henrich asked.

"Just a question. When you were at the town earlier, did you happen to see two of my people there?"

"I did. They rode on dirt-speeders just like the rest of you."

"What happened to them? I would assume that you would know since you were there when they arrived."

"They're dead."

"Dead?"

"They were killed in the store while getting the supplies they came for."

"So, you would know who killed them, right?"

"I do."

"Then who did it? Was it the clerk? Was it some shopper who had a shooter on them? Anything of that nature?"

"No. It was none of those."

"Then, who killed them?"

Henrich stared into the Scavenger's eyes and he could tell that he had some care for his two partners. Henrich understood that care and gaze over to Landon, who also looked at the Scavenger.

Henrich nodded to the Scavenger.

"I killed one. My friend killed the other."

"Oh. Oh. So, you and your friend killed my partners, huh."

"We did, and for a good reason."

"What good reason would you have in killing them? You didn't know them personally nor did you know them strategically."

"True, I did not know them in those manners. But, I do know of true honor, true respect, and true integrity. I was not about to allow them to disrespect me nor my friends here in any manner. Neither would I let them treat those back at the two with such disrespect. Today was their day of truth and the truth they could not accept. So, they made this day their last."

The Scavenger shook his head in anger toward Henrich and Landon. The Scavenger smiled as he punched Henrich in the face and punched Landon in the nose. Henrich nodded with a smirk as he looked at the Scavenger, seeing him fuming up with more anger.

"I understand that kind of strength. It's what is needed to survive in these parts."

"I'm sure you would." The Scavenger replied, returning to the others.

The Scavenger had approached them and told them about the deaths of their two partners. He pointed toward Henrich and Landon and immediately, without hesitation, the other Scavengers came to them and snatched the three of them from the table and brought them forward in front of the entire clan of Scavengers, who surrounded them in a circle. Henrich, Landon, and Beth were on their knees, facing the Scavengers. All of whom were yelling and screaming at them derogatory words and utterances.

"Look at these fools!" One Scavenger said. "How could they kill one of us!"

"I like the young man." One female Scavenger said. "But, I also like that young woman."

One of the Scavengers raised his hands up, silencing the others as they stayed quiet. The Scavenger approached them and crouched to their eyelevel. The Scavengers smirked in their faces and they only stared at the Scavenger. He nodded to them.

"Well, this must be a tough day for the three of you." The Scavenger said. "Not to mention the fact that you killed two of us today and yet, how will we get our supplies from the store."

"You go there and ask for it." Henrich said. "Unless you want to die like they did."

The Scavenger laughed at Henrich and pointed with a gesture at him. Looking at his attire, somewhat strange to see in the Land of the Survivors. Yet, the Scavengers looked at all three of them as he was forming his words in his mind before speaking them out. He nodded again and pointed at the three of them several times, before rubbing his hair and walking around them in a circle and coming back in front of them, standing over them. He clapped his hands together, rubbing them.

"Well, we can start like this first. My name is Wade, and I am what you would call the leader of the Scavengers."

"The leader, huh?" Landon asked. "I would believe you all went on your own path."

"We did at one time, but that was when chaos was circling around this place. Once I came into place and showed the people that I was leader material, everything fell into order. We all had the same goals, dreams, and ambitions in our lives and we were able to have one mind. With that one mind, we developed one accord. To live as brothers and sisters together to make sure that none of us suffer as others did during the chaos of this land."

"What do you mean by suffering in this land?" Henrich asked. "What could've happened here that hasn't happened before?"

"Change, I would say. A change that shook the foundations of many cities in the Western World. Yet, I'm not sure how the other Worlds are doing in these times, but it's not my job to focus on them as it is my duty to pay attention to where I'm at today and where I'm at is here in the Western World. Living in the Land of the Survivors."

Henrich nodded.

"I can see your reasoning, slightly."

"I'm sure you can. That is why the three of you were brought here this day. We need more recruits and the three of you would be a perfect fit for us. Especially, you, young man and you, young woman. The two of you could become great being aligned with people such as ourselves."

"Why would we side with you people." Landon said. "You seem to have enough people as it is."

"You think so? Well, from where we're all sitting right now. You guys killed two of our own to begin with and from that we will need two more to take their place in our clan. People don't fall out of the sky anymore, or come out of the ground, and neither do they get thrown up from the trees of the forests either."

"This is why we're here?" Henrich asked. "To join in with you all?"

"In a matter. But, as I've already said. You killed two of our own and we'll need two in replacements. So, if I had it my way, which I will overall, I would take this young man and this young woman as the replacements and kill you, old man. You seemed to have lived a long life as it is already. You don't need any more trouble in your life, so I would spare you from it."

"You don't even know who we are. Let alone, what we're capable of doing with our own hands when it comes to survival."

Wade placed his hands on his face, his mouth dropped. He looked at the other Scavengers before placing his focus back on the three of them. He remembered something. Something he had to ask of them that was important for his cause.

"Oh, that's right. I forgot to ask of your names, occupations, and motives of life. So, I will start with… you, young man. What is your name, your occupation, and your motive of life?"

Landon stared at Wade and gazed over to Henrich, who nodded in giving Landon the opportunity to speak. Landon understood Henrich's nod and faced Wade, who was staring at him with his brown eyes and he creepy smile that was slowly growing on his face.

"My name is Cody Landon. My occupation is being a traveler

of the Worlds and my motive of life is to see the Worlds return to their former state."

"Oh? You're a traveler of the Worlds? How so? You're only just a boy. A young man at best. How can you have the achievement to travel the Worlds at your age? Tell me, please. I am intrigued and interested in what you have to tell me."

"I was born and raised in the Northern World. When the opportunity came, I was able to leave and therefore travel across the Worlds."

"So, your mother and father just let you leave and travel the Worlds? All on your own? Is that right?"

"That is right. Some of the people up there died due to nature's power or meeting the beasts of the north. I chose to leave, and I came here to the Western World, looking to see what the other Worlds would offer me in my life."

"And what have they offered you so far?"

"So far? A greater understanding as to how the Worlds work and what will become of them in the future ahead."

"Who told you about this future ahead?"

"He did." Landon said, nodding his head toward Henrich.

Wade pointed at Henrich while keeping his eyes on Landon.

"And how would he know about the future and what will become of the Worlds?"

"Because he's one of the Warslingers."

Wade's smile turned into a laugh and he laughed at Landon's words along with the Scavengers that surrounded them. Landon looked at them and could tell they didn't believe the words that he had spoken out concerning Henrich being one of the Warslingers. Landon looked at Henrich, who turned to him and stayed silent. Landon understood the silence of Henrich. Beth stayed quiet, though she looked around at the Scavengers and sometimes would gaze her eyes toward Henrich. Wade clapped several times, regarding to Landon's words.

"You have some good jokes, young man." Wade said. "I will give you the benefit on that. You can make us laugh."

"It's not a joke." said Landon. "I am telling you all the truth."

"That's enough out of you." Wade said, silencing Landon with his finger. "Now, onto the second one."

Wade turned from Landon and kneeled to Beth, who looked at him with some small form of anger and disgust. Wade could fell her anger toward him and the Scavengers, but he could also tell that she was different from them all. Something with her was off with what they're used to in the Worlds. Wade stood up above her and pointed at her with another smile on his face.

"You, young woman. The same that I asked of Cody here. Your name, your occupation, and your motive of life?"

"My name is Beth Grasslands. I am or was a paranormal investigator from Washington D.C."

"Hold on a second." Wade said, stopping her from speaking. "What do you mean Washington D.C.?"

"That's where I'm from. I came from Washington D.C."

Wade shook his head. His finger waving at her in disagreement. He looked at her and could tell that her words were solid, but something was off about her answers.

"How can that be?"

"How can what be?"

"How can you be from Washington D.C. when we no longer have a Washington D.C.?"

"Well, I'm not exactly from this World."

"Then, would you please tell me and my clan where you from that has a Washington D.C.? Because it certainly isn't from the Eastern World, the Northern World, and neither the Southern World. Plus, you can't be from the Outer-World because you're still in the flesh."

"I'm from the planet Earth and I lived in a country called the United States of America, where I resided in the capital city of Washington D.C."

"What the hell is an 'Earth' and what kind of place is called the 'United States of America'? Hell, what is an *America*?"

"That is where I'm from. I came into this World, your World, through dimensional travel."

"I'm not understanding the big words, young lady. Can you explain all of this to me, so that I can comprehend what you're telling me?"

"I came through a dimensional wormhole that bridged Earth and your World and through that, I somehow found the wormhole and traveled through It and ended up here. Is that enough for you to understand?"

Wade nodded, proclaiming that he understood what Beth had told him about her travels. Wade understood. Somewhat.

"Fair enough, I would say. So, you're a inter-dimensional being as they would call it?"

"In this World, I am."

"My, my. Then, that explains the energy around you and the strange feelings we've been getting in our bodies since we saw you. You know we're all tingling for you and Cody of course."

"I don't understand what that means."

"That means, sooner or later. Be it today, tonight, tomorrow, or who knows when, we're going to screw Cody and you. Someday. Not sure right now, but I'll schedule it all accordingly to the day its set."

"You people are sick." Landon said. "Just disgusting."

Wade kicked Landon in the face with his boot, casing his nose to bleed more after being punched earlier at the table. Wade smiled as he let out a small sigh. A sigh of relief from the kick. He looked at Beth and wanted her to talk some more. He was very interested in her. As he reached down and had his hands go through her long blonde hair, he sniffed it, causing the other Scavengers to somewhat release a sound of awe or moan. Strangely it's what they did seeing the sight. Landon shook his head, staring at Wade in anger.

"Well, what is this paranormal investigation that you mention? You said it was your occupation?"

"That's what I am. A paranormal investigator."

"Well, I don't know what that is."

"I hunt ghosts for a living."

"Seriously? So, you get paid for hunting down ghosts, ghouls, and demons?"

"That I do."

Wade nodded with excitement. Smiling with internal joy. Rubbing his hands together.

"I want to apply for this job. It sounds interestingly good. Plus, you get paid for it and who doesn't like being paid for something they do in their lives."

Beth nodded in a way. She understood what Wade meant by his words and Wade liked how she nodded to his comments.

"And what of your motive of life? What would that be to someone such as yourself?"

"My motive in life. Is to change it for the better. To make others better than what they believe themselves to be. Even to make myself a better woman than I am today."

"I can help you with that in a hurry. Only whenever you're up for it and I know for sure that others here can help you with it as well."

Wade bowed his head before Beth, showing a sign of respect toward her. He walked over to stand in front of Henrich and as he walked he gave Landon the middle finger, to which Landon spit at Wade. Wade jumped out of the way of the spit and laughed at Landon.

"You and I are going to have some moments." Wade said. "Just you wait and see."

Wade stood in front of Henrich. Henrich raised his head up, staring into Wade's eyes and Wade stared into his. The two kept their eyes locked onto one another. Wade smiled while Henrich showed no emotion of any kind.

"You're the last one, old man. Tell me your name, your occupation, and your motive of life?"

"You're sure about that?" Henrich said.

"Either you answer them, or you die today. So, make your choice."

"Sure. I'll answer them for you."

"Excellent. Now, get on with it for me."

"My name is Randolph Henrich and I am one of the Warslingers of the Heptad."

Wade paused for a moment and shook his head. The other Scavengers stayed quiet and looked at Henrich. Wade kneeled low to Henrich's eyelevel and stared at him closer than before.

"Say that again."

"I am a Warslinger of the Heptad."

"No, you're not. You're trying to help Cody's little lie. Don't play around with me, old man."

"I am not playing around with you. I am telling you the truth."

"Is that right? Well, tell me, what is truth?"

"The truth." Henrich said slowly. "You'll never understand the truth, nor will you be able to hear it when it is spoken aloud."

"So, what of your motive of life? Is it the same as what I would believe a Warslinger to do?"

"My motive of life is to find a place hidden from the eyes and the minds of Man."

"What is that place?"

"The Haunted City."

Wade laughed and clapped his hand. The other Scavengers also laughed at Henrich's words. They did not have the belief of The Haunted City nor the belief of the Warslingers' existence. Wade nodded to Henrich.

"You're just as funny as your friend over here."

"Take it as you want." Henrich said. "But, you'll know of the truth when it manifested itself before you and your clan of Scavengers."

Wade looked closely in Henrich's eyes.

"You really believe in it?"

"Very much." Henrich declared.

"We'll see about that."

Wade walked away as the Scavengers grabbed the Three from the ground, returning them to the table where they once were. While the Scavengers sat and talked about strategy and other things of their mind during the day, Henrich gazed up toward the ski and noticed that nightfall was near. He could feel the slight chill of the night flowing through the air as the heat of the day was diminishing.

"When the time comes, let me know." Henrich said. "Let me know."

Beth noticed Henrich talking as he considered the sky. She inched over toward him, hearing what he was speaking. It was unfamiliar to her ears, but sounded like the things she's heard before in her lifetime.

"Who are you talking to?"

"A friend, Beth." Henrich said. "A very close friend of mine."

The nightfall had begun and during the night, the Scavengers would party, and they would have orgies with each other across the campsite. The Scavengers are moved the Three and placed them underneath the wooden pole, where the light would shine down upon them. As they sat on the dirty grounds, they could see the lewdness of the Scavengers. From the excessive drinking to their riotous ways.

"What in the hell are they doing?" Landon asked.

"They're living up their life." Henrich replied. "It's all that they have."

Beth watched their actions and their ways. She's seen tings familiar to those in her lifetime around people that she knew in her world.

"They're acting very similar to how people acted back on my world."

"People acted like this where you're from" Landon asked her. "Seriously? Like them?"

"It's the same. I guess people aren't different no matter what Worlds they're from."

The Scavengers continued their partying for the night hours. Henrich went to sleep underneath the pole while Landon and Beth kept watch. They looked over to Henrich, seeing him asleep as the partying is continuing. Landon started to worry for their well-being and didn't understand why Henrich would choose to sleep now in the area that they're in. Some of the Scavengers turned their sites on Landon and Beth, slowly making their way toward them. Gesturing to their private parts as well as their naked bodies. Landon and Beth tried to move, but they were tied up to the pole.

"This isn't good." Landon said.

"That I am aware of." Beth replied. "Just try to keep yourself calm."

The male Scavengers approached Beth and attempted to touch her body from all angles. She fought back with shoves and kicks while being attached to the pole. The female Scavengers approached Landon and tried to touch him. Landon fought them off as much as he could, but within his being, he desired to join them. He wanted to feel what they were feeling. His curiosity was pushing him to destroy him by joining in to their partying and orgies. Beth noticed Landon slowly fighting back and she couldn't believe it.

"What are you doing, Cody?"

"I… I'm not sure." He said. "I don't want it, but I want it."

The female Scavengers left Landon alone and approached Beth. They circled her and started breathing on her neck, touching her body. Some even placed their hands into her pants pockets, feeling her closely. She fought off the women by struggling and one of them inched over to her ear.

"You will give yourself over to us. You know that, right?"

"I will not." Beth said. "You're just a bunch of sick people. Just sick."

The female Scavenger looked Beth in the eyes and stared at her lips. Licking her own. Beth moved her head around to avoid getting closer to the woman's face.

"After I kiss you and stick my tongue in your mouth, you'll give in to me and I will have all of you. I'll placed my mouth all over your body and I will make you scream for me."

The woman inched closer to kiss Beth, but was stopped by Wade.

"Leave them be for the moment. Now isn't the time for them."

Wade nodded to Beth, signaling the other Scavengers to leave them be. Wade looked down at Henrich, who was sitting on the ground asleep. Wade laughed to himself. Seeing Henrich sleeping during a party like they're having around the campsite.

"The old man's asleep." Wade said. "How funny is that."

Wade walked away as Beth slowly sat down, trying to settle herself down and Landon slowly came to the ground, but, he was still feeling the urge to join them. He wanted to hold the women and touch their bodies. As he sat there, looking at the woman, who were partying and fooling around with each other and the men, Henrich moved his head toward Landon's direction.

"Fight the temptation." Henrich said quietly.

"How will I do that?" Landon asked. "These urges are strong."

"You're a young man. They would be strong. But, you have the option of either giving into them or tossing them away. Best you take the second option and save yourself from trouble."

Landon started to settle himself and calmed down. He looked at Beth who was calm and steady.

"What about you, sir?" Landon asked. "What do you do when you see things like this in front of you?"

"Just like I'm doing right now. Shutting my eyes and going to sleep."

"How can you go to sleep in a surrounding like this?"

"How did we sleep in the Valley of Death and in those forests? Just calm yourself and the next day, you'll be settled."

Landon nodded. He somewhat understood what Henrich told him and yet, he attempted to learn from him and understand the ways that Henrich spoke of. Henrich knew that Landon was young and that he would have these issues approaching him sooner or later.

"So, how are we going to get away from this place and keep moving?"

"In time, you'll see."

"How will I see?"

"You'll see. Just be patient."

Landon nodded and stayed quiet as the hours passed by and all three of them went to sleep as the Scavengers partied all night long until the sun arose, and the moon set before the day.

<u>III</u>

In the morning after the riotous partying of the Scavengers, Henrich, Landon, and Beth are placed once again at the table from the previous day. Wade approached them with plates of food, which were of the food stolen from the store of the small town. Wade also brought them bottles of water, which also came from the store of the small town. Wade stood in front of them as he watched them eat and drink, for they haven't eaten or drunk anything since the day before the previous day.

"I hope you enjoyed the scenery of the party from last night." Wade said. "Because there's a whole lot more on the way. I'm telling you that much already."

"What happened last night was wickedness celebrating in its own lustful actions." Henrich said. "Soon, you'll all pay for what you've done to yourselves and to others."

Wade inched closer to Henrich, seeing that his words were indeed true and were of a warning. A warning that hit Wade close, seemingly to be that Wade has heard similar words before in times past.

"And who's going to deliver the payday on us? You? Cody? Beth?"

"You'll see."

"I'm hoping I will and I hope you'll be there as well to see it fail in your face."

Wade smiled and clapped his hands together, looking back at the other Scavengers, who were also eating and drinking. Wade turned back to Henrich, before gazing at Landon and Beth.

"Later on, old man, you and I will have ourselves a conversation."

"Why would I spend more time talking to you and only to you?"

"Because it concerns your current state and it will concern your possible future. That is if you and your young partners want to leave this place without any harm to be done onto you."

Henrich only stared at Wade, who continued showing off his smile.

"Later on, old man." Wade said, walking away from the table.

Landon looked at Wade and in his heart, he was disgusted by him and if he could, he would pound Wade's face into the ground with his fists. Beth only stayed quiet as she ate the food that was presented to them and Henrich kept silent and only thought to himself of the things to come in the days ahead. Henrich kept an open mind of being set free or finding a way to escape and he did not lose any faith that was within his being. His faith had only increased since they were taken by the Scavengers. Henrich kept his eye on Wade, who was speaking with some of the Scavengers and he noticed them heading towards their dirt-speeders. The Scavengers boarded up their speeders and left the campsite. Almost a dozen of them in total. Landon watched them leave the campsite.

"Where are they going?" Landon asked.

"They're going to get more supplies." Henrich said. "That's where they're going."

After a period of hours, the dozen Scavengers have not yet returned to the campsite, but Wade approached Henrich and commanded for two of the male Scavengers to bring him to Wade's trailer. The Scavengers grabbed Henrich by his arms and brought him into Wade's trailer. An old, beaten down trailer, but was good enough for Wade to sleep in during the nights. Inside the trailer was a small table with two chairs. The Scavengers placed Henrich in one and Wade sat in the other. The two Scavengers stood by the door, just in case Henrich attempted to attack Wade. Henrich stared at Wade, who only smiled at him while drinking what appeared to be some tea. Made from within the trailer.

"I told you that we would talk." Wade said. "And now we're both here."

"Talk about what?" Henrich asked. "What is there to talk about with you that would be of any importance?"

Wade placed his cup of tea down on the table and pointed to Henrich. Wade nodded as his finger shook around, while being pointed to Henrich.

"You went on about this "Haunted City". So, tell me, what is the place and how do you know of it?"

"Why should I tell you these things?"

"Because I know honestly you and your partners want to leave our campsite in one piece and not in pieces. Besides, if what you speak of is true, I would like to reach this "Haunted City" myself and claim whatever it is to claim."

"How would you claim something that you have no understanding nor comprehension of?"

"I would bring you along with me. Hell, you can be my guide and lead the way to this City and once we're both there, you can show me where this treasure of it is bound to be kept."

Henrich shook his head, gazing back to the two Scavengers before facing Wade at the table. Wade took a sip of his tea before placing the cup down once more. Wade kept his smile as Henrich didn't smile. He only stared, and he stared with a hatred. An almost perfect hatred of Wade's well-being.

"If you were to reach the City, boy, you wouldn't make it past what's there."

"So, what is there?" Wade asked. "Tell me what is there so that I will have the understanding capable of entering the place."

"It would be too much for your mind to bear. You can't even imagine the power that the City contains and yet, you want to reach it only for yourself and you want to claim what's there for yourself."

"What else would I choose to go there for? To help the Worlds and bring them peace? Hell no. The Worlds already have enough to deal with and I will not be their savior, nor will I be their protector. I would claim what's there for myself and for my clan."

"I'm not sure how, since some in your clan refuse to believe in The Haunted City. They don't believe in the Warslingers either. I remember their laughter when you questioned Cody and myself yesterday. Their laughter proved to me of how much unbelief is within them and what it will do to them in the long run of their lives."

"I have to give it to you, old man. You know a lot of things and I have never come across someone of your age who knew as much as you do. It's almost as if you've been alive for centuries. Hell, probably ages in time."

"You have no idea."

"Of course, I don't! That's why you're sitting here before me. So, we can have ourselves a conversation and get to know one another a little better than yesterday."

Henrich kept quiet and Wade drinks his tea as the two Scavengers stayed guarded at the door of the trailer.

"These Warslingers you and Cody mentioned, how could you be one of them after what is known of their existence?"

"Things aren't always what they appear to be, boy. I've seen things in my lifetime that would bring those such as yourselves to shame and to death. I've encounter enemies that the Worlds haven't seen since their time of change."

"You're telling me the Warslingers actually existed at one time or another? Seriously?"

"They still live among the Worlds. They are only scattered due to the failings that came upon them in a mission of theirs."

"Yeah. I've heard of the tale before. A Warslinger betrayed his brethren and caused them to fail at a task greater than those that came before and from that fail, the Warslingers were scattered throughout all the Worlds, until the appointed time would arrive for them to reunite with each other and extinguished the evil of malevolency from the Worlds for-ever."

Wade laughed at his own words and Henrich's words. Henrich understood that Wade and the Scavengers believed the Warslingers and the Haunted City to be only tales of myth and legends of folklore. He knew that had no belief system within their being and he could tell they were spiritually dead. Wade drank the rest of his tea and stared at Henrich, trying to think of something to say to him. Wade snapped his fingers at an idea.

"I know you're trying to intimidate with your known knowledge of ancient stories, but, they won't help you or your partners find a way to leave our campsite. Cody and Beth will soon be a part of us and you will be an old man who will die by own hands."

"You believe them to be only stories?" Henrich said. "Ancient stories from the past times?"

"I do. That's what they are. None of them are true and speak of any logical sense of reasoning."

"So be it, boy." Henrich said silently. "You have already given me your true answer."

Wade stared at Henrich.

"Before I send you out of my trailer, do you have anything that you would like to ask me?"

Henrich thought for a moment. He remembered something. Something that he seen when they brought them to the campsite to begin with. It was in his mind and it questioned him internally. Henrich looked at Wade.

"That pit." Henrich said. "It was smoking yesterday."

"Why do you ask me about the pit?" Wade wondered. "Does the sight of it bother you or something?"

"No."

"Oh. Well, I'll tell you this much and you can determine it for yourself later. What is in that pit is something that myself and my clan have built up for months while we remain out here. We found those things some time ago and we didn't know that they would be of good use to us."

"What do you mean by those things?" Henrich asked.

"You'll see soon enough, old man."

Wade nodded to Henrich and waved his hands above his head. He commanded for the Scavenger guards to toss Henrich out of the trailer, which they do, and they returned him to the table, where Landon and Beth were still being kept. Henrich sat still while Landon and Beth looked at him before seeing Wade exiting the trailer and walking over to other Scavengers.

"What happened in there, sir?" Landon asked.

"The boy's a weak one." Henrich said. "He doesn't know what he has placed himself under and neither have the rest of them."

"Did he mention of setting us free, possibly?" Beth asked.

"He did not. He wants the two of you to join him and he wants me dead. Simple as that."

Landon looked out to the Scavengers as did Beth. Landon turned his sights on Henrich and thought for a moment to himself before uttering a word to him. Landon thought about it.

"Any plan of us making an escape?" Landon asked.

"Not now." Henrich said. "But, in due time, it will show up. That I am certain of."

Across the miles from the campsite of the Scavengers, the dozen Scavengers ride down along the pathways toward several small towns. In those small towns are people who live together, and they also have supplies of their own that come from an even greater city that is not far from their locations. The Scavengers rode along in a form of a line. As if they were indeed soldiers with a clear and intended focus. They came up to the first small town and they ransacked the place. They enter one of the homes, seeing a young couple and their children sitting down, crouched into the corner.

"Clear this place out!" One Scavenger said. "I'll take a few of the spoils if they won't mind."

The Scavenger cleared many of the homes, leaving the residents of the small town screaming in fear on the outside. Some of the Scavengers raped the women and the men. Some even harmed the children to their own pleasures. The Scavengers showed the people of the town that they were in the Land of the Survivors and they were a survivor group and they took whatever they desired.

After taking the food, the water, the weapons, along with anything else they wanted, they gave the people of the tow a warning before they moved on toward the next town, where there's been word of them having even more supplies than what was known of the Land of the Survivors.

In the second town, the Scavengers noticed the buildings were taller than the previous towns. The tall buildings intrigued them to wonder what could be kept in a place like this one. Entering the town, they brought the fear of them to the people and began to do what they did in the previous town. But, this town had a large store and some of the Scavengers entered the store. They entered with a bang and had their weapons drawn on the people.

"Now, we need all of you to stay quiet or otherwise, you will all die."

The people kept silent while the Scavengers took as much as they could from them and they loved doing it. The Scavengers even provoked the people to fight with their anger and some attempted to attack them head on, but the Scavengers were too much in number for the people and they beat down some of the towns people with their weapons to death in front of the others. A few of the Scavengers entered the tall buildings and within them, they spotted strange weapons and they looked at them. The weapons were almost ancient in appearance, but modern in usage. They looked like modern shooters, but were attached to staffs and blades.

"What kind of weapons are these?" One Scavenger said.

"Let's bring them back to the camp with us and show Wade."

"Good idea. He might know what they are."

The Scavengers jumped onto their speeders and left the town.

Two towns were destroyed and consumed with fear after being visited by the Scavengers. The Scavengers also left the same warning to the second town as they did with the first one. They were loaded with supplies, all stretched out around the dozens of them. The weapons were kept with the ones who were skilled with them and weapons like them in appearance and in usage.

Before the night had come, the Scavengers made their return to the campsite and delivered the supplies to Wade. Wade looked at them and cheered with a loud yell.

"You've all done well today." Wade said.

He looked at the weapons that were found in the tall buildings and he was intrigued by their design.

"These are strange." He said. "Very strange."

"We thought that we should bring them to you." One Scavenger said. "Maybe you would know what they are."

"Well, I'll tell you right now, I don't know about them. But, thanks for bringing them back anyhow."

"It is our duty."

Henrich, Landon, and Beth looked at them, celebrating their theft of the towns' goods. Henrich shook his head in the shame of seeing them.

"These people are something else, sir." Landon said. "What are we going to do about them?"

"As of right now, we wait." Henrich said.

"Wait on what?" Beth asked. "I'm not seeing the full picture here."

"Many don't see the full picture, Beth. Others see the picture in the form of a cloud or a puff of smoke. A few see the picture in full, with its bright colors and beautiful features."

Wade clapped his hands and gathered the Scavengers around. He stood in the middle of them and gazed out toward Henrich and smiled at him. Wade gave Landon another middle finger and winked toward Beth, who looked down at the ground to avoid eye contact with him. Wade only laughed at them before facing the Scavengers.

"My people, what you have done this day makes into only myself a happy man, but it makes us all happy people. For if it were not for you to go out there to those wretched towns and stand before those ignorant people, we would not have what we have today. It is because of their deeds that we have something to be proud of out here. What they have done is the same thing we did when we claimed this campsite for ourselves."

"What is he talking about, sir?" Landon asked Henrich quietly.

"He's giving them a speech to keep them in line with his order."

"How do you know that?" Beth asked.

"Because I've seen men like him before. All boast in themselves and desire everything for themselves. Greed and power consume them and later when the time comes upon them, it destroys them."

Henrich sat back at the table, watching Wade continue to give his speech to the Scavengers.

"With all of us united. With one mind and with one accord, we can achieve anything that we set our minds and our hands to. We have the power to make our dreams and goals a reality. Unlike many people that live in the Worlds, we know what true power is and we have claimed that power for ourselves. That power gives us the right to do anything we so desire and with that, I thank all of you and tonight, we party just as much as we did last night."

The Scavengers cheered as they began their partying once more. The night had come, they grabbed Henrich, Landon, and Beth from the table and placed them in different locations around the campsite. Henrich was surrounded by some of the male Scavengers while Landon and Beth were tossed in the middle of the partying. Henrich looked at them and seen the riotous movement of the Scavengers.

"No." Henrich said. "No."

Henrich knew what they were plotting to do, and he ran toward them, but was tripped by one of the Scavengers, who laughed at him.

"Where do you think you're going, old man!" The Scavenger

said, laughing.

They grabbed Henrich and pummeled him, while Landon and Beth were surrounded by the Scavengers. Wade watched on and raised up his hand, silencing the Scavengers. Wade looked at Henrich being pummeled and laughed. He pointed toward him as the other Scavengers looked on with laughter.

"The old man has finally got it." Wade said. "Beat him some more. We need entertainment tonight. Am I right!"

The Scavengers continued to beat Henrich with their fists, kicking him as he fell to the ground. They picked him up and held him, facing Landon and Beth. Henrich couldn't do much, as he was slow in movement. Landon tried to help him, but the circle of the Scavengers was too much fro him to slip through. Wade laughed, and he pointed to Landon and Beth. Wade gestured to two women Scavengers and they entered the circle, facing Landon and Beth. Wade smiled and nodded his head, excited.

"You two women." Wade said. "Have fun with them will you."

The women giggled sinisterly as they approached Landon and Beth. The Scavengers cheered on the entire event. Henrich raised his head up slowly. Bleeding from his face and his mouth. He could see through the large crowd that the women were about to molest Landon and Beth. Henrich stayed quiet, but he wanted to bolt through them to save them. But, his body didn't have the energy to do it.

"I… can't let this happen." Henrich said. "I can't."

The women Scavengers stood in front of Landon and Beth. One of the women started to grope Landon and he felt the urge rising again in his being. He shook himself to fight it off, but he couldn't. The woman grabbed his hand and placed it onto her bare breasts.

Landon felt the warmth of the woman's body and he couldn't contain the urge any longer.

"I can't control it any longer." Landon said. "I just can't."

Landon grabbed the woman by her waist and started kissing her, causing the Scavengers to cheer louder than before. Henrich could tell by their cheering that something was wrong. He looked up, raising his head slowly and could see Landon on the ground atop the woman Scavenger. Henrich shook his head in shame.

"Poor boy." Henrich said.

Beth watched as Landon began to have intercourse with the woman. Beth tried to back away from the other woman, but she was surrounded by the Scavengers. She cried out for Henrich to help her and as he made a step forward, he was beaten down again by the other Scavengers. Being beaten down, he could hear Beth's cry for help as the other woman approached her and grabbed her by force.

"Damn it." Henrich said softly as he could feel the kicks being put on him.

The woman took her own hand and placed it into Beth's pants and started to grope her. Beth tried shoving the woman away, but the woman's strength was too strong as she grabbed her, and she licked Beth's neck. She started to suck on Beth's neck. The woman used her strength to push Beth to the ground, where she started kissing her on the lips.

"Stop!" Beth yelled. "Get off me!"

Landon continued the intercourse with the woman and Beth was laid on the ground as the other woman removed her pants and pulled down her underwear, where she began to kiss her around her private parts. Beth tried to kick against the woman, but she was immediately held down by other Scavengers as the woman licked her body. Beth continued to scream, but Wade approached her and stared into her eyes. He placed his hand over her mouth, muting her scream.

"Shush." Wade said smiling. "It'll all be over soon."

Wade kept his hand over her mouth as the woman continued to lick and suck on her body roughly. He enjoyed seeing the moment as did the other Scavengers.

Henrich looked up and could see Landon having sex and Beth being molested on the ground. Henrich stayed down and in his thoughts, he knew he would bring vengeance upon the Scavengers.

It was only a matter of planning and a matter of time. In his being, he knew it was the time and he was prepared for it. Afterwards, Landon and Beth were traumatized by the events and Wade approached the bloodied up Henrich, who was sitting at the table.

"What are you going to do now, old man?" Wade mocked. "We already had our fun with them and we're not done yet."

Henrich slowly raised his head up, staring into Wade's eyes.

"You and your clan…" Henrich said. "Your time is over."

"How will you go about that then?"

"I will kill every single one of you."

Wade faced Henrich and smiled. Wade punched Henrich in the face and laughed with a big grin on his face.

"I hope you will try. Because as soon as we're done with them. You're dead. Now, that is a promise that I will keep."

Wade left from the table, leaving Henrich to only stare at him and the Scavengers.

IV

The following day, the Scavengers sat together, reminiscing on the night before and the actions that took place in the circle. Wade brought up the events while talking of them as if they were some funny story to himself and the Scavengers. He would occasionally look over to Henrich, Landon, and Beth, seeing them not at their best. Henrich was recovering from the beatings he received, Landon felt discouraged about his actions with the woman, and Beth was in shock, due to the actions that were done to her by the woman and the other Scavengers.

"It was a moment that we will not forget, I tell you." Wade said. "Hopefully, we will have more of them in the future ahead."

The Scavengers celebrate more and more throughout the day. A few of them were seen gathering more supplies from the forests, where they kept it hidden. Henrich could see them, even though the pain that he was going through. He kept his eyes on them always, trying to figure out a plan to get himself, Landon, and Beth free from the Scavengers.

"Cody, are you well?" Henrich asked.

Landon sat still, quiet, he kept his head down and Henrich knew that he felt ashamed of his actions the previous night. Though, Landon rose up his head and looked at Henrich. Landon started to tear up a bit, remembering what he committed with the woman of the Scavengers. He felt truly ashamed of himself and of his deeds.

"I'm sorry for what I did, sir." Landon said sadly. "I didn't want to do it, but my body was telling me to. I couldn't contain it any longer. It was just too strong for me to bear and to hold in."

Henrich nodded and placed his hand on Landon's shoulder.

"I understand what it means to fall. But, that doesn't mean that it's all over and you'll be damned for your life. You have another opportunity to make things right and you will make them right. Only if you believe you have the courage and strength to do so. Otherwise, you will never recover from what you've experienced."

"Thank you for your honesty, sir. I don't know what I will do, but I will try to do better going forward. I only hope that I will not make the same mistake again and I have truly learned a lesson about not only myself, but of the internal struggle that we all fight against daily. It really is a fight."

Henrich smiled a bit, hearing those words come from Landon's own mouth. Henrich later turned to Beth, who kept silent and she was holding herself and shivering a bit. Henrich understood her motive of silence and he recognized it from others he's seen before in his lifetime.

"Beth." Henrich said. "I need you to listen to me for just a quick moment."

Beth slowly, but surely turned her sights to Henrich and in her eyes were pain, shame, and defeat. Henrich could sense it himself as eh looked into her eyes. Henrich felt somewhat responsible for what happened to both Landon and Beth. Henrich reached out to touch Beth, but she pulled away from him and he knew why she did.

"Beth, I'm sorry." Henrich said. "There was nothing I could do to stop them. They held me down and beat me while they were...."

Beth nodded in understanding Henrich.

"I know, and I can accept your apology." She said. "But, I will ask of this one favor."

"What is it?"

"When we get set free from these bonds, I will kill them all. Somehow and someway. They all must die."

Henrich smiled.

"That I can agree with you wholly possible."

Beth turned from Henrich and looked up at the sky. Landon kept to himself while Henrich sat and thought about an idea to get them free. Later, in the night, Wade rallied up the Scavengers once more, while several brought Henrich, Landon, and Beth toward him and the surrounding Scavengers. They held them still as they stood facing Wade.

"Now, I know what some of you are thinking right now. Why have I brought these three guests of ours up front. I'll tell you why. Because we need some entertainment tonight!"

The Scavengers cheered on while Henrich stared at Wade. Landon focused his attention toward Wade and the nearby Scavengers and Beth only stayed silent and still. She didn't move an inch. Wade silenced the Scavengers.

"Now, old man. This same entertainment will not be a repeat of the beautiful sight that was last night. But, this entertainment will be either life or death for the three of you."

"What are you talking about?" Henrich asked. "What do you mean this will be either death or life for one of us?"

"Because, I'm placing you three inside the Pit."

Henrich looked at Wade, who signaled for the Scavengers to bring them to the Pit. Henrich watched on, seeing a few of the Scavengers turning around from the Pit as if they were afraid of what's in it. The other Scavengers walked on with Wade towards it. Landon and Beth also gazed their sights to what could be inside the

Pit. Inching closer, Henrich could feel heat coming from the Pit, which explained the smoke he seen before when being placed in the campsite.

"It's hot." Landon said.

"What is in there?" Henrich asked.

"Well, some old friends of ours." Wade answered. "But, I know that they will not harm us, but they will surely take a bite out of you three without any hesitation."

Reaching the edge of the Pit and having a few within it, Henrich could see what was conjuring the heat and the smoke. Within the Pit were Salamanders, elementals creatures of fire. Known across the Worlds as "Nature Spirits". The Scavengers cheered on as the Salamanders screeched out toward them and Wade. Henrich glanced over to Wade, seeing him smiling as if he was a child at the zoo. He waved to the Salamanders.

"Aren't they just beautiful." Wade said. "I mean look at them for crying out loud."

"Where did you get those creatures?" Henrich asked.

"None of your concern, old man. But, I will say that it took us some time to gather them all together to place them inside this hole that we dug. Besides, we originally dug the hole for any Scavengers or guests of ours that would've died here, but after we caught these creatures, we figured it was best to give this hole to them and now it is their primary habitat within our camp."

"You do not know what you're all playing with." Henrich said. "Those creatures possess power that will not only kill you all, but will destroy this entire land and make into a land of fire."

"That is not our concern right now, old man. But, if they do start to act up against us, we will put them out of their misery."

"You can't just kill these creatures with your methods of attack. They are smarter than you give them credit for."

"Tell me, how would you know all of this? Have you encountered them before in your lifetime?"

"I've seen many creatures in my life and all of them have the potential to do deadly things. Not only to Man, but to all the

Worlds."

Wade waved Henrich off as he commanded the Scavengers to toss them into the fiery pit. The Scavengers shove them, and they fall into the Pit, where they are surrounded by the Salamanders. Landon and Beth stood close to Henrich in the middle of the Pit, where they were surrounded by four Salamanders. The Salamanders screeched at them and their tongues slithered with fire dripping from their mouths. The intense heat was unbearable, but Henrich stood his ground.

"Just hold yourselves and be calm." Henrich said to Landon and Beth.

"How are we going to fight these things?" Landon asked. "Because I'm concerned right now."

The Salamanders of the Pit were dry-skinned, red, and thin creatures. Wisps of flames covered their bodies and within the fires around the Pit, Henrich spotted several spiritual entities roaming around in the flames. Landon and Beth measured he creatures, seeing how the lizard creatures scaly skin was protected from the flames and how their length was about five feet.

"What can we do?" Beth mentioned. "We have no weapons to face them."

"We have no other option." Henrich said, holding up his fists against the Salamanders.

Wade stood over them and yelled out a great shout. The Scavengers stood around the Pit, holding makeshift weapons of stone. He grabbed the weapons, which were made in the images of hammers, swords, and maces. Wade tossed them into the Pit, where Henrich looked up toward him as he grabbed the hammer. Wade smiled.

"Best that you have better means to face them. Now, give us what we want. Entertainment for tonight."

Landon grabbed the mace and Beth took the sword as they stood facing the Salamanders. The Scavengers began to cheer loudly, causing the Salamanders to screech and they spit out fire toward them Henrich moved out of the flame's way and swiped the

Salamander in its side with the hammer. The Salamander screech with a loud noise as its tail swiped across Henrich's chest, knocking him to the ground. Landon and Beth fought against the other three Salamanders with the sword and mace.

Henrich stood up and faced the Salamander again, this time running towards it as it spat out more fire in his direction. The flames burned through Henrich's coat and hat. He removed them, and jumped atop the Salamander. Riding it like it was a bull, Henrich took the hammer and slammed it against the Salamander's head several times. Blow after blow he slammed down the hammer. Wade kept his eyes on Henrich, looking at his fighting skills against the Salamander.

"This old man knows things that we don't." He said. "You can see it in his skills."

"Do you want us to interrogate him for you after the fight?" A Scavenger questioned.

"That is if he survives this. If he does, bring him to my trailer and I will have word with him."

"We shall do."

Henrich continued pummeling the Salamander in its head and it fell to the ground, where it began to bleed fire, a red-orange looking liquid fire in its form. Another Salamander faced Henrich and he faced it with a smile on his face. Henrich lunged toward the creature with the stone hammer in hand.

Landon took the mace and slammed it against one of the Salamander's back, though the Salamander wasn't affected by the blunt, he swiped against Landon and punched him onto the ground. Landon placed the mace in between himself and the Salamander's fiery mouth. The fire dripped onto the ground inches away from Landon's face. He grunted as he made the attempt of shoving the creature's weight off himself.

"Get off, will you!" Landon screamed, fighting against the Salamander.

Beth ran over and slashed the stone sword against the Salamanders' side, slightly cutting through its scaly skin. The

Salamander backed off Landon and looked at Beth. Its eyes showed its anger toward her and she looked around at the two Salamanders. They were prepared to pounce her and dose her with their fire. Landon stood up and attack the Salamanders with the mace. Hitting its legs and its tail.

"Take care of the other one, please." Landon told Beth.

Beth took the sword and swiped it towards the other Salamander, who backed away from the sword and spat out fire toward her. The fire touched the sword, though it did not destroy it. Beth smiled as she jumped atop the Salamander and took the stone sword, stabbing it through its back and ramming down as much as she could until the sword broke through the Salamander's stomach. The creature screamed as it fell to the ground and died. Beth pulled out the sword and jumped off the dead creature. She looked ahead and saw Landon fighting one and Henrich fighting the other.

Henrich took the hammer and destroyed the Salamander with it, until its head was flat as the ground they walked on. Landon took the mace and slammed it into the last Salamander around its body. Beth ran towards them to help as did Henrich and the three of them together slew the last Salamander. As it died, the flames that surrounded the Pit, suddenly ceased and the spirits that were within them appeared and flew into the night sky, vanishing along into the darkness. Wade stood by the edge of the Pit very still. His eyes locked on them and he began to applaud them for their victory.

"I'll be damn." He said. "They survived."

The Scavengers were silent, seeing the Salamanders killed and the Three surviving. Henrich looked toward Wade and pointed the hammer to him. Wade knew what they were about to do, he raised up his hand toward them, gesturing to them to come up the Pit and slaughter him and the Scavengers.

Beth wanted to kill them as she was covered with the Salamander's blood. All Landon wanted to do was smash Wade's head in with the mace. Henrich knew he wanted them all dead, but to try an attack on them while they're surrounded isn't a wise decision to make. Henrich picked up his hat and coat, seeing the flames on them had ceased. He put them back on, seeing Wade continuing to gesture to them.

"You have your chance to end all of us now." He said. "So, bring your asses up here and kill us all."

"I'll take the pleasure." Beth said, holding the stone sword tightly in her hands.

Henrich stopped her and she didn't know why. She looked up at them and all that was on her face was anger. Intense anger. Landon felt the same, but knew there was something wrong overall. Plus, seeing how Henrich reacted to Wade's gesture ring told Landon so much more than he already knew.

"Why are you stopping me?!" Beth yelled.

"Because if you act now, they will kill you." He replied.

"They can try."

"Beth, calm yourself." Landon said. "Listen to Henrich, please."

Beth turned to Henrich, taking in Landon's choice of words. Henrich looked her in the eyes and could see her anger. He understood her anger and why she wanted to slaughter them. Henrich held her tightly, she felt comfort with Henrich's hug. Wade watched them as the Scavengers stood quiet.

"He knows how to humble them." Wade said. "I'm starting to like this old man."

"Just wait." Henrich told Beth. "Just wait for the right moment to strike."

"Alright." She said. "I will wait for it."

Henrich released Beth and Wade signaled to the Scavengers to grab them and bring them back to the table. The Scavengers pulled them from the Pit and tied up their hands again. They took the stone weapons and placed them in a shed, where their own gear was placed. Henrich watched as they placed the weapons within the shed and shut the door. He spotted one Scavenger handing the keys to the shed to another Scavenger. He kept the Scavenger's appearance and facial details in his memory. While being brought back to the table, two of the Scavenger guards grabbed Henrich by his arms and he looked at them.

"What of me now?" Henrich asked them.

"Wade would like to speak with yon again inside his trailer."

"What for?"

"You'll hear once you're in his presence, old man."

Henrich walked with them toward the trailer and they entered it. The guards placed Henrich in the same seat as before where Wade sat in front of him. Only this time, the guard left the trailer and Wade had no tea to drink. Wade looked at how dirty Henrich was from the fights with the Salamanders. He could see the scorched burnt marks on Henrich's clothes and the blood on his face.

"I am impressed." Wade said. "Truly I am. I didn't know the three of you could fight like that."

"We did what we had to do to survive." Henrich said. "What else were you expecting?"

"I expected the three of you to be killed and eaten by the Salamanders. Who were our pets by the way and now they're dead. Thanks to you and your partners."

Henrich shook his head, looking around the trailer.

"Why am I here again?"

"Because I have something to show you."

Wade walked form the table to the back of the trailer and when he returned to Henrich, he was carrying with him the strange weapons that the other Scavengers found in the tall buildings back at the other town. Henrich stared at the weapons and he knew what they were and how they were used. Wade placed the weapons on the table between them. Wade patted them as if they were a prized dog of his.

"I was wondering if you know about these? My people found them when they scavenged a town not too far from here. They were in some tall building, just lying there. As if whoever was there left without any trace."

Henrich smirked as he looked at the weapons. Wade didn't

understand the smirk, but he took it as an insult to himself. Wade slammed his hand on the table, facing Henrich. The two men looked eye to eye and not a word was said for the moment. Wade slowly backed into his chair and sighed. Henrich's smirk became nothing.

"I believe that you know what these are and what they can do."

"How would you know that?"

"Because that's why I'm asking you right now. Tell me what these weapons are and teach my people how to use them."

"And what will I get out of doing these things for you?"

"Your freedom of course."

"You promised me that a while ago and yet, look what has happened to us."

"Because you didn't accept my agreement in joining us. You declined it, so I had to teach you three a lesson in when you decline an offer that I give to you."

"Then, you'll be delighted to know that I don't accept this agreement. Neither will I teach you and your people about these weapons and how they are used."

"So, you know what these things are, and you know how to use them, don't you?"

Henrich stared for a moment, he gazed his sights down to the weapons and looked back to Wade.

"Yes. I know of these weapons."

"So, you will teach us about them. You will."

"No, I will not."

"Give a reason why you won't teach us? Why won't you teach me?"

"Truthfully, because these weapons are far beyond your understanding and comprehension. The art of these weapons would destroy your very mind and would make you into a madman."

Wade held his head down at the table. He glanced up to Henrich as he eyes turned to the weapons. He smirked at Henrich before standing up over the table and Henrich himself. Henrich only stared at him and kept silent.

"Be that as it may, old man. But, if you won't teach myself and my people the art of these weapons, then worse things will come upon you, Cody, and Beth. You think what we did you three was bad? Hell, you aren't even aware of the things that we can truly do to you. We could do things that would bring you three to utter shame. It would destroy your inner being and it will cause you to fall and to never get back up. We can do those things and we are capable of it."

Henrich nodded. Taking in every word that was spoken from Wade's mouth. He knew that Wade was speaking some truth, but most of his words were only filled with lies and attempts at drawing fear into the room. Henrich looked at Wade. A still face and a silent one.

"Do what you have to do, boy." Henrich said.

Wade didn't like Henrich's choice of words and punched him in the face. Wade punched him again and again. But, the punches didn't faze Henrich. Wade knew that as he could see Henrich kept his eyes locked on him as he was punching him. Wade walked to the trailer's door. Opening it, calling for the guards. The guards enter the trailer and stand behind Henrich.

"Take him out of here and place him at the table."

"Will do."

The guards grabbed Henrich, returning him to the table once again. While they were walking outside, Wade watched them place Henrich at the table. He stared at Henrich, Landon, and Beth with anger. He rubbed his mouth, which was beginning to foam from his anger. He entered the trailer, slamming the door shut. Henrich watched as Wade slammed the door. Landon and Beth also noticed it by the door's sound echoing through the campsite. Henrich only smirked.

"What did you say to him, sir?" Landon asked.

"I didn't say anything to him." Henrich replied. "He wanted to know how to use something and I declined."

Landon wanted to say something, but didn't know how to say.

He looked at Henrich, who could see the words trying to push out of his mouth.

"What is it, boy?"

"I just wanted you to know that I repented of my actions. It was what I had to do to make myself clean again."

Henrich nodded with a smile on his face. "It was a good decision of you to make."

Henrich looked at Beth, who was still filled with anger, her fists clenched, she was ready to attack the Scavengers at any moment that she could.

"Calm yourself, Beth." Henrich said. "Just calm yourself."

"I am calm." She replied. "I will be fully calm when I get my hands on them."

"I know."

"So, do you have an idea to how we can make an escape?"

Henrich looked at the Scavenger with the shed key, who walked around the campsite continually and he glazed toward the shed itself. He turned back to Beth, showing a smirk on his face and Landon inched into the conversation.

"I might have a way out of here."

<u>V</u>

Randolph looked around the campsite, seeing the Scavengers walking on about their business. The night was surely coming ahead as he seen Wade speaking with other Scavengers, showing them the strange weapons. The other Scavengers wee clueless to how they worked and how they were formed. Landon looked at them and turned his head to Henrich, while gazing toward the Scavengers. Watching them as if they're about to approach them once again.

"How are we going to get out of here?" Landon questioned.

"I have an idea." Henrich said. "But, it will require to spillage of blood."

"How will that work out?" Beth asked.

"It will work out for the better. The only thing will be it must come from either one of you."

"Why one of us?"

"I've already bled for them and me bleeding again won't help out our plan. They will come and aid if it's one of you. They would leave me to bleed to death otherwise."

Landon looked around, searching for a tool that would be able to cut through their skin. He couldn't find one nearby the table.

"I don't see anything here that could cut through our skin, sir."

"Keep looking around. There has to be something capable of doing it."

Beth looked down underneath the table and found a small blade. The blade was made from glass and it wasn't sharp enough to cut through the binds of their hands, but it could slice through their skin with enough force onto it. Beth handed the blade to Henrich, who looked closely at it.

"Where did you find this?"

"Under the table."

"There was a blade there the whole time?" Landon wondered.

"The worlds are stranger than you can believe, boy."

Henrich grabbed the blade.

"This will do." Henrich confirmed. "Now, who will it be?"

Landon looked over to Beth and she does the same. Landon nodded with a straight face and turned to Henrich. He held his hands open toward him.

"Give it to me." He said. "I'll do it."

"Understandable." Henrich said. "Make sure you do it slightly around your arm and not too much. Otherwise, you'll be a dead man."

"I will keep my eyes on it."

Landon took the blade and reached toward his left forearm, cutting his flesh. Landon yelled as the blade went into his skin and the blood began to arise. The yelling caused the Scavengers to look as did Wade, who seen Landon's forearm bleeding.

"The hell is going on over there?!" Wade yelled. "What are you three idiots doing?!"

Wade ran toward them as did some of the Scavengers. Henrich seen them approaching and he nodded to Landon to cease the cutting. Landon stopped cutting himself and slipped the blade over to Henrich, who placed it inside his coat pocket. Beth turned her head as Wade and the Scavengers approached them. They surrounded them as Wade looked at the wound on Landon's forearm. He could see it was cut, but not a deep cut wound. Wade gazed over to Henrich and Beth.

"The hell is this?" Wade asked. "Tell me, what is this shit? What are you fools doing over here when we're not watching you people?"

"He just cut himself by accident." Henrich said. "That's all that happened."

Wade smirked to Henrich and the smirk immediately turned into a frown. Wade was not pleased with Landon's wound and Henrich knew he wouldn't be. Wade turned to the Scavengers in a small fit of anger.

"Go get the med kit and bring it over here." He told them.

The Scavengers left to get the med kit from the trailer of Wade. Wade stood by Landon, overseeing his forearm continuing to bleed. He looked outward at the Scavengers, who were exiting his trailer with the med kit, a blue and white box. Wade waved to them to hurry themselves up.

"Come on now!" Wade yelled. "We don't have the entire night to do this mess."

They come with the kit and hand it to Wade. Wade opened the med kit and revealed bandages, patches, and other medical supplies. Wade commanded for two Scavengers to hold Landon down as he applied the bandages onto Landon's forearm with a little bit of alcohol that was within the kit. Landon yelled for a moment in pain while his forearm was being bandaged. Beth turned away from the sight and Henrich only watched on. Staring at Wade as a predator would stalk its prey in an open field.

"Almost done with your ass." Wade said. "Just be still for a short moment, will you."

Wade tightened the bandage on Landon's forearm and the Scavengers released their grip on him. Landon looked at his forearm, seeing the bandage. Wade stared at Landon. Looking him in the eye. He gazed toward Henrich, seeing him staring back with the brim's shadow covering his eyes in the night. Wade smiled back to him before facing Landon.

"Since you decided to be a fool for the day, I have something for you tonight and you're not going to like it."

"What are you going to do to me this time?" Landon asked. "Are you going to try and get one of your women to molest me again? Because it's not going to happen this time."

Wade laughed.

"You know I would. But, you've already done that whole deal. So, this time I'm going to give the Scavengers the entire night to beat you down until they're tired of beating you."

Wade looked out to the Scavengers, who grabbed Landon from the table and brought him to their circle. In the circle were several men, who began to pummel Landon into the ground. Henrich stood up from the table, but was held down by three other Scavengers. Wade laughed at Henrich.

"You still have the fight in you. Just give up for once."

Beth looked at Wade, getting his attention. He looked at her and stared back. Seeing her anger in her eyes. Wade knew that she was not fooling around any longer. Beth slowly stood up from the table and faced Wade. Wade approached her, he held his hand up, stopping the other Scavengers from confronting her. He smirked in her face.

"What are you going to do, young lady? What can you do to me that hasn't been done before?"

Beth only stared into his eyes and she kicked him in his groin. Wade yelled as he fell to the ground. Holding his genitals tightly, screaming in pain. The other Scavengers looked at Beth and Henrich elbowed them in their faces, knocking them back. Henrich kicked them each in the head, knocking them unconscious. Landon tried to fight back, getting hits on several of the Scavengers before being crowded and jumped by many more. They yelled and screamed in his face and ears. Wade crawled on the ground, slowly standing himself up and still holding himself, trying to compress the pain. He looked at Beth and backslapped her.

"Dumb bitch." Wade said. "I should've been the one to have you myself."

Henrich kicked Wade onto the ground as he helped Beth get up from the ground. Wade looked at Henrich, who was eager to kill him where he was laying down. Wade shook his head as Henrich grabbed him by his jacket. Henrich held him up by the nearby post. Jerking him around.

"You will bring Cody back over here." Henrich said. "Do you understand what I say to you?"

"I got you, old man." Wade replied slowly. "I heard your words."

"You're going to die soon." Henrich said.

"We'll find that out won't we." Wade said with a fainting smirk.

Henrich held him and threw him to the ground, where Wade stood up and ran toward the crowd of Scavengers. He stepped into the circle, near Landon, holding his hands out to the other Scavengers.

"Cease." Wade yelled. "The boy's had his beat down for the night."

Landon stood up, wiping the blood from his nose and mouth. Wade approached him and tossed him a towel from the trailer. Landon held the towel in his hand before seeing Wade standing in front of him.

"Wipe yourself, boy." Wade said.

Landon lunged toward Wade, punching him in his face. The Scavengers came around, dragging Landon from Wade and holding him up in the air above their heads while others went to assist Wade off the ground. Wade laughed as hit spat blood from his mouth. Wade enjoyed it and stood holding his arms out toward Landon. Landon struggled against the Scavengers to approach Wade.

"Come on, boy! Come punch me again and you'll see where you will end up!"

The Scavengers dragged Landon back to the table and left him there. Wade stood by and watched. He rubbed his hands together, staring at the three of them. Henrich stood there and stared back. As did Beth and Landon. They had enough of these games and Wade knew it. He turned to one of the Scavenger guards and approached him closely.

"Tomorrow, we kill them." Wade whispered.

"By any means?" The guard asked.

"Any means necessary." Wade replied as he entered his trailer for the night.

Henrich looked at Landon, who wiped the blood from his face with the towel before throwing it to the ground. Landon has had enough of the Scavengers and ways payback. Beth wants the same as does Henrich.

"I want to beat that man down." Landon said. "I want to kill him and his friends."

"In a short time, we will." Henrich said.

"How can you be sure of that?" Beth asked. "We don't have any means to get out of these bonds right now."

Henrich reached slowly into his coat, avoiding the prying eyes of the Scavengers as they head off to sleep for the night. From his coat, Henrich pulled out a knife. Landon and Beth stood still as their eyes were locked into the knife.

"Where did you get that, sir?" Landon asked.

"I got it off the Scavenger that held me down. After I knocked him unconscious."

"So, cut us free." Beth said.

"Not right now."

Landon and Beth looked at one another. As if Henrich was crazy to hold off their chance at freedom. Beth shook her head, she didn't understand what Henrich was truly planning and neither did Landon. Henrich placed the knife back into his coat and watched as the Scavengers went to sleep. Landon and Beth noticed, and they now had the chance at being free from the Scavengers for good. But, Henrich kept the knife in his coat.

"Why aren't you cutting us free?" Landon wondered. "We have the chance now."

"We need our gear back."

"So, where is it?"

Henrich pointed to the shed across from them. Not too far from Wade's trailer. They looked ahead and noticed the lock pad on the shed's door.

"Which one of them has the key?" Beth asked.

"The one that went inside the other trailer behind Wade's."

"I'm starting to get it now." Landon said. "You're waiting till you're closer to the one with the key before cutting us loose."

"In the morning, he will walk over here and when he does. I will stab him in his neck and take the key from him. After that, we will get our weapons back and them will we kill these people."

Landon and Beth nodded to Henrich.

"Well then, I'll wait till the morning." Beth said.

Later that night, Henrich had a vision. The vision was a future that was very near. In the vision of Henrich, was a chaotic event taking place at the campsite of the Scavengers. In the vision, the Scavengers were running to save their lives. They were running from gunshots that came from the campsite and standing in the campsite were Henrich, Landon, and Beth. The three of them were all holding shooters and firing at the Scavengers. They killed many of them as others ran into the wilderness. The vision later warped itself to a field, where Henrich stood over Wade, with the shooter pointed at him.

"This is where you die." Henrich told Wade before killing him.

From the shooting, Henrich awoken from the vision and looked up at the sky, it was morning. Henrich woke Landon and Beth up from their slumber.

"Huh? What's going on?" Landon said muffled in his sleep.

"I had a vision." Henrich said. "I know how we're going to get ourselves free."

"How?" Beth asked softly.

Henrich looked up and he faced ahead, toward the shed. From the shed came the Scavenger with the key and he was approaching their location. Landon and Beth looked on seeing the Scavenger coming toward them.

"Here he comes." Henrich said.

The Scavenger with the shed key stopped at the table and gazed at the three of them. He kneeled in front of them. Dangling the key in their faces. Showing them that he is in full possession of their gear.

"How does it feel to know that I own all of your shit?" The Scavenger said.

"It feels quite well." Henrich said.

"What does that mean?"

"It means-"

Henrich quickly took the knife and stabbed it in the Scavenger's throat. He gargled on his own blood as Landon snatched the key from his dying hands. Henrich grabbed the Scavenger and tossed him behind the post, where he rolled down into a ditch nearby the campsite. Landon tossed Henrich the keys to the shed. Henrich took the knife and cut himself loose of the bonds. He then cut loose Landon and Beth. Henrich looked down at the keys and seeing how many of the Scavengers were slowly walking up for the morning. They stood up from the table, overlooking the campsite as far as their eyes could see.

"What now?" Landon said, filled with energy.

"It's time." Henrich said as they walked toward the shed.

VI

Henrich ran toward the shed and unlocked it with the key.

Slowly, opening the shed to avoid causing the Scavengers to et up from their sleep. Henrich, Landon, and Beth entered the shed and sitting against the wall of the shed was their gear. All of it. From their shooters, their knives, and other supplies they brought along with them. They take their gear and equip themselves with it as they were before being captured by the Scavengers. Beth placed the shooter that was given to her on her hip. Landon kept his shooter and knife close by and Henrich stood there with his shooters in their holsters, the blast shooter on his back and the machete within the interior of the coat.

"Are you ready, sir?" Landon asked Henrich.

"I am." He replied. "Let's make a clean sweep of these people."

As the Scavengers awoke in the morning, Wade exited his trailer and looked over to the table. Not seeing either one of the Three there, Wade started to panic and approached the Scavengers that were walking about on the campiest.

"Where did they go?" Wade asked. "Have you seen them anywhere?"

"I have not, sir." The Scavenger replied. "I haven't seen them since last night."

"Damn it!" Wade yelled. "Where are they?!"

From the shed, Henrich kicked the door down, seeing the Scavengers standing right in front of him. Henrich fired his shooter at any of the Scavengers who were in his sights. So, did Landon and Beth. The Scavenger yelled in fear and ran off from the campsite to avoid being killed by them. Wade looked on, seeing them coming from the shed. His heart had dropped in his chest and he was at a loss for words.

"No." He said to himself.

Some Scavengers attempted to take down Henrich, Landon, and Beth. Although, they underestimated their skill set with the shooters and weapons they carried on them. Henrich pulled out the machete and began slashing Scavengers left and right. Landon took his knife and stabbed many of them in their chests and their neck. Beth took her shooter and fired it, aiming for their heads. Henrich later pulled out the blast shooter and fired it. The bullet of the blast shooter went through the backs of three Scavengers at once.

"Now, you all know who we are!" Henrich yelled.

Wade stood still with his hands on his head. He gazed around the campsite, seeing it being destroyed by them. Most of the Scavengers ran into the forests that stood near the campsite. Beth watched many of them enter the wilderness. She fired several shots toward it, not knowing if she managed to take some of them down with her aiming.

"Most of them ran into the woods!" Beth said. "What are we going to do about them, Henrich?"

Henrich blasted one Scavenger in his head with the blast shooter and turned to Beth as the blast shooter's barrel was smoking.

"We go after them." Henrich said. "And we kill them all."

Beth nodded as she and Landon went for the wilderness. Henrich killed the remaining Scavengers that stayed in the campsite and he looked up toward the trailer, seeing Wade standing there. Henrich took the blast shooter and fired it toward him. Wade ran out of the fire and went into the wilderness himself. Henrich shook his head as he watched Wade run. He never seen him with that much fear in his being.

"The woods won't save you." Henrich said.

Henrich entered the woods himself and within the tall trees, echoes of screams and gunshots could be heard. Henrich knew that Landon and Beth were killing as many Scavengers that they could find. Henrich, meanwhile, searched the forest for Wade, who was hiding within the trees of the wilderness.

"Wade." Henrich said. "Show yourself. I don't recall you being this afraid of me before and yet, you ran from me."

Further into the forest, Landon shot one of the Scavengers in the leg, causing them to fall. The Scavenger he shot was the woman he had sex with the nights ago. She looked at him as he stood over her, his shooter aimed at her head. She panted for air as she was in fear of Landon.

"You remember that night?"

The woman nodded her head quickly as she could. Landon cocked his head.

"I do too." He said, taking the shot and killing her.

Beth fired as many rounds as she could with the shooter she had. Shooting Scavengers in their backs, legs, and head. She aimed as much as she could to get the perfect shots to fire. From behind, Beth was tackled to the ground by the same woman who had her way with her that night. She jumped atop of Beth, holding her down with her own weight.

"What are you going to do now, pretty girl?!" The woman yelled. "You can't get up from me. I own your ass remember!"

She went to kiss Beth and Beth spat in her face. The woman wiped the spit from her face and Beth grabbed her shooter, firing it directly into the woman's face. Beth shoved her body off her own and continued moving through the forest, killing more of the Scavengers.

Henrich continued to search for Wade, while he was killing Scavengers that he encountered. Henrich killed many of them with the blastshooter and the machete. Wade could hear the screams and cries of his clan and he didn't know what to do. He kept himself hidden from Henrich's sight as well as Landon's and Beth's if they were to come across him in the woods.

"Show yourself, Wade." Henrich yelled. "Why are you suddenly afraid of us?"

Wade kept himself silent, as his voice would give away his location in the trees. Henrich knew he would keep silent and continued walking through the wilderness, killing all the Scavengers that remained and from the numbers, there were many of them roaming through the wilderness. They ran with fear as they were hunted down by Henrich, Landon, and Beth. Some of the Scavengers knew this day would come and they weren't prepared for its arrival.

<h1 style="text-align:center"><u>VII</u></h1>

Henrich continued killing the Scavengers that fled with Landon and Beth. Their shooters were being reloaded every time they came closer to being out. The Scavengers had no other means to fight back besides their own bodies and the branches of the forest. Wade moved silently through the wilderness, trying his hardest to be unseen by Henrich, Landon, and Beth. He continued to hear his people's cries for help and Wade shook his head in shame of himself and in shame of his people.

"I thought they were stronger than this." Wade said to himself concerning his clan. "I thought they had the heart to stay strong and overcome. But, I was wrong. I was so wrong."

Landon and Beth continued killing the Scavengers that they came across. One Scavenger grabbed a branch from the ground and swung at Landon, who moved out of the branches' path and he kicked the Scavenger's knee from behind. The Scavenger fell to one knee and as the Scavenger turned his head, he only seen the barrel of Landon's shooter and the shooter fired. The Scavenger's body fell to the ground.

"Now stand up." Landon said.

Beth fired countless rounds at the Scavengers. She followed their cries for Wade's help and she could hear footsteps coming from behind her. She turned around and was grabbed by two male Scavengers. They held her tightly and yelled in her ear. They tried to snatch the shooter from her hand, but she held onto the weapon. One decided if he couldn't get the shooter, he would get something else as he tried to place his hand inside of her pants. She kicked him and bit his arm.

"Get off!" She screamed.

"Scream for me!" One Scavenger yelled. "I have all day!"

"Listen to him!" The other Scavenger said. "Scream for him and after that, you're going to yell for me!"

They knocked Beth to the ground with their own strength. But, they didn't pay much attention to her hands as she aimed the shooter as quickly as she could and started firing it several times toward them. The rounds went through the Scavengers' chests and abdomen. The Scavengers died as they fell. Beth stood up from the ground, wiping the dirt and leaves from her clothing. She took a moment to breathe before following the cries of the Scavengers. While she ran, she could also her the gunshots from Henrich and Landon, learning how to point out their locations in the wilderness.

Deeper in the wilderness, Landon fired shots at two Scavengers and after he fired the next shot. His shooter was out, and he had to reload. Yet, surrounding him were the two Scavengers as well as another one that appeared from behind him. They screamed at Landon as he tried to reload the shooter as fast as he could. One of the Scavengers ran toward him and tackled him to the ground. They stood over him, taunting him to stand back on his feet. Landon nodded and stood up. He placed the shooter on his side and faced the three Scavengers. They were impressed with his stance and they lunged toward him.

"You see this!" One of the Scavengers said. "He's not afraid of us anymore!"

"Look at this boy!" Another Scavenger said.

"You wanted a fight." Landon said. "So, let's fight like men."

The Scavengers nodded and approached Landon, who quickly knocked one of them down with a haymaker and the second one, Landon kicked in the abdomen and kneed him in his face, pushing him down onto the ground.

The third Scavenger swung at Landon, who ducked and punched the Scavenger several times before elbowing him in his forehead. The Scavengers laid on the ground, slowly moving and trying to regain their concentration. As they were doing so, Landon reloaded the shooter and killed them before they could stand themselves back up.

Henrich continued with his machete, slicing away at the Scavengers. Henrich stopped for a second and listened closely to the screams and cries that consumed the forest. He listened as closely as he could, realizing there were less screams than before.

Henrich knew that they were almost done with the Scavengers and he kept moving, killing the rest of them that were in his sights.

Around the trees, Wade moved around slowly. He managed his steps on the ground, avoiding the down branches and the leaves that sat atop the dirt.

"WADE!" A Scavenger yelled out through the wilderness. "Where are you?!"

"He's running around her somewhere!" Henrich yelled. "Don't worry about him. I'll take care of him when I find him."

Henrich moved forward, killing the Scavengers he could see through the trees. Wade followed him very slowly. Though, he was filled with both anger and sadness and he could not decide what to do. He couldn't decide to try to save his clan or to let them die and leave only himself to survive to rotationally rebuild the Scavengers in some way.

Landon and Beth ran through the wilderness, looking for anymore Scavengers that they could find and through their running, they concluded they've killed most of the Scavengers. They each understood why they've done what they did and went back to find each other while still hearing a few Scavengers within the forest and the gunshots from Henrich's blastshooter.

"He's not that far away." Landon said. "Just a few more feet."

As they ran through the wilderness, Henrich's blast shooter became louder as did the screams of the remaining Scavengers. Landon and Beth both ran toward the sounds. Passing by the trees around them, inching closer to the noise. While they ran, Wade watched them from afar, seeing the two of them running through the woods. Wade didn't know what to do anymore. He remained silent and looked around for any remaining Scavengers within the area. He would jump slight every time Henrich fired his blastshooter.

<u>VIII</u>

Running through the wilderness, Landon bumped into Henrich, who fired the blast shooter at a fleeing scavenger. Landon looked ahead, seeing the Scavenger lying on the ground with the hole in his back. Henrich reloaded the blast shooter as Landon looked around.

"Where's Beth?" Landon asked.

"She's out here somewhere." Henrich replied. "She can handle herself. No need to concern yourself about her whereabouts."

"That I can understand."

Henrich and Landon ran further out together, looking for the last Scavengers. Beth, running through the forest looked ahead, seeing them running in front of her. She nodded as she followed them through the wilderness. As she followed them, Wade followed her, moving quietly in the wilderness. He knew he lost many of his people and he couldn't do anything about it, but he kept following them. Somewhat intrigued by their actions and their way of using the weapons.

Henrich tossed Landon another box of ammo for his shooter and while Landon placed the box in his pocket, they stopped in front of the two male Scavenger Guards from Wade's trailer. Big in size according to muscle and height to Landon's eyesight. The two men weren't afraid of Henrich and Landon nor were they afraid of the weapons they carried on them. The men beat on their chests while staring at them.

"How do we take these two down?"

"Simple." Henrich said, firing his blast shooter at one of the Scavengers. Blowing his head clean off.

The other Scavenger watched as his partner's head was blown from his body and he ran toward Henrich and Landon in anger. While he ran, a shooter sounded through the forest and killed the Scavenger from the side. Henrich and Landon looked over to the side where the shot came from and there was Beth, standing next to one of the trees with the shooter in her hands. Henrich nodded toward her as she waved to him and Landon. She approached them.

"I would guess you've done your best to get revenge." Henrich told her.

"I did what I had to do to survive." She replied. "How many do you think are left remaining out here?"

"Not that many. Wade is still around. So, we can count him."

Not too far from where Henrich, Landon, and Beth are talking, a Scavenger moved stealthy through the wilderness and as he ran from their location, The Scavenger ran directly into Wade. The Scavenger paused and hugged Wade, hoping to find some relief. Wave hugged him back. They were both in fear of the Three.

"What can we do, boss?" The Scavenger said.

"Nothing we can do now, my brother." Wade replied. "Only thing we can do is stick together."

"I hear you, sir."

Wade looked around for the Three, not seeing them anywhere near his location in the forests. He looked at the Scavenger, seeing him in constant fear for his life as he would turn around to look. He would turn constantly and would not stop. He looked as if he was in shock, but free to move around.

"So, where are the remaining brethren?" Wade asked.

"Most of them are dead." The Scavenger said. "There's probably only three of us left out here besides you, boss."

Wade nodded. Taking in the information that he knows. He patted the Scavenger on his right shoulder, trying to relax him.

"Just stay quiet and follow me."

The Scavenger nodded and after he nodded, his brains splattered onto Wade. Wade wiped the blood from his face and looked ahead. Seeing the Scavenger on the ground, dead by a shooter. In front of Wade, stood Henrich, with his shooter in hand.

"I've finally found you, boy." Henrich said.

Wade ran for his life and Henrich followed him as did Landon and Beth.

IX

Henrich, Landon, and Beth chased down Wade, who ran from them within the wilderness. Wade ran out of the wilderness and returned to the campsite. He looked around the site, searching for anymore Scavengers. There were none. Within the woods, Henrich spotted two Scavengers. He pointed Landon and Beth to their direction.

"Go after those two." Henrich said. "I'll deal with Wade."

Landon nodded and went after them. Beth stopped Henrich, before looking at Landon running.

"Leave some of Wade for me." She said.

"Fair." He replied.

Beth ran behind Landon. Henrich continued chasing down Wade and discovered he reentered the campsite. Henrich shook his head at Wade's choice of decision.

"Boy. You haven't learned anything in this short time." He said. "You are on your last hour."

Landon and Beth chased down the last two Scavengers. They fired shots at them, causing the Scavengers to run even faster. While they ran, they exited the forest and appeared on the pathways. The Scavengers looked around at the dusty road and from the other side of the pathways appeared Henrich's horse, which stampeded one of the Scavengers, killing him from his stomping. The other Scavenger watched on and took off running. He has lost hope in surviving. Landon and Beth appeared, seeing Henrich's horse sanding over a dead Scavenger and seeing the one Scavenger running down the pathways. Landon raised up his shooter, aimed for the Scavenger. He gazed over to Beth and lowered his shooter. He turned to Beth.

"Your shot."

Beth smiled as she aimed her shooter and fired, killing the Scavenger in the middle of the pathways. She sighed as she, Landon, and Henrich's horse went back to the forest to find Henrich. At the campsite, Henrich fired at the trailers and the tents that stood. He used the blastshooter to shoot at the vehicles that surrounded the campsite. Wade hid himself around the camp.

"Just do yourself a favor and end all of this." Henrich said. "You're wasting precious time here."

Wade stayed quiet, only hearing the shots from Henrich's shooters and blastshooter. He moved slowly behind his trailer. From the forest, Landon and Beth return to the campsite with Henrich's horse. Henrich looked behind himself, seeing the horse, which ran toward him. Henrich embraced the horse.

"I knew you would be back son." Henrich said.

Landon and Beth approached Henrich and the horse. He seen them standing there and pointed around the campsite. They looked on.

"He's here somewhere." Henrich said.

"Where could he be?" Beth asked.

"I am not sure about that. But, he's here and he won't leave this place."

"Why won't he leave?" Landon asked. "There's no one else here with him anymore."

Henrich looked at Landon and pointed around the campsite again.

"It's his home. It's all he's had and it will be his burial ground."

The horse gallop toward the trailer and they followed the horse. The horse circled the trailer. Giving Henrich a hint. Henrich nodded and kicked the trailer door open. He entered the trailer, but there was no sign of Wade. From the outside, Wade took off running. The horse galloped again as Landon and Beth turned around, seeing Wade running away.

"He's running off!" Beth yelled.

Henrich exited the trailer, seeing Wade running away from the campsite. Henrich looked at Beth. Seeing the shooter in her hand and her fingers twitching toward the trigger.

"Beth, you have your opportunity." Henrich said. "Take the shot."

"Yes sir." She said, aiming at Wade.

Beth pulled the trigger of the shooter and fired it. The bullet flew toward Wade and went right through his leg. Wade yelled as he fell to the ground, holding his leg. Beth placed the shooter to her side, Henrich and Landon stood by her, seeing Wade yelling and holding his leg in pain.

"You did good." Henrich said.

"Thank you." She replied. "What of him now?"

"I'll finish him off."

Henrich approached the down Wade and Landon and Beth followed him. Wade looked on as they approached him. He did what he could to back away from them as much as possible. But, his body was in so much pain, he couldn't not move from them. Henrich stood in front of him and Wade was in fear.

<u>X</u>

Henrich stood over Wade. Landon and Beth watched on while the Warslinger's horse stood still next to Henrich. Wade looked at the horse and looked at Henrich. He looked at the two of them again. He gazed to Beth and Landon.

"Where did that horse come from?" Wade asked.

"It belongs to me." Henrich said. "The horse is always close to my locations."

"That can't be possible."

"How come?"

"Because horses of this nature only belonged to Warslingers." Landon said.

"I told you I was one of them as did Cody."

"How? They're all supposed to be dead according to the stories told."

"The stories never tell all the details." Henrich said. "We are scattered across the Worlds, but in time, we will come together once again and bring a balance to the Worlds."

Wade nodded.

"Good luck with that." He said.

Henrich reached to his right holster, where he pulled out the shooter with the Heptad engraving marks. Wade looked at the shooter and he finally believed Henrich to be a Warslinger.

"Now, do you believe?" Henrich asked.

"I guess I do." Wade replied. "So, what of me now? Warslinger of the Heptad?"

"It's very simple, boy. Your life is over. Time for you to enter the Outer-World."

Henrich pulled the trigger of the Heptad shooter, killing Wade right in his campsite. While Wade's body laid on the dirt, Henrich, Landon, and Beth set fire to the Scavengers' campsite. Destroying all that belonged to them.

"Now, we can continue forward." Henrich said, getting atop his horse.

While the camp was burning, Landon spotted one of the dirt-speeders and took it. He rode on the speeders while Beth rode on the horse with Henrich. They left he campsite, which was set ablaze. Returning on the trail of the pathways, they went on about the journey toward The Haunted City.

"Do you know what else lies out here?" Beth asked.

"We'll find that out once we get far enough." Henrich replied.

<u>XI</u>

Leaving the destroyed campsite and the dead body of Wade behind and on the other side of its mighty structure, Henrich, feeling slightly relieved, traveled on horseback along with Landon and Beth. Traveling several miles from where they were, nearby the wilderness and Scavengers' site. They traveled further, on their way toward a place to gather more supplies for the long journey. While on the pathways, they came to a halt when bystanders approached them. Two of them, both were men, dressed in torn clothing. They carried wooden sticks in their hands, yelling and screaming for help.

"We need help!" One screamed.

"What is your problem?" Henrich asked.

"We just need to warn those who are traveling on this pathway to turn around. It's not safe down there."

"What is down there that makes the two of you afraid?"

"It's not safe down there." The second one said. "So, do yourselves a favor and turn around."

"Back there is only a destroyed campsite and a lot of dead bodies." Henrich said. "Nothing more and nothing else."

"Better a mountain of dead bodies and a demolished campsite than what's down there. I'll tell you that for sure."

Henrich nodded. Landon and Beth stayed quiet, seeing the bystanders walking themselves around them in a circle. They kept their hands to their side, next to their shooters. The bystanders continued to circle them, waving their sticks in their air like they were signs at a protest.

"Gentlemen, if you don't mind, we're on a journey and we do not want to be halted any longer."

Henrich went to move forward ahead and one of the bystanders decided to stand in the way of the horse. The horse shook its head, its mane flying around as Henrich stared at him, who stared back. Henrich nodded as he jumped off the horse and approached him. The bystander kept his ground, looking at the approaching Warslinger. Henrich wasn't intimidated by either one of the men and neither was he intimidated. Though, he appeared to be.

"Why won't you move out of the way?" Henrich said.

"Because you're not going down that pathway."

"Why not?"

"Because you shouldn't."

"That's not an answer, boy. Now, move out of our way or we'll make you move."

"Is that a threat? Are you threatening us right now?"

"Take it however you see it." Henrich said, getting atop the horse.

The two bystanders stood in front of them. They didn't; move, holding their sticks out in the way. Henrich nodded to them and he gazed to Landon and Beth. Landon looked at the bystanders, so did Beth. They turned their sights to Henrich, who looked back at the bystanders. The bystanders stood boldly in front of them. Their faces showed no emotion as it did previously. That confirmed to Henrich that they were playing a trick on them the entire time.

"What now." One bystander said.

"You're going to have to move us out of your way."

Henrich nodded to them, taking in their words.

"That's fine." Henrich said. "That's fine."

Henrich pulled out his shooter and fired it at the two bystanders. Killing them each with shots to the head. Their bodies fell to the ground. Henrich looked over to Landon and Beth.

"We keep moving." Henrich said, as they went pass the dead bystanders and down the pathways to continue their journey toward The Haunted City.

<u>XII</u>

Continuing from the bystanders they've met. They discover there to be a small village up ahead. Henrich noticed the small buildings that slightly resembled tents and hovels. They moved forward and while they came closer to the village, they could see the people that dwelled there, and they were immediately in fear of the Three. One child looked up at Henrich and ran off into the village, hiding from his sights.

"That child surely feared you." Beth said.

"I take that as a compliment." Henrich replied. "Most of these people might fear all of us. They know that we're different from them."

They decided to enter the village. Upon their entry, the inhabitants stared at them as if they are spirits to be opposed to the ones unseen. Henrich stopped as Landon and Beth seen a man approaching them. He was dressed in a mixture of sackcloth and animal skin clothing. His face was painted with red and black coloring and his hair was long, down past his shoulders, reaching his elbows. The man bowed his head before Henrich.

"It is an honor to see one of you." The man said.

"What do you mean by that?" Henrich asked.

"It doesn't take a strander or a knowledgeable man to know who you are and what you do."

The man knew Henrich to be a Warslinger of the Heptad as he looked past Henrich to Landon and Beth. He bowed to them. Showing his respect toward them as they were in allegiance with Henrich. The Warslinger looked at the village and seen its people. Young and old, men and women, ranging from all nationalities known to the Generations of Man.

"Before we came here, we ran into two men who were warning us of a city ahead." Henrich said. "What of this city they spoke of?"

"Come with men and settle yourselves down." The man said. "I can tell that you three have been through some rough times as of late. It shows within your eyes."

They listened to the man and followed him in the village. Moving past the others that lived there, they nodded and waved to them. The man led them to his base of operations within the village, which was a small shack. The shack was made of bark from the trees of the wilderness. Henrich could sense a power coming from the shack. It was familiar to him.

"What is of this structure?" Henrich asked. "I can sense something here and its embedded in the wood."

"This shack was built with the wood of the wilderness that sits in the Valley of Death. I had some of my people come along with me and we took down some of the trees. Though, we had to fight out way out of the forest against those shadowic beings that lurk about. We overcame and returned here to build many of these homes for the people."

"Most of the homes are built with the same wood from the Valley of Death?"

"Yes. We could've gone into the wilderness nearby. But, whenever we made the attempt. We were harassed and sometimes ambushed by a group that called themselves the Scavengers. They gave us no other choice but to travel down toward the Valley of Death and take some of the wood from there."

Henrich looked at the man and gazed around the village once again. Landon only stared at the man, taking in the words he spoke to them. Beth stood there, silent, but listening closely. Her ears were wide open to the conversation.

"Maybe the Scavengers are the reason why I can feel your pains." The man said. "Even your clothing bears the mark of their touch."

"You won't have to worry about them anymore." Henrich said. "They've been taken care of. All of them."

"Is that correct that I hear." The man said. "You killed them all. Every Scavenger that there is? They're all gone now?"

Henrich nodded.

"That is the case." Henrich said. "We took care of them before coming down the pathways and finding your village. We killed their leader and burned down their campsite. Leaving nothing of theirs to remain standing."

The man nodded and clapped his hands. He was happy to hear the news of the Scavengers' destructive end. He rallied up his people, telling them of the news of the Scavengers. The people of the village turned to Henrich, Landon, and Beth and began cheering them. Thanking them for saving them from any more harm. They only nodded and held their hands up to the cheering. The man stood there, smiling as he watched his people be happy and cheer.

"Please, come with me. For I know you will stay for the night as the sun is already showing signs of its setting phase."

Henrich looked up at the sky and saw that the sun was showing signs of setting. Unusual to him, knowing that only several hours have passed since the previous night. Henrich agreed to stay at the village for the night. The man led them to a empty shack, where

Henrich, Landon, and Beth will stay for the night. Inside the shack were several cots and a table for eating. Henrich looked at the place and nodded. He felt comfortable within the shack.

"How will this do for you, Warslinger?" The man asked.

"It will do just fine for me. We have to thank you for this."

"There is no need. You have done enough for us in eliminating our enemy of the land. This is the best that we can do for your service."

The man left them inside the shack as they prepared themselves for the night.

As the sun set and the moon arose, the inhabitants of the village partied for the night and the party was unlike those of the Scavengers. The village's party was one of praising and thanking. They continued to thank the Three for killing the Scavengers and sparring them anymore trouble ahead. The people danced with each other and they were happy. Landon and Beth watched them dance with smiles on their faces. Signs of joy.

"They seem like much better people, don't you think?" Landon said.

"They appear to be." Beth said. "I haven't seen any problems with them as all since we've been here."

As the party was going on, Henrich walked with the man throughout the village. Speaking with one another concerning the Scavengers, their leader Wade, and other events that prelude their current conversation. The man spoke of historical events that Henrich knew of, but didn't know that had traveled across the Worlds, hitting the ears of all who would listen. The history that contained information of the Warslingers and their legendary activities.

"I take it that you haven't come across your brethren yet?" The man asked.

"I haven't seen any of them in ages." Henrich replied. "I can only wonder when we will cross paths again.

"When you all do, you will know why you've been brought back together again. In time, it will all come to you as it did to those who came before you. It is something that happens in the Worlds. The universe itself binds these events together and most of the time, repeats itself. Many of the generations of Man believe it all to be a fairy tale of sorts. Though, I have concluded it all exists. All that we know is true."

"May I ask, where did you encounter this historical information?"

'I spoke with someone who lived ages ago and traveled the Worlds for thousands of years. The one who taught me how to survive out here in this land. He taught me how to build these shacks and homes for the people, he taught me wisdom and how to apply it and he taught me of the times before and the times to come."

"The times to come?"

"Yes. He told me some small details concerning the future the Worlds have ahead of them."

"So, what is of their future?"

The man smiled, and he placed his hand on Henrich's shoulder. He looked at Henrich, knowing him to be seeking answer and yet, he knew that the answers were already on their way to him. Just not at the precise moment. The man nodded to Henrich, while looking around the village, seeing the people continuing to dance and praise.

"This is not the time for you to know, Warslinger. Though, that time is not too far from you. It is coming closer than you think."

"Sorry to ask of this. But, I never got your name."

"My name is Necuametl. Many only call me sir, master, friend, brother, or father."

"Your name sounds familiar to my ears. Is it your birth name?"

"It was. Yet, eons of time have erased it from the minds and records of Man. When I became the leader of this village, the people only referred to me as the titles I have previously told you."

Necuametl looked up at the moon, seeing its bright feature above them in the sky. Henrich also looked up toward the moon. Necuametl smiled.

"Something isn't it. How that large object was placed there to have its ruling during the darkness and how the sun is in place when we are in the morning of the light."

Henrich nodded. Acknowledging the lights of the orbit.

"It is something to behold. In a way of matters."

"Why are you out here, Warslinger? Where are you heading?"

"I am going to The Haunted City?"

"The Haunted City? Why would you choose to do that?"

"I need answers."

"What sort of answers are you seeking from the mystical place?"

"Answers that contain details on eternal life and all of existence."

"You sure you're prepared for it when you enter into the City? Are you prepared to face those that lurk around the Kingdom of the Gate and who has dominion over the place within the Outer-World?"

"I have no other choice but to head there and find the answers that I surely seek."

Necuametl nodded. He understood Henrich's drive and ambition to reach the City. He once had the same energy and vigor as Henrich does. Though, that was a very long time ago. Henrich could tell that Necuametl was somewhat ageless. Maybe immortal. But, who could know by his physical appearance. As that of a man in his middle ages of life.

"Time for me to sleep." Necuametl said. "It was a pleasure to speak words with you, Warslinger of the Heptad."

"Same here, sir." Henrich said. "It was truly an honor to speak with one who knows much about the Worlds."

"I've traveled much. Therefore, I know much."

They shook hands and walked separate ways within the village. The partying had settled down and everyone entered their homes and shacks to sleep for the night. During the night in the late hours, Henrich arose from the bed, seeing both Landon and Beth sleeping. He walked outside of the shack and sat down in one of the chairs that stood out by the shack on the side. Henrich sat down. Outside by himself as he thought about all that he has been through on his journey toward the City. He remembered the words of Necuametl and what he had told him. Henrich kept believing in his mission and he had faith to back him up.

Henrich closed his eyes and as they closed a scream could be heard not far from the village. Henrich's eyes opened, hearing the scream. He stood up from the chair and walked out of the village, following the screaming. Henrich came to the end of the village, where a small field was located. In the field, Henrich could see three men of the village standing around a pillar of fire. The screams were coming from the pillar. Henrich was hid behind a tree and looked closer, seeing a man, being burned alive on the pillar. He screamed for his life, but his throat was damage to lower his voice. The three men of the village however were chopping off parts of his body that were being burnt up and they began to eat them.

"I'll be damn." Henrich said to himself.

Henrich now knows that the people of the village are in fact cannibals. Henrich makes a run for it, returning to the shack to awaken Landon and Beth. One of the men turned around and spotted Henrich running. Necuametl yelled as he and the other two ran after him. Henrich, returning to the shack finds himself surrounded by the people of the village and standing by them was Necuametl. Henrich looked and saw the door of the shack being kicked open and out of the shack bolted Landon and Beth, who were being held by two of the men. Henrich stared at Necuametl, shaking his head.

"What in the hell is going on?" Henrich said. "Why are you burning up and eating people of your own village?"

"Warslinger, we need what we need. There isn't much meat to be found out here in this land. So, what I have done is set up a lottery of sorts. Whoever's name is chosen from the barrel will be tied down to the pillar and they will be burnt. As they're being burnt, we will cut off the limbs of their body and eat them. For we need to eat if we seek to survive."

Henrich looked around at the people. He was in shock and he was angry. Staying in a place he thought could've been comfortable and peaceful turned into a place of hell and evil. Landon and Beth stared at Henrich, who looked toward them. Nothing he could say to them due to himself being in a small form of shock. Necuametl looked at Henrich and nodded his head to him.

"You're angry and I understand why. If I were to tell you of this when you arrived, you would've killed us all and I couldn't allow that action to be taken. Besides, you killed all the Scavengers. Even though they were our enemies, you killed them, therefore, making us starve to death. Until now."

"What are you planning to do with us?"

"Yeah." Landon said. "You could at least give us a hint as to what you're about to do with us."

"We're going to place the three of you onto the pillar of fire. You're outsiders and outsiders have a different flavor to them as opposed to those who live out here. Trust me, my people have told me a lot about how they taste."

Necuametl signaled to the men, who held Landon and Beth to take them to the pillar of fire. More of the men grabbed a hold of the Warslinger and brought him along. Necuametl walked with Henrich. His countenance didn't change, and he was still the same man who Henrich spoke to hours earlier during the partying and praising.

"All of your praise for us, it was for show? A mockery?"

"No. It was sincere. We were truly thanking you for what you did to the Scavengers. We needed them gone. Even though, we would've eaten them all into extinction. But, due to your actions, we no longer have that luxury to accomplish. Therefore, we must eat your flesh."

"There's no need for all of this." Henrich said. "Listen to me and know there is no need for this to happen."

"There is a reason for why we must do this, Warslinger. We

must eat if we want to survive and eat we shall do."

Walking through the trees as they see the pillar standing before them, still ablaze from the recent kill, whose body was decimated by the people pf the village as they ran for it, pulling the body apart and eating anything they could get their hands on. The people ate as if they haven't eaten in days. Henrich could tell by the way they were munching own on the meat of the person. Necuametl stood by and watched as the people ate one of their own. It didn't bother him. For as he said, they must eat if they want to survive.

"I hope you're ready for this, Warslinger. You're all next in line to burn."

<u>XIII</u>

They stood out in front of the pillar of fire. Which smoked continually as they increased the flames by tossing in more of the wood from the trees. The same trees that came from the Valley of Death. Henrich looked and could hear screeching coming from the fire. The screeches were those of the shadowic entities that were trapped within the wood. Henrich thought to himself of the wood and of the people. Only a spirit of their kind would transform people to eat one another. The Warslinger has come across those kinds of spirits in his past. Necuametl kept his eyes on the three, seeing them struggling to get free from the hands of the people of the village.

"Tell me, how long has this been going for? How many days or weeks or months or years?"

"This has been going on since the inception of our village. After we built the homes and shacks, we suddenly had the urge to eat the flesh of other generations of Man. It consumed us like a fire consumes the wood. It burned in our bodies to taste the flesh of another human being and we listed after it like animals."

"You people are all sick!" Beth said. "Just sick."

"Maybe we are, madam. But, we must eat to survive."

"Enough of that." Henrich said. "You have a decision to make right now."

"And what is this decision that I must make?"

"Either you can set us free and let us be on our way or you can all meet your ends by my hands and theirs."

"So, you're threatening to kill us all? Is that what I'm getting from you, Warslinger of the Heptad? You're saying you're going to kill us if we don't let the three of you live. Then, if we let you go, where will we get our food for the days ahead?!"

"I do not know. But, I am sure that you'll stumble across some dead bodies along your searches and maybe you'll see an animal around here that you can feast on instead of feasting on other humans."

"I will not take in hand your decisions of choice, Warslinger. For this day, one of you will first be burned and after that the rest will follow. Enjoy your final moments, Warslinger of the Heptad because it is your last."

"We'll see about that." Henrich said.

Necuametl gathered the people of the village together and they surrounded the Three as they inched closer toward the pillar of fire. The pillar burned with black smoke and the wood that was burning, within the smoke and fire could been seen the shadowic entities levitating into the sky, they were being burnt alive themselves and could feel the heat. Necuametl pointed toward them and pointed to the pillar of fire. The people of the village cheered on the event.

"This is your final day! Say your goodbyes to one another as you each will become food for our stomachs."

Necuametl's hand gestured toward Landon, who the men brought forward.

"Enough of this!" Henrich said.

Henrich jerked himself from the other men, kicking them and punching them. He pulled out his shooters and blasted them each in their heads, killing them. Henrich turned to Beth and shot the shooter behind her, killing him as well. The people of the village took off and ran, leaving only a few of them remaining with Necuametl. Landon was set free and he ran toward Henrich and Beth stood by him. Each of them with their shooters in hand, facing down Necuametl and those who remained with him.

"What will you do now, Warslinger of the Heptad? Kill us or be killed?"

"I'll take your second choice of words." Henrich said. "Sorry about what I am about to do. But, you caused it to happen on your own."

"Take the shot. End my life and those of my own."

Henrich nodded and fired the shooter. The bullet went through the air, but stopped in midair by Necuametl, who held the bullet by a form a levitation. Henrich slowly lowered his shooter, seeing him holding the bullet.

"You possess such power." Henrich said. "How?"

"I told you earlier, I have traveled much. Therefore, I know much."

Necuametl waved the bullet back to Henrich, who moved out of the bullet's path. The bullet flew and ended up inside of a tree. Henrich looked and shot more shots toward him, who caught each of them and held them in the air. Henrich shook his head. Staring up at Necuametl and seeing the twirling, levitating bullets above him.

"This can't be happening right now."

"I'm afraid it is happening, Warslinger. Now, you will learn what it means to be one within my shoes."

Necuametl threw the bullet toward Henrich and he moved out of their way once again, but this time, Necuametl lunged toward Henrich, spearing him into the tree, holding his throat tightly. Henrich attempted to fight Necuametl's force, even if he was too powerful. Powerful enough that he had to have something on him that gave him the enhanced strength. Across the field, Landon and Beth fought against the men that remained. The men were unlike the Scavengers in terms of fighting. The men moved around like animals. They were faster than usual. Their attacks much stronger than the beating from the Scavengers.

"There's something with these people!" Landon said. "Something isn't right with them at all!"

"Maybe they're connected with something!" Beth said. "Something that has to do with this pillar of theirs!"

"You want to try and knock the thing down or something?" Landon asked.

"We could give it a shot." Beth said. "If you're in for it."

"I am."

Landon shot the shooter at one of them, Necuametl entered and dodged the bullet by jumping into the air like a panther and coming back down on the ground. Others climbed the trees and sat above them. Silent as the nocturnal creatures. They searched for them and they gazed up toward the sky and could see the men in the trees as their eyes only glowed in the darkness of the night. The men came down from the trees and lunged toward Landon and Beth. Trying to bite them on their necks. They held them off as much as they could and the Warslinger was still fighting Necuametl, who was unharmed by any punch or kick that Henrich delivered to him. Necuametl was in a way, invincible.

"What did you do to yourself to gain this strength?" Henrich asked.

"I was taught how to harness such power and yet, you've never managed to do the same thing. You and your Warslinger brothers only used the weapons that were given to you that you never thought of the possibilities of other ways to combat your enemies. Such a shame."

"Maybe it is a shame. At least I am still capable of standing up when I'm knocked down. Therefore, I have yet to give up and I will not cease myself in doing so."

"That's good to hear. That way, you will die a fighting man and a honest man. Only a few in the generations of Man can speak those words and remain a memory in the minds of Man."

Henrich kicked him and there was no harm done. Necuametl punched Henrich and knocked him to the ground. Necuametl kicked Henrich in the side, causing him to fly in the air and impact into one of the standing trees. Necuametl shook his head.

"This is a sight to see. A Warslinger being destroyed by my hands. Hands that aren't even worthy to touch your garments, let alone clean them."

Landon and Beth continued to fire at the roaming men, who ran around them. Landon approached the pillar and went to touch it. But, backed away from the pillar as it was still on fire and its heat was intense. Landon also noticed the blood and some flesh that were left lying on the pillar. The smell was terrible, and it stunk up the area in only a matter of minutes. The closer one approached the pillar, the stronger the stench became, and it was one to avoid at any cost.

"We can't get close to it!" Landon said. "It's too hot to touch and it is covered with blood."

"What else do you have in mind?" Beth asked. "Come up with something and let me know about it."

"Sure thing."

Henrich reached over to his back, raising up the blastshooter. He fired it at Necuametl, who backed up a bit from the impact. Henrich looked and noticed Necuametl's movements after the blast. He nodded.

"It's a start." Henrich said, firing another blast to Necuametl.

Henrich stood up, firing several more blasts from the blast shooter at Necuametl, he continued to back up as he was being hit by the blasts. Necuametl waved the smoke from the blasts away from his eyes and he could see Henrich running toward him and in Henrich's hands were the blast shooter in his right hand and the machete in his left hand. Henrich lunged toward Necuametl with both weapons. Shooting the peashooter and swiping the machete. Necuametl stepped back and looked at his chest, which was cut from the machete.

"I see that I've breached your strength." Henrich said.

"For the moment, you have." Necuametl said. "But, that doesn't give you the sign of a possible victory."

"No. It does not. What it gives me is a chance to prove to you that I can, and I will kill you."

Henrich continued his attacks against Necuametl while Landon and Beth had started to kill some of the men with their shooters. Aiming for their heads, they killed them as they could get a good aim. They still haven't come up with a plan of what to do with the pillar of fire, which was still burning, and the stench still covered the area. The stench had grown to where Landon had covered his face with his shirt and Beth did the same, using both her shirt and her hair. The stench had approached the Warslinger and Necuametl. Henrich covered his face and Necuametl did not. Necuametl breathed in the stench as it made him feel empowered.

"Continue with your attacks, Warslinger. Face me and see what becomes of you."

"As if I have a choice." Henrich said.

Henrich fired the blast shooter again and swiped the machete across Necuametl's body. Cutting his chest and neck. Henrich later took the blastshooter and slammed it into Necuametl's face. Necuametl dropped to one knee, where Henrich stood over him with the blastshooter pressed down on the back of his head. Necuametl only applauded Henrich for his actions.

"Very good." Necuametl said. "You have proven what you are capable of and what you must do in a situation of this sort."

"What do you mean by all of this?" Henrich said. "Why not be honest with us when we arrived here?"

"As I told you before, you would've done the same to us as you did to the Scavengers. You needed to be led in like an animal towards its food."

"I'm truly sorry for what I am about to do." Henrich said, with his finger on the blastshooter's trigger.

"I know you are, Warslinger of the Heptad." Necuametl said quietly. "I know you are."

Henrich took the shot and blew Necuametl's head off his body. The people of the village were watching, and they were in silence. Their leader is dead and Henrich stood over his body. Henrich looked at the people and shook his head. He was disgusted with them as he looked over, seeing Landon and Beth trying to take down the last man. Necuametl went to lunge at them and from behind Henrich took the shot, killing Necuametl. His body fell to the ground, blown in half. Henrich approached the pillar with the machete and started chopping it down. The pillar of fire trembled and shook until Henrich used the blastshooter and shot it. The blast caused the pillar to fall and once it hit the ground, the fire within it ceased and the stench was evaporating from the air.

Henrich faced the people of the village and stared at them. They looked at the Three and were more fearful of them than before. Landon and Beth looked at the children that stood by and were sad for them as opposed to those who were adults that stood by. They now had no leader and were left stranded in the Land of the Survivors.

"What will you people do now that your leader is dead?" Henrich said. "How will you survive in this land now with no one to give you the way to move forward?"

Henrich stood in the middle of the village with the people surrounding him, Landon, and Beth. He pointed the blastshooter at them and they were not as afraid as before. It intrigued Henrich and he noticed that something was taking place within the people.

"I will leave you all here to handle this matter yourself." He said, walking away from the village. "For I will not be here to see your decision be made."

Henrich approached his horse, which was standing by the entrance to the village. He went atop the horse with Beth, Landon rode on the speeder and the Three left the village, leaving the people of the village to decide their fates. As they left and went back on the pathways, they could hear screams of many. Henrich didn't look back as he already knew what decision the people of the village made. From the village itself arouse a fire. The fire was great in size and it engulfed the entire village. The fire lit up the areas nearby in the night. Henrich, Landon, or Beth never looked back to see the flames. They moved on as the village was destroyed by the fire that came from the people of the village and all of them died in the fire.

<u>XIV</u>

They rode along the pathways as the sun began to rise. Traveling miles and miles from the Scavengers' campsite and the village of the cannibals. Coming to a field nearby a mountain. Further down the pathway during the day, they could see someone standing in the middle of the pathway. The horse ceased. Landon stopped the speeder. Henrich looked at the strange man, who was dressed in little armor and a lot of black leather. He carried with him a shooter of his own. Made of black metal.

"Who is that?" Beth asked.

Henrich jumped onto the ground, slowly walking towards the strander. He recognized him from somewhere before. Somewhere very, very recent according to the locations. Henrich pointed toward him with a confused look on his face. Henrich looked as if time has reversed itself while they were on the pathways.

"This can't be possible." Henrich said. "We saw you earlier."

The strange man who stood in the middle of the pathway is the real Mercenary Man. Known as Marco Desthain and he smiled at Henrich.

CHAPTER FIVE

THE WARSLINGER vs. THE MERCENARY

I

The Warslinger stared and he stood silently toward the real Mercenary Man, Marco Desthain. Desthain looked at Henrich with a smile on his face. He turned his sights toward both Landon and Beth and waved. They didn't wave back, but they were in fear. A small amount of fear. Henrich only shook his head.

"I know what you're about to say to me, Warslinger." Desthain said.

"And what am I about to say?"

"You're about to ask me am I Judas Arkdragon from the field near the Valley of Death."

"How do you know about that?" Henrich asked.

"I keep tracks of things regarding the incidents of the Worlds. I've been keeping tabs on you across every turn you've made under the direction of my master."

"Your master? He's this Tubal King that I keep hearing about."

"Yes. The Tubal King is my master and I am his servant. I live and breathe to do whatsoever he commands me to do. That's why I'm standing in your presence at this very moment, Warslinger. The Tubal King has been watching you ever since you became one of the Heptad and he's seen your successes and your failures."

"The scroll which was given to me by those vampires back in the desert lands? It's all true? There's a bounty on my head after all?"

"In a manner of speaking, there is. Again, I'm the Mercenary Man and my job is to take bounties and complete them under the orders of The Tubal King. Which led me to you. If my master never spoke of you, I wouldn't be out here in your way this day."

Henrich didn't move, but his hands were close to his holsters. He was ready to fire at Desthain at any moment possible. Landon and Beth stood back from the two, giving them both the space that they needed. Desthain kept his smirk on his face and his hands were laid close to his holsters. They stared each other down like animals.

"Now, look, Warslinger. I understand that seeing me, the real me, right here is kind of shocking, but what Arkdragon did, it was all a test."

"Why a test? Why not it could've been you that I saw and that I shot."

"Because, The Tubal King wants to know more about your feats and your skills. He sent Arkdragon to confront you in my own image. Surely, I don't like it when someone decides to dress like me or even shift themselves into myself completely. But, it was what the master required of Arkdragon and he delivered and proved a lot about you that even you have yet to understand."

"You believe me to expect that you, this Arkdragon, and your Tubal King know more about me than I know of myself?"

"Exactly." Desthain replied quickly. "Because, after your Heptad were separated and scattered across the Worlds, each of you lost something that you once had. Now, all of you are slowly regaining that lost art and you don't even know what to do with it. Do you?"

Landon approached Henrich from the side, his eye locked on Desthain who stared at him. Desthain pointed out to Landon.

"That young fella right there." Desthain yelled. "Is he this Cody Landon guy that I keep hearing about?"

Landon looked at Desthain and stood facing him.

"That is my name." Landon said.

Desthain smiled at him.

"Tell me this, boy, do you really want to throw your entire life away?"

"How am I doing that?"

"By hanging around that man. He's a Warslinger and they get people killed or they have people being seduced by the malevolency of the Worlds and of the Worlds not known."

"I will not go to that side of life." Landon said. "I will remain good in my days."

"You can say that now. But, when tragedy comes your way and more calamity and destruction is shown due to your actions, then you'll know if you're on the good side of things. But, I already know your future, boy. You will be utterly destroyed by what is to come in your lifetime and that event will turn you toward the malevolency, where you will become another servant in a long ass line to The Tubal King."

Landon disagreed. Shaking his head at Desthain. Desthain expected Landon to tear up for the moment, but there were no tears in Landon's eyes. There was only anger and a mission. Desthain looked at Landon and liked how he didn't cry. He nodded to him in respect.

"See, you're already on that path, son."

Henrich pushed Landon aside and faced Desthain. The two men locked eyes and they've had enough of the talking. Each of them were ready to start firing at each other and they were counting down the seconds that came before and the seconds that followed.

"I'm going to kill you." Henrich said. "Then, I'm going to reach The Haunted City and I will kill your Tubal King."

Desthain smiled back at Henrich, pointing toward him in a gesture.

"You know, I figured you would say something of that nature. Which reminds me of why I'm here this day. Randolph Henrich of the Warslingers of the Heptad, you have a choice to make this day. Either you can live and bow to The Tubal King and work in his service or you can die and go into the Outer-World as a man who never finished his mission to begin with. Make your decision."

Henrich looked at Landon and he looked at Beth. They nodded to him with a smile on their faces, seeing that he's already made his decision. Desthain awaited Henrich's answer, holding his shooter in his hand. Desthain waved the shooter around, counting down the time.

"I'm waiting for your answer." Desthain said. "Give it to me right now."

Henrich nodded and stared into Desthain's eyes from where he stood. The horse slowly backed away from the spot, causing Landon and Beth to follow. Desthain watched how they were moving away from Henrich and seen that he was only standing there, still and not moving an inch of his body. Desthain laughed and pointed his shooter toward Henrich.

"Your answer?" Desthain asked.

"My answer." Henrich said. "One of us shall live and one of us shall die."

"You expect that to be an answer to my question?"

"It is my answer."

Henrich pulled out his shooter and began firing at Desthain. Desthain ran from the area, into the field, where Henrich ran after him. Landon and Beth watched the two men enter the field and they followed as did Henrich's horse. While they ran, they could see Desthain firing back at Henrich as he continued to shoot. The two men were trying to kill one another and that was their only goal.

II

Henrich ran after Desthain as fast as his legs were able to move at the running speed. Desthain kept his pace up, while continuing to shoot at Henrich. Henrich would dodge the rounds and fire back at Desthain, who's armor had protected him from the bullets.

A few feet behind them, Landon, Beth, and the Horse made their way to catch up to them as they ran through the field. The field was vast in its length and thee only thing that was seen across the field was a mountain and the mountain was astounding in its size and structure. Above the mountain were clouds of darkness and clouds of light. They emitted off a strange energy that came down to the field and the closer they were by the mountain, the more powerful the energy became.

"You won't be able to catch me, Warslinger!" Desthain yelled loudly. "Because once I vanish from this place, you won't be able to know where I'll be coming next. Either way, I will find you again. Somewhere and sometime!"

"Why wait then, when you have the opportunity right now!" Henrich replied. "Stop running and face me like a man!"

"I like your kind of speech, Warslinger of the Heptad. You sound like those bastards that came before. All talk and no show."

"I have the ability to show you what I can do, Mercenary. But, it appears to me that you refuse to see what I can do since you're running afar from me and from my shooters."

"Listen, Warslinger. Did it ever occur to your ass that I don't want to get shot? Maybe I don't want to die this day or any other day."

"You've fired back at me!"

"True. Very true." Desthain said.

Desthain continued firing at Henrich, who kept firing back as they both ran through the field, stepping over the tall growing green grass. Some of the grass in the field were dead or dying as their color was fading away. Mostly due to the mountain ahead of them and the energy that comes from it. Henrich pulled out his second shooter and fired it toward Desthain. Desthain looked back, seeing Henrich with two shooters.

"That's called cheating you know!" Desthain yelled. "But, I like your style, Warslinger!"

Desthain smirked and continued firing himself. Landon and Beth kept up with them, watching them shoot their shooters at each other. They didn't want to interfere in the shootout between the Warslinger and the Mercenary. Although, they wondered how much running they could keep up out in a vast field.

"How do they do that?"

"They're both skilled at what they do." Beth said. "Otherwise, one of them would be dead already."

"They can't continue running like this for the entire day. They'll tire out."

"Leaving only for one of them to take the shot and end all of this."

Beth stopped as did Landon, both watching Henrich and Desthain from afar off. They looked at one another as the Horse galloped from behind them. Beth shook her head, rubbing her hair back from her face as the wind began to pick up. Landon thought to himself within his mind. There was something they could do to assist Henrich, but what they could do was uncertain within their own selves. Landon turned to Beth and she looked at him. Both with questions concerning their current situation and yet, neither one of them had an answer to speak to the other.

"What do we do?" Landon asked. "What can we do?"

"There must be a way to stop Desthain from running."

"How do we stop him from running? I'm not getting all the corners here."

"There has to be something lying around out here that could stop him for a moment. Something that will temporary cease him from running away even further out."

Landon looked ahead to the mountain, seeing the clouds above it and seeing the lightning flashing within them. He pointed to the mountain, seeing Desthain running towards it as the shooter shots continued to echo throughout the field. Low rumbles of thunder roamed across the sky. Landon kept his finger pointed to the mountain, Beth looked at him, then gazed toward the mountain.

"Appears Desthain is heading for that mountain."

"Why would he go there?"

"He probably has some stuff there that he intends on using

against Henrich and us."

Beth looked at Henrich. She smiled, and he just stood there. Unsure of what to say as he didn't know why Beth was smiling. He shook his head at her confusingly and waved his arms out.

"Why are you smiling?" Landon asked. "Is there something funny about all of this that I should be aware of?"

"No, but I have an idea." Beth said. "Come on."

They ran after Henrich and Desthain as the thunder grew louder in sound and the lightning started to increase in its surroundings. The field wasn't as safe as it was before as the lightning has caused some parts of the field to set themselves on fire. Now, they all were running in a field that was burning. Burning slowly, as the fires themselves spread out quickly.

III

The shooting continued with Landon and Beth following them. The lightning increased in its appearances and in its strikes as the field slowly became a blazing field of fire. The thunder rumbled in the sky, louder than it previously roared before. The clouds that sat atop the mountain have overtaken the field and the mountain. Something taking place between the Warslinger and the Mercenary, other things were being handled according to both of their deeds. While he chased down the Mercenary Man, Henrich would occasionally look up to the sky, seeing the lightning and hearing the thundering that was going on around him. He looked back behind him, seeing Landon, Beth, and his horse behind him as well as the growing fire of the field.

"If I don't take you down, Desthain, the flames of this field will do so!" Henrich said. "They are growing quicker than I would imagine a flame to grow out in a place like this!"

"I wouldn't be worrying about the fire, Warslinger!" Desthain yelled. "I would be concerned with surviving against me in a shootout. Remember, one of us will die this day and one of us will live. I believe that I will have the second option!"

"Only if your Tubal King finds a way to help you out here! Though, I don't that he, himself would show up to face me. He already knows of his fate when I have it in my hands!"

"You're a complete and utter fool to believe that The Tubal King is in fear of you! you're only a man and he is something much more!"

"I've heard that before!"

Desthain made a turn, and in front of him stood several sets of trees and the lightning bolts were striking the trees, setting them ablaze, but the trees entirety would not burn. The trees stood tall themselves, taking the strikes of the lightning. Only burnt branches fell from the trees. Desthain ducked from the falling branches and Henrich done the same. Landon and Beth watched as the tree limbs were burning.

"What is this plan of yours, Beth?" Landon asked. "Because I'm wondering how it will works concerning where we're standing right now."

"I have it in the works, Cody." Beth said. "Don't worry yourself about it. I have it all under control."

"We'll see about all of that."

They continued to follow Henrich and Desthain. Running toward the mountain, Desthain looked back, dodging another bullet from Henrich's shooters. Desthain spotted Landon and Beth not too far behind them. He smirked and closed his eyes while running, mumbling something to himself.

"I need assistance." Desthain said. "Send them to assist me, please."

From around Landon and Beth, the ground started to quake, ceasing them from running forward. They looked around themselves and the surroundings, seeing the dirt fly up in the air and from the ground arose six being wearing black cloaks and hoods. Their skin was pale, and they appeared to be hungry.

Henrich turned his head around and gazed out to the field and could see the hooded figures standing in the field, in a circle. Within the circle, Henrich could see the hooded figures all surrounding both Landon and Beth.

"Again." Henrich said.

"How are they out here, Desthain?!" Henrich yelled.

"My master sent them to help me!" Desthain said. "Not too worry, you are my only true goal now. Your allies will be just fine being food to The Tubal King's vrylolakas."

The vrylolakas snarled at Landon and Beth. They stood together aside Henrich's horse, surrounded by the hooded vampires. They could see the fire in the field was increasing and there was no way out of the circle for them to make an escape. Their rotten teeth were shown to them. Beth looked at them, remembering information from Earth. She continued to stare and knew they were vampires.

"Wait, these are real vampires." She said. "I didn't know they existed."

"So, they don't have these things on your World, do they?" Landon asked. "Because if they don't, I'm moving over there when I find a portal."

"People dress up as them. But, not in the manner as these."

The vrylolakas screeched their voices out toward them, causing them to cover their ears from the siren-like sound of their screams. The vampires moved around them, they pulled out their shooters and stared to take shots at them. One of the vampires ran up toward Landon in the circle, Landon seen the vampire coming and shot the vampire in the face as its body fell to the field. The vampires tried to latch onto them, but their strategy of alignment was too smart for the vampires to keep up with, even at vampire speed. They looked at each other after taking more shots toward the vampires.

"We're pretty good at this." Landon said.

"For the moment."

Henrich used the blastshooter, blowing the heads off of the vampires. The vampires didn't hesitate to stand by and watched. Each of them lunged out toward Landon and Beth. Henrich's horse stomped some of them into the ground to where their bones were shattering from the weight of the horse and the strength of the ground.

Henrich paused for a moment and looked back to Landon and Beth. He stood, seeing Desthain running for the mountain and watched Landon and Beth fight the vampires with their weapons. He seen how they were studying his own move set in a way. Henrich pulled out the blastshooter from his back and fired it outward, the round from the blastshooter traveled across the field, leading to a hit in the back of one vampire. The vampire fell and turned into ashes. Landon and Beth witnessed it and looked up, seeing Henrich standing afar off from them.

"Take them out!" Henrich yelled.

"Yes sir!" Landon replied, shooting the vampires.

They continued killing the vampires one by one. Afterwards, the horse stomped onto one of the vampires, leading to Beth to shoot it in the head. Only two vampires remained for them to kill off. The vampires weren't afraid of them and didn't bother to count the dead ones that laid around them on the field. The flames increased on the field to where Landon and Beth could feel its intense heat coming near them. One of the vampires went first at Landon, but was unable to grab him by his shoulders as Beth shot the vampire first. Landon raised his leg and kicked the vampire on the ground and shot him in his head. They stared their sights on the last vampire. They smiled as Landon blew the head completely off the last vampire, with only scraps of its brain and other remains laying on the ground.

"That's all of them." Beth said. "What's next?"

Landon turned, seeing the horse running to Henrich as the fire of the field started to grow and it headed right where they were standing. Beth noticed the flames and she started backing away. Landon could see the flames were already on their trail, growing fast and consuming all the field.

"We have to go!" Landon said, seeing the flames coming.

They ran from the sight as the fire consumed the remains of the vampires to where only ashes laid. Henrich stood and seen Landon and Beth coming his way, both were smiling, looking out to Henrich. Henrich turned back and could see Desthain near the foot of the mountain. He nodded.

"You're not that far from me, Mercenary." Henrich said.

Desthain stopped to catch his breath from the running. The running had somewhat made him slow and the heat of the flames were not helping him in any sort of way. He understood that and kept going. While he made his short stop, Desthain wiped his forehead of the sweat and his looked out behind him. Seeing Henrich with Landon, Beth, and the horse. Desthain laughed and raised his hands up to where they could see him. He waved them in the air, getting their attention.

"Did you believe the vrylolakas were all he had to offer me?! There's something else that I was given to cease you from stopping me!"

Henrich, Landon, and Beth stood still listening to Desthain's words and from behind them came a loud nose. They turned to see a choiros. Henrich shook his head as did Landon.

"Not another one of these damn things." Henrich said.

The mutated pig screeched at them as it ran toward them with its large tusks. They fired at it with their shooters, leaving Desthain only to smile at the sight of it as he continued moving forward to the mountain. Henrich kept firing and raised the blastshooter, shooting the rounds toward the mutated pig. The blastshooter blew off one of the pig's tusks, causing the estranged creature to stumble for a moment. Henrich gazed back, seeing Desthain at the mountain.

"He's at the mountain." Henrich said. 'I will go after him."

"What about us? What are we supposed to do?"

Henrich pointed to the choiros, which regained its movement. It shook its head as blood poured out from the broken tusk and blood covered its face and the fur of its body. The smell of the creature increased due to the amount of blood that was coming from the broken tusk. Henrich nodded to Landon and Beth.

"Finish that unclean creature off."

Henrich took off, leaving them to finish off the choiros. They fired several more shots toward the creature as it screeched in pain. The mutated pig ran toward them with force. They moved out of its way and continued firing at the creature from the ground.

"It's not working!" Landon yelled.

"Go for its eyes!" Beth said. "We can blind it."

They aimed for the eyes and took the shots. Landon's shot missed, but hit the creature in its side and Beth's shot went through he pig's right eye. The pig stopped running and tumbled itself over onto the ground, covering it in its blood and fur. The pig kicked around a bit, trying to stand back up. From behind Landon and Beth came Henrich's horse, which stomped the pig until the pig was dead. The horse did not hesitate to stop as it ran toward the mountain. Landon and Beth looked at each other, wondering if the horse knows something that the two of them aren't aware of.

Henrich continued to chase down Desthain, who has already climbing the mountain. Henrich shook his head, seeing the Mercenary Man climbing up the mountain. Henrich climbed the mountain himself with Landon and Beth following them. They stopped and gazed to the mountain, which was unlike the field, silent. There wasn't any noise coming from the mountain. The only noise that could be heard was of the thunder and the flames behind them around the field. The clouds still covered the mountain, but there was no thunder roaring from above the mountain. Beth looked to the top of the mountain, staring at the dark clouds. Some parts of the clouds were white, and others were a dark gray. But within the middle was a dark blue and black.

"What do you think is up there?" Beth asked.

"We can only know if we reach the top." Landon said. "Probably where they're headed anyway."

"What of the horse? How will it reach to the top?"

Landon looked at the horse.

"Trust me, there's something with this horse that is not as natural as many people would believe."

"What do you mean by that? I don't see anything unusual with the horse."

"You haven't been around it or Henrich long enough. I know, it will take some time for you to see what this horse is truly capable of. Should've been enough when it stomped those vrylolakas and that choiros back there."

"I'll figure it out somehow." She said, walking to the mountain. Landon nodded.

"I'm positive you will figure it out. Not sure how though."

<h1 style="text-align:center"><u>IV</u></h1>

Climbing the mountain, both Henrich and Desthain, they come to the realization that something sits atop the mountain. Desthain laughed as he climbed the mountain, gazing down to the field, which was consumed by the fire. The thunder continued to roar, lightning flashed throughout the sky. Henrich followed up the mountain. Far below them were Landon and Beth, who climbed the mountain. Slower than both Henrich and Desthain, but they were sure of themselves to reach the mountain just as the Warslinger and the Mercenary were sure to reach the top.

"We can make it up there." Landon said. "We have no choice but to."

"Basically, we shouldn't look down." Beth said.

"Now, why would you do that anyway. Unless you wanted to see how far a fall that would be. I would suggest that you keep your eyes upward and focus on climbing this rock."

Beth gazed down, seeing that Henrich's horse was gone. Landon looked at her as if she was crazy. He shook his head, seeing her looking down at the field.

"Are you going to jump or what?" Landon said.

"I'm not going to jump, alright. I just wanted to see if the horse was still down there."

"Tell me, then. Is the horse down there or not?"

"It's not down there."

"Then, let's make our way to the top. No telling what the two of them will do to each other once they reach it."

Several more feet to climb and Desthain could see Henrich below him on the mountain. He laughed to himself, pulling out his shooter and firing it at Henrich. Henrich hid beneath a nearby cliff to avoid the shots from Desthain's shooter, which was continually firing. Henrich decided to fire back, hitting the tocks on the side of Desthain.

"Good one, Warslinger!" Desthain yelled. "Good one indeed!"

Desthain climbed and reached the top of the mountain. Henrich followed and after climbing a few feet himself, he also reached the top. Henrich stopped and seen Desthain standing in front him. They were surrounded and covered underneath the clouds, seeing only a form of light and darkness. Sitting atop the mountain was a mirror, made of crystal. The mirror glittered from the light emitting from the clouds around it.

"You don't know what this is do you?" Desthain gestured. "This is far beyond your means, Warslinger of the Heptad and you know it to be the truth."

Henrich pointed at the mirror with his shooter, monitoring Desthain's movements as he looked at the crystal structure that stood with marble sides.

"What mirror is that?"

"One for only the few of Man to see. Not everyone in existence is capable of seeing what the mirror can show."

"What can this mirror show to those who approach it?"

"It can show the past, the present, and the future. Along with alternate realities and other Worlds that are not known to the generations of Man."

"How do you know about all of this, Mercenary Man? Who taught you these ways of knowledge and handed them to you to keep? Who gave you the time to learn all these things?"

"The Tubal King taught me, Warslinger. He taught me of the mirror, he taught me of the knowledge of the Worlds, and he taught me how to use this mirror to see not only my past, present, and future. But, his own timeline as well. He wanted to know about the alternate realities and Worlds that are not known. So, with this mirror, he was able to know about them and through it, he learned much. The Tubal King possesses so much knowledge that he passed some of it down to his servants. Myself included as I know a lot about the mirror and of the times to come."

"How am I to believe the words you are speaking to me?"

"Because I know them to be the truth, as you only know them to be lies because you haven't seen everything that you're meant to see. There are times ahead for you, Warslinger, where you will come across places and people who are not like those of your past."

The Warslinger stared deeply at the mirror. His shooter still raised up in his hand, pointed at Desthain. Desthain took his shooter and aimed it directly at Henrich, who noticed Desthain's movements. The two had themselves at odds. Both with their shooters pointed toward the other. They stood across from each other several feet away. The wind blew across them as the clouds rotated above them while the light fought its way to escape from the darkness in the sky. Landon and Beth reached the top and stood still, seeing the two aiming their shooters at each other.

"We should help him." Landon said.

Beth stopped him by grabbing his arm. He looked at Beth and she nodded to Henrich. Landon looked forward, seeing the mirror.

"Let Henrich deal with this himself. He knows what he's doing."

Desthain's smile grew bigger on his face and on Henrich's face was no emotion. His eyes were locked on Desthain's own eyes. Their shooters didn't flinch in their hands and they were still as the mountain itself. Desthain had to laugh, seeing himself and Henrich standing atop the mountain next to a crystal mirror. It was something he had yet to behold the sight. But, seeing the

Warslinger standing in front of him, Desthain felt that he truly lived up to his name of being the Mercenary Man.

"When are you going to take the shot, Warslinger?! Take it now!"

"I will take the shot when I'm ready." Henrich said. "The time is almost here, Mercenary Man."

"I'm sure it is. Because, after I kill you and your partners and your damn horse, I will take your carcass to The Tubal King, who will rejoice at your death and then you will know that The Tubal King is one of his word and the King of the Worlds."

"How about I tell you of another alternative. I will kill you. Then, I will see what this mirror must show me. Then, I will travel across the Worlds to enter the Outer-World. Once I enter and approach the Kingdom of the Gate, I will slay your Tubal King and enter The Haunted City, where I will get the answers that I seek."

Desthain nodded and shook his head to Henrich. Taking in his words of the decision. Desthain waved his shooter around, though it's still aimed toward Henrich's chest.

"May the best man live."

"As I will." Henrich replied. "Take the shot, Desthain."

Both men pull the triggers of their shooters and shots fired across the mountaintop. The sound echoed through the clouds, blending in with the thunder from above. Landon and Beth could only watch from a distance as they couldn't even tell who was shot as both men were standing still, their shooters were aimed at one another.

V

The Warslinger and the Mercenary stood with their eyes locked onto one another. Landon and Beth looked on, seeing the two men standing still with their shooters drawn onto each other. Neither one of them made any movements after firing the shots at each other. Desthain smiled and from his chest, blood slowly began to drip. He looked down at his chest, seeing that the round from Henrich's Warslinger shooter went straight through his armor, pierced his chest and went through his heart.

"Wow." Desthain said, as he slowly fell to his knees on the mountain.

Henrich placed his shooters in their holsters as he walked toward the downed Desthain. He kneeled low to his face and stared at him. Desthain continued to laugh as he was in pain. A pain that was increasing growing in his chest as more blood began to come from the bullet wound. Desthain couldn't take the pain internally, but he tried to keep himself up. Although, his body thought it best for him to lie down on the ground, He stayed on his knees, holding his chest.

"You never cease to amaze those, Warslinger. I didn't know you had it in you to do such a task. I should've known because of the actions you've done in your past. Now, those things are worth seeing again, aren't they? You can be honest with me since I'm about to pass over into Outer-World."

"It was between either you or me and it seems that I came out the victor."

"For the moment, maybe. But, you should look ahead and see what your future will bring to you."

"Through using the mirror."

"By using the mirror. Yeah. Go ahead and do it. See what is in store for you and those who follow you in your footsteps."

Desthain fell to the ground, losing his breath and feeling the cold of the mountaintop. Henrich walked over his dying body to the mirror. He faced it, only seeing his own reflection. He looked back at Desthain.

"How does this work, Mercenary Man?"

"You speak the word."

'Tell me the word."

"Why should I? You already know the word."

Henrich looked and thought for a second. A word, what could be the word, Henrich thought. He searched through his mind for

the word and nothing was coming through for him. He approached
Desthain, who was already near-death.

"What is the word?!"

"You… already… know…it." Desthain said, losing his
consciousness.

Henrich watched as Desthain died atop the mountain from the
shooter. Henrich looked around, searching for anything that might
have the word Desthain was speaking to him about.

Finding nothing, Henrich becomes enraged. Not only at the
deceased Desthain, but himself as well.

"Damn it!" Henrich said.

Landon and Beth approached the angry Henrich. He looked at
them, shaking his head and gazing to the mirror. Landon looked at
the mirror and looked at Henrich. He looked at them again and
took another look at the two. His mind was racing, but at a decent
pace than Henrich's mind. Beth didn't understand what Desthain
meant by a word, though, she was capable of tagging along with
them to figure out the word that was needed to start up the mirror.

"What about Heptad, sir?"

Henrich spoke the word to the mirror and the mirror was still
and silent. That word didn't work. They took the time to think
again. Landon thought for a second, searching his mind for words
that he's heard since tagging along with Henrich. Beth even
searched her mind for words that she could remember in her head.
She approached Henrich with a word on the edge of her tongue.

"What about Warslinger." Landon said. "Or you could try
Tubal King or something like that."

"What do you have?" Henrich asked Beth.

"Why don't you try, *genesis*." She said. "Try genesis."

Henrich nodded and stepped forward to the mirror. He stood
completely still and looked directly into the mirror. He took a
breath and he spoke the word, "Genesis" and from the mountain
arose a light. The light flew around them several times before
entering the mirror itself. The mirror began glowing a bluish purple
and a wormhole appeared within the mirror. They gazed at the

mirror, seeing its light shining upon them.

"What the hell is going on?" Landon wondered.

"It worked." Henrich said. "Beth, it worked."

"The word was just there for a second." She said. "I guess I picked the right one."

From the mirror arose a voice. A voice with the sound of a woman in a mature age. The voice echoed over the mountain and it was unheard of in their ears as neither of them have heard a voice like the one of the mirror. The mirror started groaning as it became brighter than it was before. They used their arms to block the blinding light from their eyes.

"Speak your name." The mirror commanded.

"Randolph Henrich. Warslinger of the Heptad."

"Randolph Henrich of the Warslinger of the Heptad, what do you seek to know on this day?"

"I seek to know the future and my place in finding The Haunted City."

"Is that all you seek from me?"

"That is all that I seek from you."

"Very well, Randolph Henrich of the Warslingers of the Heptad. What you seek, you may not see. For what you will see is what you will find."

Henrich nodded.

"Show me the visions of the future, mirror."

"As you command."

The mirror busted open and through it brought about images which surrounded Henrich, Landon, and Beth. The three of them could see the images and they were sights of the future to come. They looked at them as they came across their eyes. One image that appeared first was of a town. The town was in the middle of nowhere and standing on the field were people.

An amount of people that was unseen in the location. The people were dressed in all black and standing in front of them was a man wearing both black and white garments. Henrich didn't know who they were, but he knew they were a part of his future toward

The Haunted City. In the image, the man standing before the people spoke and they could hear his words.

"From this day forward, those who oppose us will learn why those who disobey later disappear from The Secret World!"

The image later showed the leader of the people, beheading others with an axe and the people stoning others against a stone wall. The leader stood out in front of his people, who praised him as if he was their savior in the Worlds. The image faded away as another image appeared before them. This image was of a city. The city was a large metropolitan city. Within the city walked around people, but they were enhanced with robotics arms, legs, chests, and heads. The city was Mega City and the people who lived there were in fact transhumanists. Further into the image appeared a woman. Henrich knew her.

"Cara?" He said. Seeing her walking on the sidewalk of Mega City as large autonomous vehicles passed by down the streets.

"You know of her?" Beth asked.

"I met her some time back." He said. "Before I met Cody. I met her. She said she was going to Mega City. I wondered if she was on good terms."

"Well, now you know."

The image of Mega City faded out and the third image appeared before them. Showing them the lands of the Eastern World. Walking about on the land that appeared to be made of stone and wood, they could see a pair of people crouched down together. The people were suffering, suffering of their current condition.

The image shifted to two individuals, a young woman and a young man. Both were dressed in unusual attire. Different from those that Henrich is familiar with. They carried with them katanas and other blades while they approached several men who were dressed up as samurais and slaughtered them where they stood.

"What happened there?" Landon asked.

"It hasn't happened yet, boy." Henrich said. "But, it will. Soon."

The image of the assassins faded and came the fourth image. This image showed an old castle and Henrich knew that castle. He's been there in the past. He walked forward near the image, getting a closer look. He shook his head, seeing the castle again and in the image, he could see an army standing outside of the castle being led by a man, who was known to be close with a certain Warslinger in the past, who was led by a woman dressed in a black and red dress. The woman wore a crown on her head as the army embraced her and worshipped her.

"She couldn't have." Henrich said. "Not her."

"What's wrong?" Beth asked. "Do you know her?"

"I do. I see what she's done to my brother's castle."

In the image, standing next to the woman, who took a seat is another man. Only, this man is dressed in the exactly same attire as Henrich. Equipped with the trench coat and hat. Henrich knew the man, because he was a Warslinger of the Heptad. Henrich balled up his fist and he was in anger once again.

"How could he betray us like this!" Henrich said. "How could he do such a thing to his brethren? Those who were there by his side! Who protected him against all the obstacles that we came across and this is what he does to us!"

The image shifted again, showing Warslinger Knight Arthur Pendragon speaking with a man only known as The One from Albion. They were speaking about a certain area as they each pointed toward the direction of the land they stood on. Henrich noticed the location and knew it by heart. They were pointing toward the west.

"He's still alive." Henrich said. "I knew he could survive the attack."

"Who is he, sir?" Landon asked. "The older man?"

"He is one of a trustworthy ally." Henrich said. "Good to know that he still lives.

The image disappeared, and the fifth image appeared, showing a pair of witches and warlocks sitting together and the image shifted to where the witches were altering all of reality and they were destroying all the Worlds. Henrich knew that the witches were powerful, but they couldn't contain that much power to alter the Worlds. The witches were laughing amongst each other. In the image appeared a werewolf, which lunged out onto people in a valley, killing them with its claws and gnawing on them with its fangs. The image shifted to a sight where a witch sat at a table, in her hand she held a tarot card. On the card were the Warslingers. She took the card and tossed it into a fireplace.

"I didn't know that witches and warlocks truly existed." Beth said. "I had some belief that they did exist among people, but I've never seen one before."

"Now, you have." Landon said. "In a way."

"They know of us and they know we're still alive in the Worlds."

The image evaporated, and the sixth image appeared and within this image were all the Warslingers of the Heptad with others and in front of them stood The Haunted City itself. But, in between the Warslingers and the City, was an enemy to come, who was shrouded in a dark fog. The fog was black as the night sky and within the fog, the enemy knew all the Warslingers and it desired to see them dead at the gates to the City. The image turned into a war, where the Warslingers and those who came to help battled the forces of the malevolency and the dark fog in front of The Haunted City.

The battle was intense to the point that beings of the *benevolency* appeared from the sky to assist the Warslingers and those who allied with them. The fight ended with raining fire.

"I will make it to the City." Henrich said.

"It looks that way, sir." Landon said. "Must be something to witness."

"For the time being. Until we get there, it's another story all in of itself."

All the images come together in a ball of light and banished into the mirror. The mirror's light slowly dimmed out. Henrich approached them mirror, looking at the images that he witnessed.

Landon and Beth also looked at the mirror and seen the images within. The images still held them in its grasps. The images were of the future to come and even though, they were of the future, they can be altered be certain actions that could take place.

"This is your future, Randolph Henrich of the Warslingers of the Heptad." The Mirror declared. "You have seen what is to come."

Henrich, Landon, and Beth backed away from the mirror, seeing the images faded away. The mirror sat quietly.

"So, what now, sir" Landon asked.

"Now, you all sleep." The mirror spoken.

A loud gong sounded from the mirror, causing a drift to come upon them as they fell to the ground and were in a deep sleep. The mirror itself evaporated as it entered a portal. The portal looked as if it was heading into another realm of existence and the mirror fell into the portal, to which the portal was closed afterwards. Only thing that remained on the mountaintop was silence and silence was surely needed.

<u>VI</u>

Henrich awoken from the deep sleep and he looked up toward the sky. The clouds were gone and only the dawning sun was there. He stood up and gazed over to the field, where the flames were and there were no flames. The fire had ceased, and the grass was green as if it never was set ablaze. He looked down, seeing Landon and Beth asleep and the body of the Mercenary Man gone from the mountaintop as was the mirror itself. He understood that the mirror had to be removed to another location to avoid others coming to the mountain. Henrich turned around, seeing his horse. He nodded to the horse to which the horse gallop to him.

"How did you get up here." He said.

On the cold grounds of the mountaintop, Landon and Beth also awoke from the deep sleep. They stood up slowly, looking at

Henrich who was looking at them. Landon rubbed his head.

"What happened?" Landon asked.

"I am not sure. But, we've been granted the energy we needed."

"That and some silence." Beth noticed. "Finally."

Henrich nodded as he looked outward toward the direction that they needed to go, which was on the other side of the mountain. While Henrich looked toward the direction, he could see something far ahead of them. What Henrich was seeing was a structure of a city. Though, the city seemed strange to be where Henrich was looking. Landon also seen the city, pointing out to it.

"What is that place, sir?" He asked.

"I know that city." Henrich said. "Though it isn't a city that dwells in the Worlds of Man."

Beth approached them and seen the city herself. The city didn't have a modern looking appearance as there were no skyscrapers known as they are of the modern world. She looked at its buildings and they were of a gothic nature. They appeared to her as a city in the time of the Victorian Era back on Earth. She was amazed by it. Though, she could feel an uneasy feeling continuing to look at the city.

"Why does the city give me the chills? I don't know why."

Henrich turned to her and pointed out toward the city that sat in their eyesight. He knew what the city was and where it was. His heart could feel the city and what was sitting inside of it. Landon believed it to be a city that sat in their direction where they would have to gather up some more supplies for the journey.

"That city." Henrich pointed. "Is where we are going."

"What do you mean that's the city we're going, sir? I thought we were heading to The Haunted City?"

"We are." Henrich said, looking back at the city. He pointed toward it and kept his finger in the air.

"That is The Haunted City."

Landon and Beth looked at one another. Both were confused as they stared at Henrich. They shook their heads and shrugged their shoulders.

"What do you mean that's The Haunted City?" Beth asked.

"Because it is and we're getting a preview of it." He said. "Best to take it all in."

They stood together atop the mountain as the horses stood next to Henrich. The Three looked out to The Haunted City. The place where they were heading. Knowing after seeing the visions of the images, they each know there is a long journey to be had before stepping foot on the grounds of The Haunted City.

MYSTERIOUS WAYS

Moving on across the Western World, leaving the mystical mountains, the Warslinger led his new allies into the deeper parts of the revelations. Moving on from their previous encounters with foes and otherworldly scenarios. Calm and collective. More of a unit. Cody and Beth have agreed to align themselves with the Warslinger on his quest to reach The Haunted City. After seeing a glimpse of the fabled location atop the mountain. The mountain is now known as the Mount of Divination.

While they walked down the straightened path, which they knew was a road due to the tire tracks and horse prints in the dirt. Cody could see something in the horizon further out. Objects near reaching the clouds. He pointed it toward them.

"Sir, what are those?"

Henrich glanced up and saw the objects in the sky. From his eyesight, they appeared as sharp needles standing above the ground, almost touching the first heaven. Beth took a step forward, shading her eyes from the sun with her hand.

"Are those buildings?"

"Yes." Henrich said. "They are."

"What place is further down?" Cody wondered. "Is that where we're heading next?"

"If it's in our path, then yes. If not, we continue moving on."

After miles of walking, they came to a stop. Taking a moment to relax and rest, Henrich turned to his right and saw the city closer. He could see the buildings which stood tall. Cody glanced at them, looking at their height.

"I've never seen such structures before."

"Seriously?" Beth said. "You've never seen skyscrapers"

"No. What are these skyscrapers?"

"They're buildings, boy." Henrich said. "Just buildings. Although, they're not called skyscrapers anymore. Hell, they haven't been called that in almost four hundred years."

"What do they call them now?"

"Breachers of the Heavens in the Western World. Domebreakers in the Eastern World."

They continued their move toward the city ahead. Very familiar, yet old. Old due to the amount of years which have gone by since its inception. Henrich was there when the city was founded as he stood there now at its end. Or so it may seem to be. Finally, their walk had ceased as they stood in the entrance to the city.

"What was the name of this place?" Cody asked.

"Now, Old Los Angeles." Henrich declared. "A place once called a city of angels. Now, it's a resting place for the lost, the weary, and mostly, the wicked."

II

Walking through the dirty and trash-filled street of Old Los Angeles, the city has become a rest stop and a salvage point for nearby everyone who can survive the time within. Building have crumbled into rubble. Others stand tall as their once attractive appearance has faded into a plain dusty tower.

"What is that stench?" Cody looked around, covering his face.

"It's the river." Henrich replied. "It's dead."

"What's happened here." Beth wondered, looking at the city's destruction. She continued looking and saw cracks throughout the ground of the city.

"What are all these cracks?"

'A great *worldquake* came through here during the time of the War of the West." Henrich stated. "Destroyed much of whatever was in its way. People evacuated without notice. Many died. Few managed to survive and fled to the nearest region."

"And what of the rest of this place?" Cody asked. "The buildings and such?"

"Time." Henrich said. "The movement of time has transformed this place into what it's become. During my youth, this city was a prosperous place. Yet, that was all before the War of the West."

"Where I'm from, Los Angeles thrives. It's a big city. Resembles this one, but fully functioning."

"Must be pleasant." Henrich said.

"I wouldn't call it pleasant. But, it's lively."

"How many wars have there been?"

"Too many to count. I was in most of them."

"You fought in the Shooter War?" Cody asked.

"I was a front liner in that war. Very young. Eager to do the killing when it was necessary."

"And what are you now?" Beth wondered. "Are you still that same young man or are you more mature?"

Henrich sighed and shrugged.

"Little bit of both I presume."

Upon walking, Henrich caught the wind of several men scattered through the area. Five of them, dressed in ragged clothing. Torn pants and worn-out boots. They smelled of the old city. The stench of oil and must covered the area. Henrich slowly moved his hands toward his shooters. Landon spotted the hand motions and signaled toward Beth as the men inched closer.

"Well, what do we have here." One man gestured. "A couple of stranders."

"We're just passing through." Henrich said. "We desire no trouble."

"Sorry to hear your plea, good sir." Another man said, approaching Henrich. "But, you're in our city and here, we make the rules."

"And what rules to you imply to stranders?"

"We take what they have and, usually, kill them. Very simple."

Henrich nodded, looking at the men surrounded. Landon gave Henrich a nod and so did Beth. Henrich nodded back before turning toward the man in front of him.

"Now, what do you three have to offer? Water, food, herbs?"

"Perhaps, they can lend us the young woman." One man spoke from the distance. "We haven't had a new woman come through these lands in months."

"That will not happen." Beth said.

"Oh, she speaks."

"Don't take her lightly." Henrich said. "Don't take any of us as such."

"Nobody's taking anyone lightly. Just give us something of yours and you can pass."

"Not giving any of you anything. Except for one word of advice."

"A word of advice?" the man shrugged. "What advice?"

"You reap what you sow."

"I wh-"

Before the man could finish, Henrich fired a shot at the man's head. Landon and Beth turned to the men behind them and fired shots of their own. Henrich turned toward the others and let out blasts, killing the small gang. After the shotfire, silence stilled the air.

"This was on them." Henrich proclaimed. "Not us."

The three continued on their journey as the vultures appeared from the air and covered the bodies of the dead men.

III

Walking further through the city, something caught Henrich and he grabbed quickly to what it is. He moved with more speed; a vigilant look covered his face. There was no expression. Only focus. Cody and Beth paced themselves to keep up with the Warslinger.

"Sir, what is it?" Landon asked. "Why are you moving at this pace?"

'There's something here. Something in the city."

"Like what?" Beth wondered. "A portal out of here?"

"No." Henrich stated. "Something more. I haven't sensed it since the Battle of Astolat."

"Astolat?" Landon said. "It's fine and well."

"Now it is."

"I don't know what either of you are speaking of. But, what is Astolat."

"A place." Henrich said. "A tale for another time."

The Three made their move through the city. Not one stop was made nor was a break. They each moved with focus and speed. Unified in their mission to find whatever it is which has caught the attention of the Warslinger. They passed by more gangs, prostitutes, beaten-down shelters which stood empty, apart from a few homeless remaining in its shadows.

Still moving, a man indivertibly bumped into Henrich. He neither flinched nor hid himself. He stood bold, just as the Three. However, his focus was on the Warslinger and it was unsettling to Cody and Beth. Henrich has been through these situations' countless times. It was nothing to him.

"Pardon me, sir." The man said, raising his head.

"Your eyes." Cody said.

The man was elderly and blind. He stood before them, dressed in what would assume rags and a coat. His unkempt hair flowed with the sudden gusts of the air. Henrich stared at the man and the man did the same to the Warslinger.

"Your essence." The man said of Henrich. "It is familiar. Ancient-like."

"And you can tell from?"

"On your sides, the shooters. Their power can be felt."

"Wait, you can sense the shooters?" Landon said. "How's that possible?"

"Appears this man has seen many things in his life." Henrich said. "Tell me, sir, how you've come to learn of a Warslinger's arkshooters?"

"I used to travel a lot in my prime years. I've seen the wonders of the Eastern World. The structures of Old Egypt and the Temple of Old Jerusalem. I lived in Old London before it became New London. I'm sure you're understanding my words well."

"I am" Henrich said. "But, we're not here to hear stories. We're tracking something down and it is of great importance we discover the source."

"You sense it as well." The man said with a smile. "Good. I am not the only one."

"Do you know what it may be?"

"I have a clue. I am not sure it is direct."

"How about this. Where were you when you felt it as its strongest?"

"Almost out of the downtown area. Near the outside points of the city."

Henrich nodded.

"Great." Cody said. "Let's get a move on."

"As we should." Henrich said. "Thank you for your aid, elder."

The elderly man bowed before Henrich. His hands and face flat on the concrete grounds. Cody and Beth stood still, confused. Henrich kneeled and help the man to his feet. The man seemed to have been crying as he was on the ground. Not of sorrow or sadness, but of hope.

"Why bow before me?" Henrich wondered.

"It has been a long time since I've encountered a servant of El. Forgive me if my behavior was out of place."

"No need. Only do not bow before me or any other Warslinger.

We're just servants as you said. If you choose to worship El, worship him in spirit and in truth."

The man nodded as the Three went their way.

IV

Walking along their projected path, tracking the source of the aura, Henrich started to notice their sudden exit of the downtown region. Due to the fact of staring at a deserted road ahead. In the distance, there were no tall buildings. Skyscrapers only stood behind them. Quiet and motionless. They could only see fields of half-dead grass and withered trees. A combination of light sand and soil covered the ground.

"Where does this road lead?" Cody wondered.

"We'll have to find out." Henrich replied. "The source is coming from along this path."

"I have to ask, what is this source?" Beth questioned. "Is it some kind of paranormal thing or something larger?"

"Where you're from, they would call it a paranormal occurrence. Here, it's a spiritual matter. One of a dire need."

"How dire are you talking?"

"A serious matter." Henrich professed. "Plus, it reminds me of things I've felt in my youth. Training and growing in this life. Sources like this were always around. A constant hesitation to all who served the benevolency of the universe."

"You know, you're going to have to tell me more about your world." Beth gestured. "It's very, mystique compared to where I'm from. Yet, very similar in a lot of ways. Almost as if this world is my world's future or vice versa."

Henrich turned to Beth. A sudden urge to speak something in his mind. He looked down at the sandy soil and back up toward Cody and Beth.

"Better you wait for the day to come and be prepared, rather than the day comes and you're not ready. Besides, this could all be a test for you. Or a purpose."

"What purpose is it for someone or something to take me from my home?"

"A higher purpose. For good or for evil. Only you'll know when the test is complete."

"And you know this how?"

"I've seen many like you before. Mindset-wise. Never have I ever encountered someone from a world you've spoken about. A place where there's paranormal investigators and go looking for trouble with the malevolency."

"There's a lot of things the people should know about the world they live in."

"And yet, how many of them disagree with that statement?" Henrich asked. "Many. Only a few can manage this knowledge. Seeing as how you've not gone crazy proves you're one of the few."

Beth nodded with respect. A calmness came over her.

"I appreciate that."

"I'm only being honest." Henrich replied. "Come on, we need to keep moving."

They continued their journey, following the aura. Ironically, Cody and Beth could not see what the Warslinger was keeping his focus on. A strange, violet trail of mist covered the air above them. His eyes were focused on it and marked it for an easy track to the source.

V

The deserted road is well, deserted. No sign of life seemed to be around the area as Henrich tracked the source. The surrounding areas were still. Not a sound nor a chirp of a bird, nor a bark of a dog, a screech of a cat. Nothing. Only complete quietness except for the wind bristling against the trees and grass.

"The breeze is nice." Beth said.

"It's to keep us cooled down." Henrich said. "Felt the same breeze when I was in the desert on this journey."

"I'm just curious as to where they come from." Cody said. "Like where a breeze starts and where does it end?"

"A question for another time, eh." Henrich grinned.

After walking several miles, not distant from downtown Old Los Angeles, they come across a sign. The sign detailed a location covered with people and life. Written in *Old Tongue*, yet Beth approached the sign.

"You can read that?" Cody asked.

"Yeah. It's English."

"It's what?" Cody said.

"One of the past languages of this World." Henrich professed. "I can read it as well."

"Wow. You have to teach me."

"I will." Henrich said.

Beth read the sign. She looked ahead, her eyes on the deserted road and what's ahead.

"The sign says there's a church down this path."

"Might explain the source." Henrich said. "then, we'll go there. See what's ongoing."

"Didn't that mirror warn you of some kind of church." Cody referenced. "It all sounds familiar."

"That's why we must go. To confirm the mirror's prophetic words."

"I understand. I guess."

They passed the sign and continued further, seeking to reach the church of the sign.

FINDING THE CHURCH

Following the trail and the aura source above, the surroundings increasing with trees. While they walk, Henrich showed a peculiar expression, taking notice of the area. It seemed to appear somewhat familiar to his memory.

"What is it, sir?" Cody asked.

"This place. This area, it's appearing familiar to me. I've been here before. Long ago."

"Then, you know where we're headed." Beth said.

"We're reaching the San Fernando Valley."

"The Valley?" Beth said. "It's still a dwelling place in this World?"

"Not sure. But, this trail and the source are coming from that direction."

As they walked, a bright flash of light appeared before them. Nearly blinding them of the path. Henrich raised his arm to avoid the light and just as quickly as it appeared it vanished. They each looked and saw someone standing before them. A young man. Wearing the clothes of a vagabond with a weathered fedora the colors of dried bark. Cody and Beth were unaware as to who the young man could be. Henrich, however kept his gaze keen.

"I've heard of you." Henrich said. "The Jumper."

"That's what they call me nowadays? Man, I would've preferred something more creative."

"Who are you?" Cody asked.

"Pardon my manners, I am the Kroger Kid."

"Kroger Kid?" Beth said. "Like from a grocery store?"

"What?" The Kroger Kid gestured. "No, I travel between worlds."

"Really." Cody said.

"He travels across the Four Worlds." Henrich added. "It's how he gets from place to place within seconds."

"Hold on, Warslinger. I can also travel to worlds outside of the Four."

"Then, let me ask this question. Have you traveled to the Outer-World? Have you seen the City?"

"Have I? It's a place of great spiritual power. But, it isn't designed for me."

"How come?" Beth wondered. "I'm sure there's a reason."

"I'm the kind of guy who does things on his own terms."

"Why bother us to begin with?" Henrich asked.

"Because I heard about a Warslinger who went through the towns of Savel and Hevoc. I noticed the Cailleach was no longer doing her little tests near the Valley of Death. Those dirty Scavengers are all dead and the Mercenary Man's body was found in another dimension."

"You've seen all of this?"

"I might have been hiding behind corners and suchlike. Maybe."

Henrich shook his head. "Why are you here now?"

"Because I know what you're seeking and where you're heading. That source does take you somewhere. But, it's best you do not do what you did to Savel or Hevoc."

"I had no choice."

"We all have choices, Warslinger."

"And yours is to stop my journey to reaching the City?"

"Why yes." The Kroger Kid giggled. "I can't let you pass."

"I wasn't asking for a pass."

Henrich pulled out his shooter without hesitation and fired. The Kroger Kid illuminated himself, vanishing in a blast of light. The three looked around and unnoticeably, the Kroger Kid returned behind them,

"I have to lure you away in one shape or another!" The Kroger Kid yelled with excitement.

Henrich looked to his left and spotted his other shooter was gone. He stared at the Kroger Kid, who was waving his shooter in the air after snatching it from Henrich's side. The Kid took off into the woods, laughing maniacally.

"Seriously." Beth said.

"He took your shooter, sir." Cody said. "What are we going to do?"

"Get it back." Henrich replied as he ran after the Kroger Kid into the wilderness.

"Ah, man." Cody said, following the Warslinger and Beth.

II

Henrich ran through the forest after the Kroger Kid, who would appear and reappear in certain locations. Cody and Beth followed fast on their feet. Henrich fired a shot every time the Kroger Kid appeared. While he continued to vanish with a quick flash of light, Henrich moved faster with every step. Shooter firing. Cody did the same as did Beth.

"I've never seen him move that fast." Cody mentioned.

"He wants his gun back." Beth replied. "What would do think he'll be doing?"

"Wait. Gun? You mean his shooter."

"Yes, that's what I mean."

The Warslinger continued firing shots at the appearing Kroger Kid, who proceeded to mock him as they moved through the trees.

"It might take you all night to catch up!" The Kroger Kid yelled.

"You're a nuisance!" Henrich said. "A pain!"

"I've heard worse!"

The Kid vanished once more and appeared before Cody, tripping him onto the ground and teleporting behind Beth, shoving her against the nearby tree. The Kid vanished with only a laugh echoing through the forest. Henrich caught up to the two, helping them up.

"He tripped me." Cody said.

"You'll be fine." Henrich replied. "Beth, how are you?"

"Just a scratch. It's nothing."

While they spoke, the Kid appeared above them, sitting in the tree. Giggling.

"Here's the thing, stranders." The Kid said, getting their attention.

"Not again." Henrich said, raising up his shooter and firing.

The Kid snatched the bullet from the air and returned it to Henrich's shooter. Right in the chamber.

"Did he just give you the bullet back?" Cody said. "And put it back in the shooter?"

"I have skills, my boy!" The Kid said.

"Give me back my other shooter and let us on our way."

"I'm sorry, Warslinger. As much as I respect you and your kind, I cannot let you bother the World beyond this forest. For the Valley has seen better days since their union."

"What union?" Henrich wondered. "Who's waiting on the other end of this forest? Who's dwelling in the ruins of the Valley?"

"Ah, now that is a conversation for another time."

The Kid raised his right index finger and Henrich's shooter was returned to his side. Henrich looked and grabbed it, holding now both shooters aimed at the Kid. Cody held the blast shooter and Beth grabbed the machete from Henrich's coat. The Kid applauded the team.

"Looks like a new Heptad is resurging from my point of view."

"You will let us pass." Henrich proclaimed. "Or else, you'll wish you could teleport to a place of peace permanently."

"More threats." The Kid laughed. "As long as you're in this region, near the Valley, I will not cease to stop you."

The Kid gazed up toward the afternoon sky, seeing the sun. He pointed toward the sky.

"Appears the sun will be going down soon, you're in this forest, and I will not let you pass. Therefore, you have two options before you. Return to where you came from or spend the night in these woods and wish for a better morrow."

Henrich stared at the Kid with intensity. Cody and Beth remained still. The Kid didn't take his eyes off the Warslinger and neither did he. Henrich took the shot with both shooters and the Kid disappeared once more. Henrich placed the shooters to his side, turning to Cody and Beth.

"Looks like we're camping here for the night."

Later in the night, after setting up camp with the equipment they carried in Henrich's bag, the three sat together under the dark sky and stars above. The silence of the wilderness and the still wind. A fire was kindled for heat as the surroundings gravely dropped.

"This world is strange." Beth said. "Very."

"So, it doesn't get cold where you're from?" Cody asked.

"It does. But, not on a day like this. It's usually warm. Somewhat cool."

"Your world isn't that different from ours." Henrich said.

"Then, let me in on it. Tell me about this place. Your Worlds."

Henrich nodded and drew closer toward the flame. Holding his hands over the fire.

"At the beginning of time, our sense of time, the Master known as El created everything from our world to yours and others beyond. Here, He created *Adamah* and it combines the Four Worlds. Afterwards, he created the stars, the heavens and the five seas. Four surround the Four Worlds and one sits in the center of them all; *Tsaphon* is the sea of the north, *Teman* is the sea of the south, *Qedem* is the sea of the east, and *Maarab* is the sea of the west. Together, they form *Tehomayim*, the great sea of the Worlds. The center sea is called the *Sea of Tabbur*, which signifies the connection of the Four Worlds. The Worlds themselves are as follows; *Yaphean*, the Northern World. A place of sheer winter and diverse kingdoms. From Anchor Bay to Old Camelot and what is now New London. Then, He created *Khamain*, the Southern World. A land filled with kingdoms and lush landscapes. The home of Old Egypt and the Amazon City. A place of beauty. Next was *Shemia*, the Eastern World. The land where El placed His name. The home of Old Jerusalem, my home and Mount Sinai. The land which is the birthplace of the Warslingers of the Heptad."

"I didn't know you were from Old Jerusalem." Cody said. "You've seen its fall."

"I was there when it fell. The moment where we lost. The defeat of the Heptad. The end of the Warslingers. Betrayal and unjust ones claimed the land soon after. That day was named the Fall of Old Jerusalem."

"And what of the other World?" Beth asked. "The Western one?"

"You speak of *Arzareth*, the Western World. Which we are currently placed. The land where the Warslingers were dispersed. A place of prophecy. Yet, there is one more world. The realm where the spirits dwell and judgment is set. The realm where The Haunted City itself sits amongst the Gate of the City and the Kingdom of Order. That place is called *Ruachayim*, the Outer-World."

"Then, what happened next?" Cody asked curiously.

"After the Worlds were formed, to keep the seas from overtaking them, El created a boundary made of steel-like ice and called the place

Qeramah. Then, before Man walked upon the worlds, the animals were formed. Yet, there were also those above. The Sons of El, a group of spiritual beings. We know them as the Seraph."

"You mean like angels." Beth said.

"Yes. One deemed himself worthy of ruler ship. A war broke out in the Outer-World and he was defeated. Upon his downfall, his essence and dark spirit spread throughout the Four Worlds and the Malevolency was born, eventually consuming the generations of Man which came after. An opposition to El's Benevolency. That is why the Warslingers of the Heptad were created. To combat the forces made from the spread of the Malevolency."

"So, you've seen a lot during your years." Beth said. "Which brings me to a question. How old are you?"

"How old you do perceive me to be?"

"You look as if you're in your mid-forties. Perhaps early forties."

"There's no way he's in his forties." Cody said. "Impossible."

"What do you mean? He looks forty to me."

"Because I'm in my mid-twenties."

"No, you're not." Beth said. "You're at least sixteen. Maybe seventeen."

"He's in his twenties." Henrich said. "I'm certain."

"I don't understand. People in my world look much older in their mid-twenties. Then, how old are you if you're not in your forties?"

"I've been around for over five hundred years." Henrich said. "Humans age much slower in the Four Worlds than yours I'm assuming?"

"Very much so."

Henrich looked up, still seeing the aura trail in the air glowing in the night hour. He also sensed the magic of the Kroger Kid lurking around the trees.

"Best we get some sleep."

"What of that Kid?" Beth wondered.

"We'll deal with him in the morning."

The Warslinger put out the fire and sleep fell upon the three.

III

They awoke right at the brink of dawn. Henrich stood tall, gazing toward the morning sky and looking around the trees for the Kroger Kid. Beth and Cody rose up from their slumber, seeing Henrich gazing around the area.

'What is it?"

"Seeing if he's around." Henrich said. "He's watching us. I'm sure of it."

"Well, he can't possibly keep us in this forest for long." Cody added. "I mean, what's the worse he could do to us?"

While talking, the sound of a breaking branch echoed through the forest. Henrich caught the sound quickly while Cody and Beth talked. Henrich approached them, waving his hand.

"Something's out here." Henrich said steadily.

The Warslinger reached and raised up his shooter. He looked around and the sound increased. Moving closer. Cody and Beth stood up, holding weapons of their own. Henrich turned back around, following the sound and could see what it was. It was approaching them fast.

"There it is." Henrich said.

"There's what?" Cody asked, turning around to see what Henrich saw. "Oh no."

"What is it?" Beth asked.

They found themselves staring at three scorpions. Larger than Beth had ever seen. A dark brown with a hint of gold in their shelled bodies. Their eyes burning violet and the tips of their tails sharp as blades. Henrich and Cody took steps forward with their shooters. The scorpions hissed with fury and their tails slammed against the ground, tossing dirt and leaves into the air.

"What are those?!" Beth asked.

"Dire Scorpions." Henrich said.

"Like the wolves?!"

"Yes."

Henrich fired several shots toward the scorpions, but their hollow hide was too dense for the bullets to penetrate. Cody turned to Beth with haste, dropping his weapon.

"Hand me the blastshooter!"

Beth tossed him the shooter and he fired a round toward the first scorpion. The blastshooter proved effective as it burst the shell on the top of the scorpion. The shell slid off with pus. Cody fired rounds toward the other two, blowing one's claw and the other's tail off. The scorpions screeched with agony.

"What's next?" Cody asked. "We keep shooting?"

"We'll have to get closer." Henrich said.

Henrich pulled out his machete and ran toward the first scorpion. He jumped up as the claws reached out to snatch him. Henrich raised the machete and impaled it into the creature, killing it with the blow. The scorpion fell to the ground as the other two ambushed Henrich. Cody ran after him and fired another round from the blastshooter into the scorpion's face, blowing it off as it slid from the body. Henrich grabbed the remaining one's tail and used it to impale the scorpion itself. The Warslinger stepped back as the scorpion fell dead by its own tail.

"That's it." Cody said. "We won."

"It seems." Henrich replied.

"Are those things native to this place?" Beth asked, looking at the bodies in awe.

"Dire Scorpions don't belong here. They're mostly found in the Eastern World. In Old Egypt."

"Then, how did you three end up here?" Cody asked.

"The Kroger Kid." Henrich replied. "He brought them here. To distract us. To cause us to stumble from our mission."

"You're telling me there's more of these and other creatures as big as this?" Beth asked.

"A lot more." Henrich said. "You would be amazed at the creatures within the Four Worlds."

Cody looked around the trees and approached Henrich.

"Do you think he's watching?"

"I know he is."

Henrich stepped forward and looked around.

"Kroger Kid!" Henrich yelled. "I know you're watching us, and you saw what we did and what we're capable of. Either you return to me my shooter and let us pass. Or, you will suffer the same fate, if not worse like your pets from Shemia!"

The burst of light reappeared in the trees above them, Henrich looked, spotting the Kroger Kid moving through them as if he was running on air. Henrich pressed forward, grabbing his gear and ran after the Kid. Cody and Beth followed.

IV

Chasing the Kroger Kid through the forest, the eyes of the Warslinger were locked onto the young man. The Kid raised his hands and threw energy balls of light toward the three, stumbling them from the chase. No matter, Henrich proceeded past the light, for his eyes were not shaken nor blinded by the brightness. Beth had to pause, and Cody stumbled in his running, nearly tripping himself.

"We need to keep up!" Henrich yelled.

The Kid threw more energy balls and once they were in the air, Henrich raised up his shooter, firing rounds into the balls, causing them to explode and spreading the brightness of the light.

"That's not possible." The Kid said to himself, still running and teleporting.

"I can hear you." Henrich responded. "This game of yours is over."

The Kid moved and vanished into a tree in the midst of the forest. This tree was larger, thicker in size. The branches were nearly long as the tress standing around them. Cody and Beth caught up to the Warslinger, staring in awe at the massive tree.

"What is this?" Cody wondered.

"The Kid went inside the tree." Henrich said. "He's not leaving."

"How can you be sure?" Beth asked. "I mean he did show us he can teleport."

"Because this tree is his home. He dwells in it."

"I don't understand."

"The outer layer appears as a mammoth tree. But, the interior, is like a home. A mansion for his kind."

Henrich kicked the tree, causing it to rattle. He kicked it again, shaking the tree. Henrich backed up and ran shoulder first into the tree and the door opened in front of them with a creak.

"How did you know the door was there?" Cody asked with

confusion. "I mean, I didn't know trees have doors."

"Only these trees, my boy." Henrich answered. "Kroger Kid! Come on out! Let's finish this!"

The three stood guard, weapons in hand as the Kid stepped foot from the tree. His hands up in the air, a grin on his face. Not one of a humorous nature.

"This game of yours is finished," Henrich said. "it's over. Return to me my shooter and let us pass."

"I can't let you pass. You'll ruin what they have!"

"That is not your place to decide what happens and what doesn't. The aura is strange and unusual to this place."

"They're seeking to help people. They have faith."

"And it is my duty as a Warslinger of the Heptad to search such places and discover what truly lies within those walls."

"I know. But, they seem happy."

"Seeming happy isn't a sure answer to peace."

The Kid nodded, showing respect with a hint of resistance in his body. Cody gripped the blastshooter as Beth held the handle of the machete tightly. The Kid snapped his fingers.

"There, you have your shooter back."

Henrich reached down and pulled out the shooter, he began searching it for rounds. The Kid held his hand up in a pause.

"Don't fret, Warslinger. I didn't take any of your rounds."

Henrich gazed with a nod, placing the shooter back into its holster.

"May we now pass?" Henrich asked.

The Kid sighed. "Fair enough."

The Kid waved his hand and the aura presented itself within the forest, however its appearance was greater, and the energy was stronger. Henrich looked up and saw the location of its origin.

"Don't worry, Kid, we won't harm anyone." Henrich said. "Anyone innocent."

"I know you won't, Warslinger. I know your kind."

Henrich signaled for Cody and Beth to leave the forest with him. They walked away as the Kid watched them leave.

"One more thing, Warslinger." The Kid said.

Henrich turned around to face the Kid.

"This isn't our last meeting. We will meet again. Someday."

"That, I am certain of." Henrich replied. "Peaceful nights and blissful days, Kid.”

“May you prosper in years.” The Kid replied, returning into the tree. The door shut and the tree itself vanished into the light. Leaving an open space in the forest.

The three continued following the aura, until they could hear voices, multiple voices talking to each other and once they exit the forest, they saw the source of the energy. Henrich took a step forward, Cody looked ahead and approached the Warslinger.

“Sir, what is this place?”

“It’s a church community.” Beth said. “I’m familiar with these places.”

“A community, you’re right.” Henrich said. “But, this one, with the aura, there’s something very spiritual happening here.”

THE SECRET WORLD

I

The three stood in front of a gated community. Filled with people of diverse appearances and sizes. Cody had never seen the likes of such unification. Beth, on the other hand has, yet, not as it's portraying right before her face. Henrich stared, looking at the people. He found no arguing, no selfish nature, no signs of betrayal. All he saw was love. A love of humans coming together in a world lost to itself.

"This place is incredible." Cody said. "And we haven't even entered it yet."

"Are we even sure we want to go in?" Beth added.

"The source of the aura is coming from this place." Henrich said. "best we find out what it is and continue on our way."

While they stood in awe, the gates opened. Upon their opening, a man approached the three. Dressed in the clothing of a Catholic priest. He was a middle-aged man. He stood facing the Warslinger, gazed him down and up and nodded.

"I see we have new members."

"I wouldn't call us members of your community." Henrich said. "What is this place, truly?"

"Why follow me and I'll explain everything in the form of a tour."

Henrich turned, giving Cody and Beth a look. They nodded as the Warslinger turned back to the priest. He nodded with a hand gesture.

"We will follow."

"Wonderful." The priest said. "By the way, my name is Father

Naillain."

"Father?" Henrich said. "There is only one father."

"I know what you're going to say and please, I will explain everything in the tour."

"I will be listening closely."

Naillain nodded. He walked before them as they entered the community and the gates closed soon after.

11

Passing through the gates, they startled and somewhat marveled at the scenery around them. The amount of people staggered Cody, never seeing such since their incident with the Scavengers, however, these seemed more benevolent. Beth respected their hospitality and greetings. Henrich walked beside Naillain.

"How did all of this begin?" Henrich asked.

"Began right around the time the air changed and the Worlds shook."

"I'm aware many places fell. I assume this one right after the worldquake?"

"Yes. I lived not far out of the limits of the city. I saw many of the towers fall upon the streets. Taking away the lives of the scattered. There was nothing I could do but pray."

"And did you receive your answer?"

"I did. But, at the cost of some relatives. They didn't take heed to my warnings of the quake's coming. I told them something was happening across the Worlds. They ignored me. Despised me. Until the day the quake shook."

"How do you know they're gone?"

"I went to their homes. Found them under trees and swallowed by the ground. I knew then, I was on the right path."

"And this path led you here? Being a preacher to those who seek answers?"

"Yes.

They continued to follow Naillain through the community. Seeing gardens, homes, trailers, and facilities. People were living together in what some would call true harmony and prosperity.

"Is there a place here for all these people?" Beth asked.

"Everyone you see here has a roof over their heads and food in their homes." Naillain replied. "No one is of need of anything."

"And you guys grow your own food?" Cody asked. "I saw the cattle over by the gates. Figured they're your meat source."

"Your right. Although, there are some here who live the life of vegetation, no discrimination here."

"I'm not surprised at that." The Warslinger said. "Many sought after food once the tragedies ceased. Vegetation was all that was left in most places."

"We found the cattle trapped in an old farm far from here. We picked them up and brought them here. They breed and bring forth more cattle."

Bleating sounds come from nearby, Henrich turned, seeing a pair of goats passing by. Cody laughed.

"You have goats too?!"

"We do."

Cody went over and petted the passing goats, laughing. They continued walking and stopped in front of the church. A large building with a steeple on top.

"This is where we worship."

"Worship who?" The Warslinger asked.

"The God of the Worlds." Naillain answered. "He's the one who answered my prayers. Gave me this land and brought these people to me. He has a great purpose for my life."

Henrich nodded.

"Good of you to keep in tune with the spiritual."

"It's what we all need in this World."

"I see."

Naillain opened the doors and gestured for his guests to enter.

"After you." Naillain said.

They entered the church, but there was something off in the air. Henrich looked up and the aura was gone. A peculiar nature of such.

III

Inside the church itself were dozens of people. Some were praying, others were fellowshipping, and a few were talking amongst each other. Naillain escorted Henrich, Cody, and Beth inside. Walking down the aisle, greeting the people around them with kind words.

"Everyone seems generous." Henrich said.

"Because they are." Naillain replied. "This is the perfect place for such a harmony."

Upon the greetings, they are brought by Naillain toward a woman, who was tending a family. Naillain stood firm, as did those around him.

"Brandi." Naillain said.

The woman turned around to see him. She smiled and nodded.

"Yes sir?"

"I would like to meet our new guests."

She approached them and extended her hand with a smile on her face.

"Hi. My name is Brandi Bush."

"Beth Grasslands."

"Cody Landon."

"Randolph Henrich."

Brandi looked at him and a quickening came into her spirit. Her smile grew as she looked into the eyes of a Warslinger.

"You're one of them?"

"One of what?" Henrich asked.

"A warrior from the East. The ones who helped in the Battle of Astolat all those years ago?"

"I was involved in that event. It was during my younger years."

Brandi looked at Cody and Beth. Measuring them.

"Now, you." Brandi said to Cody. "You're not from the Western World, are you?"

"Not exactly. I come from the Northern World. It's where I was born."

"I can tell by the way of your speech."

Brandi turned to Beth and turned her head.

"You… you're not from around here either are you?"

"I'm not from any of these places you're all familiar with."

"What does she mean?" Naillain asked the Warslinger.

"She come from another world. Not one of the Four."

"Can't be." Naillain replied. "That would mean…"

"There are other Worlds out there besides our own."

"It goes against our word of law. Our history."

"It doesn't go against them. It confirms them."

"So, where are you from?" Brandi asked.

"I'm from a world called Earth. From a city known as Washington D.C."

"D.C.?" Brandi said. "You have an operating D.C. in your world?"

"Yes."

As they spoke with her, Henrich looked over toward the right of the church and saw an older man, wearing clothing which resembled the Eastern World. Henrich knew there was something peculiar with the man and proceeded to approach him.

IV

The Warslinger approached the older man, greeting him with a handshake. The man stared and hugged Henrich.

"It is time I've gazed upon another." The man said.

"Another what?" Henrich asked.

"One of you. From Old Jerusalem."

Henrich nodded slowly.

"I didn't get your name."

"My name is Abraham."

Cody and Beth approached Henrich and Abraham. The older man greeted them with the same hug he gave the Warslinger. They themselves, weren't sure of what to make of it.

"You're very affectionate." Cody said.

"It's gentle." Beth added. "A sense of love and peace."

"I see you're with the Warslinger."

"We are…" Cody said, looking at Henrich.

"Don't be afraid." Abraham said. "I know of many things. But, if you don't mind, I would like to speak with the Warslinger myself."

"Of course." Beth replied, nodding to Henrich and walking away with Cody.

"Why do you need to speak with me?"

"Because there's a lot to discuss. Follow me."

Henrich followed Abraham to a secure and quiet area. Cody and Beth spoke with others within the church. Abraham brought Henrich to a quiet spot in a corridor of the church and the two sat down in the chairs near a window.

"First off, let me say how it is a true privilege to speak with a Warslinger again."

"Again?"

"I, myself as you can tell, come from the same landmass the

Warslingers dwelled."

"Why are you here in Arzareth?"

"I came across the sea sometime after the Fall."

Henrich nodded and sighed. He looked up toward Abraham, seeing the story in his eyes. The words echoing through his ears.

"You were there when it happened."

"I was. Seen everything that transpired."

"You saw the Fall of the city. The end of our tribes and the desolation of our purpose."

"Your purpose was not destroyed. You know this better than the common folk."

"What I know is after the fall, all the Warslingers were scattered. Dispersed across the Four Worlds. I ended up in the desertlands. Traveled through some small towns, came across some peculiar creatures and humans. That trail led me here."

"I can see this isn't the destination. Only a crossroads in your journey."

"It is."

"What are you seeking? Where are you headed?"

"To the Haunted City."

"The Haunted City? Why seek such a place? After all the things you've seen. The blessings you've been given, why go there?"

"Because I need answers."

"You already have that access."

"I've tried. It seems after the fall and our dispersion; everything has gone silent. The City is outside the Four Worlds. It's the perfect place to uncover everything. Why the city fell and why we failed."

Abraham sighed.

"Perhaps, when you reach the City, will you be content with the answers you'll be given?"

"Do I even have a choice."

"You do. You can accept the answers given or decline them and walk away."

"It's a start to a conclusion."

"And yet, how do you intend on reaching the City? The Outer-World at least?"

"There are portals. Gateways throughout the Four Worlds. I intend on finding one and gaining my entry into the City."

"What of the Gate?"

"The Gate of the City will not be a problem for me."

"And this Tubal King?"

The Warslinger stared at Abraham. A knowing.

"How do you know of that name?"

"Because it's an ancient one. Far past the time before you became a Warslinger."

"Then you are aware of his lieutenant?"

"Arkdragon? I am aware."

"How?"

"I lived in the same areas as you did. I was there when you were but a boy and became a man. I am here now, speaking to you as I did my own sons in times past."

"I don't know what to make of all this."

"Make of this in what form?"

"Speaking to you concerning these things. I haven't spoken to anyone in this manner since before the Fall."

Abraham nodded with a smile.

"Then, it is time your journey begins."

Abraham stood up from his seat and Henrich followed.

"I do know what is truly happening here, as do you."

"There's something off about the Priest and this place. The energy around here seems benevolent, but dark."

"You will have those answers soon. But, for right now, see what you can learn and when the time comes, you will know what to do and I will be there by your side."

The Warslinger agreed with a nod.

"Good. Let's return to the others."

"I wonder what they're all up to?" Henrich wondered.

"Naillain is about to perform an exorcism."

"Exorcism?"

"You will see."

V

Abraham and Henrich returned to the congregation, finding them sitting down upon the pews while Naillain stood at the podium. The Warslinger spotted Landon and Beth, he walked toward them and sat down, Abraham sat behind them as they looked on.

"My family, we have been brought into this tabernacle to cast out a particular spirit from one of our own. Now, I will not point out who this individual is, but as I speak and proclaim the powers of the true god, this spirit will show itself and it will be cast out."

Abraham leaned in toward Henrich.

"You're familiar with all of this, aren't you?"

"I am." The Warslinger replied. "But, in a different way."

Naillain continued, "Now, we have three visitors who have come from the outside and this is the perfect time for them to see what truly dwells in the Four Worlds."

Without a notice, Naillain began yelling out with a loud voice for the spirit to come out and show itself. He screamed it further and continued speaking the phrase. Right after the first minute, a young girl arose from the pews, screaming and shouting from her lungs. Cursing out Naillain, although he continued speaking his words as the spirit moved with the young girl, trying to reach the podium, but was held down by others in the congregation. Cody was sheer afraid, Beth was startled.

"I see you have not budge." Henrich said to Beth.

"I've had my fair share of these things. Frightened me when I first saw it. Now, I know it's only part of the greater battle."

"What is happening to that girl?!" Cody asked.

"That's not the girl." Henrich said. "What you're seeing is a spirit, a demon who was masquerading and dwelling within the girl."

"And it's upset?"

"Upset for the fact it has to leave her." The Warslinger confirmed.

"She is being delivered and set free."

Naillain walked down from the podium and toward the girl. He yelled with a loud voice for the spirit to be cast out and to leave the area. The spirit put up a fight with Naillain and those around him. However, when the spirit caught a glance of Henrich. It froze."

"Come out of her!" Naillain yelled.

The spirit screamed and went silent. The girl fell to the floor. The room was quiet. Yet, above them, the spirit roamed and moved through the air, making its way toward Old Los Angeles, still screaming and enraged. Inside the tabernacle, the girl arose, and the congregation cheered.

"She has been set free!" Naillain cheered.

"Where has the demon gone?" Cody asked.

"It's moving through dry places." Henrich replied. "Seeking rest."

"Will it ever try to return?"

Henrich sighed, looking at Cody.

"They always will."

Sometime later, Henrich remained in the tabernacle with Abraham. The older man could sense something was going on with the Warslinger.

"Why have you chosen to remain in here?"

"The Priest." Henrich said. "Naillain, what god does he speak of?"

"Well, from what I've learned, he believes he serves El, the God of Salvation."

"And does he?"

Abraham shook his head.

"I don't think so. He does serve a god. Only thing is, I haven't been able to discover which one."

Henrich nodded.

"Give it time. It'll reveal itself to us."

"And what will you do when that time comes?" Abraham wondered.

"As I've always done. Finish the work and proclaim El as the true god."

CONVERGENCE

I

Abraham gathered the Warslinger, Cody, and Beth into a room separated from the congregation. Abraham sat them down as he sat in front of them. Looking at the door and taking in a breath.

"What Naillain is about to do may frighten you."

"Frighten us how?" Beth asked.

"He's seeking to convert the three of you into this congregation."

"What's wrong with that?" Cody wondered. "Everyone here seems happy. At peace."

"This place is an illusion." Henrich said. "I noticed it before the gates opened. The aura in the air brought us here. Because the energy isn't a part of the benevolency."

Beth turned to Abraham. A keen look on her face.

"Then, why are you here?"

"Because it is part of a greater plan." Abraham replied. "Far greater than I can speak of."

"And Randolph is a part of this plan?"

"Indeed. He's always known. Yet, he didn't suspect it would bring him to a place like this. Nor meet someone such as myself. Yet, this reality brings people to many peculiar places. To meet peculiar people."

"But, Naillain's way of doing things, appears to be off." Henrich said. "Deeply, I know he means well. Yet, I can only wonder where he received such a message."

"Ask him when he has some time to himself." Abraham replied. "I'm sure he will give you the answer you're hoping."

"I will. Don't worry, I won't cause a disturbance of any kind."

"I know you won't." Abraham smiled. "You're not that kind of man."

11

Naillain stood before his congregation. Speaking on the great things and miracles which have occurred since their fellowship began. Henrich, Cody, and Beth sat in the back of the tabernacle with Abraham.

"The things of which the Worlds have suffered, will no longer matter in the end." Naillain proclaimed. "Because, what's about to come, will shake the foundations of the Four Worlds and they will never be the same."

"He speaks with eloquent words." Henrich uttered.

"You know the types." Abraham replied. "Very talkative."

"Eventually, we will all be caught up together in the Outer-World of Ruachayim and we will remain as one for all eternity."

Naillain looked toward the back of the room, seeing the three visitors. He extended his hand out to them for all the congregation to see. The people turned to glance at the visitors, Cody waved. Beth nodded. Henrich grinned.

"It is with great honor for us to have these three guests in our tabernacle. Fellowshipping with all of us. For they have come from the outside and have seen the tragedies thereof."

Henrich leaned in toward Abraham, keeping his gaze upon Naillain, who's now walking back and forth in front of the congregation.

"The words he's using, I've heard them in such manner before."

"Because he took them from the ancients. Naillain is only following what he learned while out there in Shemia."

"He's been to the Eastern World?"

"Of course, it explains why he knows much about the spiritual differences and the quickening of the Four Worlds."

The Warslinger sat back. Uneasy feeling within him. Abraham could feel it as well. Cody and Beth were unaware of the circumstances taking place. When Naillain would speak, the energy of his words went out to

252

the congregation. Entering their minds and altering their motives without ease. Henrich waved his hand in front of Cody and Beth.

"What was that for?" Cody asked.

"Protection." Henrich replied.

"Protection from what?"

"You'll soon know."

III

Naillain walked down the aisle of the congregation, making a stop at Henrich, Cody, and Beth. He smiled. They grinned. Abraham sat back and watched.

"I believe it's time you three become official members of this family."

"Wow." Cody said. "Already?"

"I have a general feeling you were destined for a place like this. The Worlds only dream of it."

Naillain extended his and out toward Cody. Cody went for a reach and quickly sat back. Naillain nodded with a stern look. Uncertainty crept upon him. He shook himself and focused on Beth. Speaking to her the same words he spoke to Cody. Beth nodded.

"Do you accept?" Naillain asked.

"This place is special. One of the best places I've come across in this world of yours. But, with all due respect, I must decline. I must return to my world. It's where I belong."

"Naillain stepped back. Nodding slowly.

"That I see." Naillain said. "Much respect to your wishes."

Naillain moved over and stood before the Warslinger. Their eyes locked on one another. Naillain searched Henrich's spirit and was unaware of the Warslinger doing the same. Naillain nodded.

"Do you accept?"

Henrich was silent. He looked over to Cody, Beth, to Abraham, and out toward the congregation. All were awaiting a response from the Warslinger of the Heptad.

"No." Henrich replied. "I do not accept."

The congregation let out a loud gasp and Naillain turned to them, signaling them to be silent. They obeyed their shepherd as he turned back to Henrich. He looked at Cody and Beth. He couldn't understand the true purpose of their decline.

"Why?"

"We're on a mission." Henrich said.

"A mission? It must certainly cannot be higher than what we're doing here."

"It goes forward. Answers must be found for everything that has happened. Everything that has took place across the Four Worlds."

"That a genuine fact?"

"It's a reality."

Naillain nodded. A grin showed upon his face. He pointed toward the Warslinger. While glancing gat the window, seeing its past dark.

"Tomorrow, the two of us shall speak. One-on-one."

"What do you wish to speak on?" Henrich asked.

"Your purpose in the Worlds. My purpose. To see if they are intertwined."

"And if they are?"

"Then, my theory is correct, and the balance is near set."

Naillain turned away and took one step forward. He stopped and turned back to Henrich. He scouted Cody and Beth before focusing on the Warslinger. He could sense something around them.

"There's a barrier around the three of you. Its power is highly strong. I've never come across such a power before."

"Means we're in good company."

"Company with whom?"

"I'll tell you in our talk on the morrow."

Naillain nodded.

"I'm looking forward to it."

The congregation cleared out, leaving on Henrich and Abraham inside. Cody and Beth returned to their rooms.

"What will you tell him?" Abraham asked.

"Everything." Henrich replied.

KNOWING THE TRUTH FROM THE LIE

I

A gunshot rattled across the plains, the arkshooter was held still. Holding it was Henrich. His eyes focused, his mind clear. He took another shot across the plains, eventually hitting his target. A scarecrow. Henrich showed a smile of gratitude, placing the shooter back into its holster. He turned around, finding himself standing before his master. Wearing his dark red robe, carrying his sapphire staff. His grey beard gave off a presence of the ancients. A presence of a master.

"Young Randolph, I see you've improved your range."

"Yes, Master Moses. I managed to hit the target this time."

"That I am aware."

Moses escorted Henrich from the plains, toward the small temple. Inside were others, dressed in garb familiar to Henrich's own duster and hat. Some wore leather vests, robes, and diadems. Henrich sat with Moses at the table to eat. Two plates were placed before them by a handmaiden. She was fair to look at. She carried within her a meek and quiet spirit. This pleased Henrich dearly. For there were hardly any in the region which they sat.

"Don't let your eyes wander, boy." Moses said. "For at best, you'll slip and fall."

Henrich caught himself. "Yes sir."

The two ate their bread and meat as another figure approached the table and sat with them. Henrich looked up at the visitor, raising his head from his plate. Seeing another one of his masters. He nodded his head in respect.

"Didn't expect to see me here, did you?"

"No, Master Noah." Henrich said. "I thought you were still in Old Jerusalem."

"I had to come here for duty. It is why yourself and Moses are here as well."

Henrich paused himself, wiping his mouth.

"How's Arthur and Charlton?" Moses asked.

"Being kept occupied with Joshua and Daniel. They've been sent out toward Damascus. Signs of an estranged sphinx were found. Troubling the villagers. They can't sleep nor leave their homes."

"They'll clean out the area." Moses said. "Send the spirit away."

"A sphinx in Damascus?" Young Randolph uttered.

Moses turned toward the young Warslinger. Seeing his enthusiasm in the others' mission. Yet, Moses knew he had to keep him focused.

"You remember why we're here don't you?"

"We're here on a mission?"

"Yes." Moses answered. "Take a look over there."

Henrich looked out in the distance. What he saw was a city. A large one. Standing around the city were three pyramids. One higher and larger than the other.

"What do you see?" Noah asked.

"I see a city of marvelous wonders. I see the pyramids of old. The one our ancestor constructed."

"What else do you see?" Moses asked. "Look closer."

Henrich gazed his eyes closer and what he saw was a shadow looming over the city. The skies above the pyramids seemed clear to the natural eye, but in the spiritual realm, there was a darkness. A malevolent darkness.

"Evil." Henrich said. "I see evil."

Moses nodded.

"That is why we're here in Old Egypt. To uncover what this evil is and destroy it before it spreads further out into the Four Worlds."

"I understand."

"So, is the boy ready?" Noah asked Moses.

Moses turned toward Henrich. He smiled and nodded.

"He's proven himself to me and to El. The boy's ready."

11

Henrich arose from his bed, raising up and looking around the room. Sunlight shining through the windows. Reflecting against his duster and hat. Only seeing Cody and Beth still asleep. He sat up and rested on the side of the bed, reflecting on the dream. He smiled at the memories. His mind warped from the past and to the present, remembering where he is. He stood up and dressed himself. He left the room. Outside waiting was Abraham.

"What are you doing here?" Henrich wondered.

"Figured I would escort you to Naillain's office. He's waiting for you."

"This early in the morning?"

"Indeed. He said he couldn't sleep. His mind was set on the discussion between you two. He has theories and demands answers."

"Demands?"

"I know it sounds forceful. But, they are his wishes."

"And what if he doesn't like the answers I give him?"

Abraham sighed with a gestured expression. He already knew the outcome and the results which would follow.

"Then, he may kick the three of you out or even try to kill you. For being trespassers who seek to do this place harm."

"And what are your thoughts on all of this?"

"I know the truth. When the time comes, I will be standing on the side of justice and victory. Defeat will be on the other end, hoping for a spot."

Henrich nodded with a grin. He extended his hand toward Abraham. He looked down at the Warslinger's hand and instead hugged him.

"Everything is going according to plan."

"We'll see." Henrich said.

Henrich walked down the hall, making a left turn, finding himself facing the office of Naillain. Henrich took a moment and exhaled. He approached the door calmly and as he went to knock, the door opened. As it opened, he saw Naillain sitting at his desk, staring.

"Come on in." Naillain said.

Henrich entered the office and closed the door behind him. The office was silent. Not a sound. The two stared at one another. Naillain stood up from his desk and approached the Warslinger. Looking him down and up.

"It seems the two of us have something to discuss."

"I'm all ears."

Naillain nodded.

"Good. Good." Naillain said. "Let me first begin by acknowledging your rank as a Warslinger of the Heptad."

"So, you're aware?"

"I've been aware before you even approached our gates. You see, I have a keen eye and a traveling spirit."

"Do tell."

Naillain sat at his desk. He gestured toward Henrich to sit and the Warslinger sat down, facing Naillain at his desk.

"You're not the only one here who's had the pleasure of traveling across the Four Worlds. Seeing their wonders and their marks."

"You call it a pleasure?"

"Oh, yes."

"Is seeing the lives of many perishing and suffering considered a pleasure in your field?"

"Depends on who are the perished and suffered. I can only aid those who are like myself. Like-minded and serve the same god."

"You believe you serve *El*?"

"I serve the God of the Worlds. He brought me to this land. This Silicon Valley that once was. He gave me the tools to reconstruct its foundations and in doing so, I have gained a following, a congregation. A family."

"And the exorcism you performed? Was that of your god's power?"

"Yes. Who else can cast demons out of human beings besides him."

"Yet, a foul spirit cannot cast out demons."

Naillain paused. His face became stern. His intent had changed. This is what Henrich was expecting.

"It appears we serve two different gods." Henrich added. "For the

God of the Worlds is the ruler of the Malevolency."

"That so?" Naillain questioned. "And where did you learn of this?"

"From my mentors."

"You speak of the originals?"

"They taught me in their ways. It's how I became a Warslinger. A member of the Heptad."

Naillain cocked his head, standing up once more from his desk. Henrich moved and Naillain paused him with caution. No harm. No sense of attack. Henrich understood and kept still. Naillain approached the closet and opened its doors. Upon the opening, Naillain pulled something from the shelves, something large. He turned toward the Warslinger to reveal a weapon. Henrich recognized it well. By its design most importantly.

"Do you know what this is?"

"I do." Henrich replied. "Where did you get it?"

Naillain placed the weapon on the desk, wiping the sheath clean. He removed it, unveiling a sword. The blade was forged in pure gold, the hilt made of carbuncle with a small emerald set in the middle of the hilt and a sapphire placed at the bottom of the handle. The blade itself was thin, with a small thickness in its core. The tip pointed and the sides sharpened. Henrich knew what kind of sword he was looking at and was astonished in his spirit.

"I retrieved this during some excavations over in Old Egypt. I figured someone of your stature would recognize such a weapon."

"It's a *purgesword.*"

"Ah." Naillain uttered with a smile. "And what is a purgesword?"

"A blade not from the Worlds. Made for the Seraph."

"This blade belongs to them who are not like us. This explains a lot. The detail. The forging. The stones within. Tell me, how much power do you believe rests inside this sword?"

"Too much for one of our own."

"I don't believe that."

"Doesn't matter what you believe."

"I think it does. I now have the sword. Therefore, I should be able to use it when necessary. For example, I could use it now and kill you. Then kill your two other friends."

"You wouldn't get the opportunity."

"You're willing to test that boast?"

"The test was proven when we first met. I've seen your kind before. Come off benevolent. Seeking friendship, trust, and love. But in reality, you desire control, dominance, and severity."

"I'm not like those you've met before."

"You're all the same." Henrich confirmed. "It's in your nature to repeat the actions of your ancestors."

Naillain slammed the sword onto the desk. His temper grew, yet, he stood back and took in a breath. Relaxing. Henrich kept his eyes focused.

"My congregation cannot see me like this."

"Then, tell them the truth. Tell them what they need to know about you. About this place."

"I will tell them what I choose to." Naillain rebuffed. "They're under my guidance. Not yours. They will do as I say. As I command. In a sense, I am God here."

Henrich cocked his head. Staring at Naillain, while glancing at the purgesword.

"You know something, 'Father' Naillain? You talk of those in the past. Same demeanor and stature. Such like yourself tried to end the Warslingers, to erase them from the Worlds. Yet, I can speak on the opposite. For the Warslingers have always triumphed over their adversaries. For that reason, I can say, the Warslingers will be gathered again. The Heptad will be restored. All will be done at the sound of the last trump."

"And where did you here this fable?" Naillain questioned. "From one of the books in Old Jerusalem?"

"Moses, my Leader told me." The Warslinger replied. "Proclaimed it from the mouth of El."

Naillain took in the words of the Warslinger, he approached the door, opening it. Henrich stood up.

"Best you leave while I get my thoughts together."

Henrich walked toward the door to exit. After taking one foot forward, Naillain placed his hand on the Warslinger's shoulder. Holding him steady. The Warslinger was prepared to retaliate, for his left hand was already set upon his shooter.

"Best to tell your friends of our discussion, for I fear neither of you will remain here for long."

"Is that a threat?" Henrich said.

"Take it however you please."

Henrich stepped away as Naillain slammed the office door.

III

Henrich walked down the hallway, seeing Abraham, Cody, and Beth waiting for him. From their expression, they knew something was off. By the way Henrich walked toward them, they knew something had happened. Something dark.

"Take it didn't go well." Abraham said.

"It went as we expected." Henrich replied. "We have to warn these people."

"You saw it didn't you?"

"How did he retrieve the sword?"

"He did tell you of his excavation days, did he not?"

"He mentioned it."

Abraham nodded. "We both know the sword doesn't belong to him. Nor to this place."

"It belongs to the Seraph who wielded it."

"What happened?" Beth asked.

"Naillain isn't the man his people believe him to be. He's using them to gain his own purpose."

"That's not good." Cody said.

"He turned the truth into a lie." Henrich said. "That is all I needed to know from him."

"How are we going to warn them?" Beth wondered. "We can't just bombard them with words about their leader going mad."

"There's a way it can be done." Henrich said. "Just give me a little bit of time."

"And what should we do until then?" Cody asked.

"Prepare." Abraham said, nodding to Henrich. "Prepare for what is to come."

Henrich nodded back, walking away from the three and to the outside.

IV

Stepping foot on the outside, Henrich saw the congregation. How the people seemed happy and content in their current state. Yet, the Warslinger gazed up toward the sky and above him, he saw what had brought him to this place. The aura had returned and was set over the entire congregation. Over the community landscape. Its energy was dark. It was and is malevolent. As the aura slowly descended onto the people, their faces were shaped and formed differently. The life which was present in their eyes had faded away. The peace from within had vanished.

"Their will is lost." Henrich said to himself. "Their minds erased. Gone."

The people turned their focus toward the Warslinger, who was standing amid them. The congregation began to form a circle around Henrich. He was aware of their motives and their potential goal. He knew Naillain had done this. More than likely praying to the God of the Worlds to send destruction upon Henrich, Cody, and Beth. Slowly, reaching to his shooters, Henrich was prepared to protect himself at all cost. As his hand gripped the handle on the shooter, his head was jolted up toward the heavens. His eyes became clear white. The people stopped in their movement. The Warslinger was frozen still. After several seconds, Henrich regained control of himself. Shaking himself back to steadiness.

"It is time." He uttered, moving with quick pace to find Cody, Beth, and Abraham.

SALVATION OR DAMNATION

I

The Warslinger bolted through the door, startling Cody and Beth. Henrich looked around for Abraham and he wasn't there.

"He went off to find someone." Beth said. "What is going on?"

"We have to leave this place."

"Why?" Cody asked.

"It is not what it seems."

Henrich grabbed the rest of his gear. He commanded Beth and Cody to get their stuff immediately. As they made the moves, the doors shattered. They looked back, seeing the congregation. No longer their peaceful selves. Just energized bodies. No life was set in their eyes.

"What's happened to them?" Beth wondered.

"The aura we followed here returned and fell upon them. Taking away all we once saw."

"Then, where's Father Naillain?" Cody asked.

"He's responsible for this. He's not the man he claimed himself to be."

"Then, let's stop him and save these people."

Henrich shrugged. He knew he wanted to, yet, knew it wasn't the determined call.

"Can't. we have to leave now."

"Why in a hurry?"

"Death is coming to this place. From the sky, death will rain over this community. All that will be left is the remains of the dead and the rubble of a fevered dream."

Cody looked over to Beth. She turned to him in response.

"He's right." Cody said. "We need to leave."

Beth sighed.

"Look, I know I'm not from around here. But, I need to understand what you mean by death coming from the sky."

"Fire." Henrich proclaimed. "Fire will rain upon this place. Scorching everything and everyone."

"Then, how will we know it's close?"

"Start by watching the animals. Then, watch your steps as you exit this place."

Beth nodded. Henrich nodded back.

"Good. Let's get going."

Meanwhile, Naillain hears the rumblings of thunder in the distance. He rushed over to the window in his office, gazing outside to see dark clouds making their way toward the area. Red lightning flashing within them.

"This cannot be!"

Naillain ran out of his office and toward the cellar. Opening the hatch, he dove in and rushed toward what sat beneath the congregation grounds. A large statue. An idol of the God of the Worlds. A large figure made in gold, standing at near thirteen feet in height with the physique and facial appearance of a man, yet with the wings of an eagle and the eyes of a lion. Naillain bowed before the statue. Paying obeisance.

"I've done all you asked of me. Why is that storm headed here? What is the cause of all this?"

The statue gave off the sudden appearance of smoke. Naillain keened his eyes to get a better look and what was standing in the smoke was a shrouded figure. Cloaked in a black hood and robe.

"It is you." Naillain said with joy. "Please, help me."

"I cannot interfere with such events." The shrouded one spoke. "However, I can give you the source of this circumstance."

"Tell me."

"The visitors. They are the cause."

"The Warslinger and his fellow travelers?"

"They are not the visitors you seek. They desire to destroy all you have built here. Everything. From the buildings, the homes, the livestock, the plants, and even your precious and faithful congregation."

"I cannot let that happen. Tell me what I must do to spare all that I have built under your name?"

"Rid your land of them by any means and the storm will clear."

"And that is all I must do to keep this place protected by your great power and mercy?"

"That shall be all. You have my word."

The shrouded one evaporated with the smoke. Naillain nodded continually, sweating profusely. He wiped the sweat from his forehead and contained himself.

"Rid of them. Yes. I can do that. Yes. I know a way."

Henrich, Cody, and Beth were nearly out of the main building. On a quick turn down a hall, they ran into Abraham and Brandi, who were in a way waiting on them to arrive.

"I was hoping to see you." Henrich said. "We have to go."

"I know."

"You know?"

"I had the vision as well. Same as yours."

"Then you know what's about to happen to this place."

"Indeed. Which is why I must come with you. Brandi and I."

"Why?"

"This path you walk on, it includes the both of us. Trust me, Warslinger."

The Warslinger gave a nod to Brandi. She nodded back. Henrich shook his head, putting on his hat, reaching for his shooters.

"Then we need to get going."

"Yet, you're forgetting something." Abraham gestured.

The Warslinger thought and remembered. He turned toward Cody and Beth, telling them he will return. Abraham kept watch over the group as Henrich returned to Naillain's office. Kicking in the door like it was nothing, he was surprised to find Naillain not inside. Henrich looked around on the desk, it wasn't there. He knew, approaching the closet. He opened the doors and grabbed what he came for.

"You do not belong here." Henrich uttered, putting on the sheath of the purgesword. He walked out of the office, returning to the group with the sword's handle seen over his right shoulder. Abraham nodded with a smile.

"It is coming to pass."

"Let's go." Henrich said.

Reaching the outside of the community, the congregation bolted from all corners. Henrich fired off some shots. He continued firing rounds, until from the ground, black hands and claws came up from the ground. The stench of sulfur engulfed the community. Demons arose.

"Demons!" Brandi yelled.

He paused and reached for the sword. Pulling it from its sheath. The sunlight sparked the golden blade. The congregation and the demons came rushing at him and the Warslinger did what he had to do. Swiping and slashing his way out of the Secret World. Demons clawed against the blade, cutting themselves in the process. Henrich was amazed and continued killing the demons which came toward him in rage. Cody and Beth fired off some shots as well with Abraham and Brandi reaching the community gates.

11

The five make it to the main gate. Yet, the gate is locked and stood strong.

"What are we going to do?" Cody asked.

The Warslinger looked around and from the sky, the thunder roared, and the dark clouds had arrived over the Secret World. Immediately after the thunder, a red lightning bolt came down, striking the church of the community. Setting it ablaze.

"It is happening." Henrich said.

Naillain appeared from the main building, witnessing the church building on fire. Burning down faster at a rate unnatural. The flames had a strange roar to them. As if they themselves were alive and eating the church. Naillain ran toward the front entrance to the church, the doors blew opened by the strong flames, letting out a hollowed screech. Sounds very familiar to a woman's scream in fear.

"No. No. No!" Naillain screamed in anger. "You said you would preserve this place! You gave your word!"

The five watched on, seeing Naillain in a venting rage. Slamming his fists into the dirt.

"What's he going to do?" Beth asked.

"Watch." Abraham said.

Naillain fell to his knees. Nothing left. Nothing to live for. This is what he thought of himself. What had become of his community, he became himself. For if the church was burning, he had to burn with it. In doing so, Naillain arose on his feet and walked into the burning church. Not a thought nor a motion of retreat. Naillain was hopeless. He had nothing else to live for in the Four Worlds. He stepped into the fire. Disappearing into the flames, some of his congregation had caught sight of him and followed along.

"They're killing themselves." Brandi said.

"They chose to die with their leader." Henrich added. "Nothing more."

The rest of the congregation ran amok throughout the community grounds. The sounds of scorching screams echoed from the burning church. Mixed in with the crying howls of the those who remained. Beth looked around and noticed all the animals were gone. Every last one of them.

"They're gone." Beth said. "Just like that."

Henrich felt a peculiar presence of calming in the air. He looked up and made a move on. Abraham also felt it and looked over to the Warslinger. He knew what was to come and turned back to the gate, seeking a way out.

"Then, you know what's about to happen." Henrich said.

A heavy gust of wind came from the east, knocking over the gate, pushing it into the ground, the five ran over the gate remains and stood outside of the grounds. They continued moving further away from the area While doing so, a large whirlwind appeared from the sky and slammed into the grounds directly. Destroying everything and everyone. Due to this, the fire and the whirlwind mixed as one and once the five made it to a stopping point, they saw a flaming whirlwind and people flying into the air, some burning in flames, other not. Cody was astonished, Brandi was in terror, Beth was amazed. Henrich and Abraham paid respect.

"So, everything that was there… the people, the homes… they're all gone?" Beth asked.

"Yes." Abraham said. "Everything. There's nothing left."

"That's a lot of things gone." Cody added. "Just in mere seconds."

Brandi sighed. She approached Abraham and hugged him.

"Thank you for telling me the truth."

"It was only my duty."

Brandi walked toward Henrich and hugged him as well. He hugged back.

"I'll be willing to tag along. If you'll allow."

"You're on the other end of the grounds." Henrich replied. "You're already with us."

"The whirlwinds are the favorite tools of El." The Warslinger proclaimed. "When the darkness comes and calmness covers the air, it is time."

III

After moving miles away from the ruins of the Secret World, the five continued on their journey. The Warslinger was back to focus on his mission, to reach The Haunted City. During their short travel, they encountered some minor remains from the community grounds. Two brown horses and one dirt-speeder. Cody took the speeder. Abraham and Brandi took one of the horses while Beth took the other. From the wilderness appeared Henrich's horse. The same one from time past.

"Where has that horse been?" Beth questioned.

"He comes when needed." Henrich replied with a smile.

Cody approached Henrich, starring hard at the purgesword.

"I have to ask. What kind of sword is that?"

"It belonged to the Seraph. I guess now, this one belongs to me. Which reminds me."

Henrich pulled the machete from within his duster and handed to Cody. Cody grabbed the machete.

"You're giving it to me?"

"I no longer need it." Henrich said. "Besides, you need something else to wield when in a fight. Something extra."

Cody nodded, looking at the machete.

"I appreciate this."

"Where are we off to, Warslinger?" Abraham asked.

"Back on course. I need to reach the City. I need my questions answered and my fate determined.

They all rode off from the Silicon Valley that once was. Yet, in the trees, watch on the Kroger Kid. Rubbing his hands together with a grin covering his face.

Later during the day and the travels, Henrich remembered all the mirror had spoken to him. He was sure to believe what it told him, and he would encounter all it said. While traveling, a rushing sound came from above, they stopped and looked to the sky, seeing a large craft flying overhead. With two large wings spanning feet apart. Its body oval-shaped with a circle in the front and back. No windows on either side, only in the front. Glowing neon lights on both its sides and on the wings. The sound it gave off was close to the beat of a humming drum mixed with a horn. With speed that surpasses anything they've met. Cody stood off the bike.

"The hell was that?!"

"A techno-craft." Henrich said. "This far out? Strange."

"You've seen one of those before?" Beth said.

"I have in my travels."

"Then, you know where they're from." Cody said. "We need one, man."

"That's a difficult task." Abraham said.

"How come?"

"Because the location isn't a friendly one." Henrich said. "Yet, it would make our travels from the valleys, ruined cities, and religious communities look like a child's tale. A shepherd's walk across strait pastures in narrow corners."

"What is this place?" Beth asked.

"They call it Mega City. A metropolis built and filled with cybernetic and technological marvels, and, it's where we're headed."

GLOSSARY

This is a short glossary of words, meanings, beasts, weapons, vehicles, and locations revealed so far across The Haunted City Saga through The Legendary Warslinger and Redemption of the Lost

Adamah: The name of the World as a whole. Combining all four worlds. Named after the first human to walk upon the world.

Arkshooter: The revolver pistol shooter wielded by the Warslingers of the Heptad. Made from the gold and wood as the Ark of the Covenant.

Arzareth: The Western World. Also known as the Western sector of Adamah.

Benevolency: The true good of the Worlds. A bringing force of peace, love, and hope.

Blastshooter: A shotgun hybrid of the shooter.

Bull-Lion: The mutated beast with the body of a bull and the legs and tail of a lion.

Choiros: The mutated furry hog with large tusks from its mouth. Its size is of a small beetle vehicle.

Demons: The spiritual creatures who roam the Four Worlds due to the Malevolency.

Dire Scorpions: Large sharpened insectoids. Significantly larger than the traditional scorpions from Shemia and Khamain.

Dirt-Speeder: The primary source for fast travel across the landscapes of the Western and Southern Worlds.

Ghouls: Spiritual entities which roamed throughout the Valley of Death.

Ghosts: Spiritual entities of the previous life. Capable of traveling across worlds and dimensions.

Green Man: A plant/human hybrid. Its body covered in foliage, oak leaves, and small branches. Its face is covered with a beard made of grass.

Heptad: The significant title of the primary Warslingers. Meaning "seven".

Hevoc: A small semi-deserted town. Known for its encounter with Randolph Henrich.

Horse-Spider: The mutated beast with the body of a horse and the legs of a spider.

Khamain: The Southern World. Also known as the Southern sector of Adamah.

Lamia: The demonic creature which takes the appearance of a young girl. When in true form, it appears reptilian in nature.

Land of the Survivors: The land occupied by Wade and the Scavengers.

Leprechaun: The dwarfed species which lives across the Western and Northern Worlds. Usually sighted by the presence and scent of gold.

Maarab: The West Sea.

Malevolency: The true evil of the Worlds. Capable of corrupting all life. Whether material or spiritual.

Minotaur: The hybrid man/bull beast whom resides in the labyrinth of the Dark Forest.

Mount of Divination: The mountain of which Randolph Henrich defeated the Mercenary Man and received a glimpse into the future from the Mirror of Fate.

Old Camelot: The ancient city of Camelot. Led by Knight Arthur Pendragon, a Warslinger and King of Camelot. It was taken siege by Morgana Pendragon during the Fall of Old Jerusalem.

Old Egypt: The remains of Ancient Egypt. The land hasn't changed since the ancient periods.

Old Jerusalem: The ancient city of Jerusalem. Still intact from its ancient days. The dwelling place of the Warslingers of the Heptad.

Old Los Angeles: The remains of what was Los Angeles, California. Only several buildings remain standing after the events of the War of the West.

Phantom Dog: The supernatural beasts that surrounds death. It's red eyes are always remembered. Seen by Randolph Henrich in *The Legendary Warslinger*.

Purgesword: An ancient sword made from the fires of the Seraph. Lost during the Fall of Old Jerusalem, later taken by the Secret World, later retrieved and carried by Randolph Henrich.

Qedem: The East Sea.

Qeramah: The ice wall surrounding Tehomayim and the Four Worlds.

Red Demons: Stronger Demons. Malevolent entities with the scent of sulfur. They primarily roam in packs. Smaller in nature and much faster in speed.

Revolver Shooter: The standard shooter in the Worlds.

Ruachayim: The Outer-World. Also regarded as the spiritual realm outside of Adamah.

Salamanders: Elemental creatures of fire known as the "*Nature Spirits*".

Sapphire Staff: The legendary staff carried by Moses The Leader.

Savel: A town reminiscent of pilgrimage and full of secret sodomy.

Sea of Tabbur: The center-ocean between the Four Worlds.

Shadowic Creatures: Supernatural creatures whom dwell in the shadows and have enhanced abilities connected to the darkness.

Shemia: The Eastern World. Also known as the Eastern sector of Adamah.

Shroudoks: Shadow insects that reside wherever there's little light present.

Sphinx: The estranged creature mentioned by Noah in Damascus. Its appearance is half-man (head), half-lion(body), and half-eagle(wings).

Strander: A fellow traveler. Usually from a foreign location.

Succubus: The feminine sexual creatures that feed on the energy of Man.

Techno-Craft: Large and quick skycrafts made in Mega City.

Tehomayim: The Full Ocean which surrounds the Four Worlds.

Teman: The South Sea.

The Dark Forest: The supernatural wilderness set at the end of the Valley of Death.

The Haunted City: The titular city. The location where Randolph Henrich searches for truth concerning the universe.

Tsaphon: The North Sea.

Valley of Death: The desolate land covered as a desert.

Vrylolakas: Druid-Like Vampires. Some fought against Randolph Henrich in *The Legendary Warslinger*.

Warslinger: A holy knight and warrior. Usually born and trained in Old Jerusalem. Servants of El, enhanced with spiritual abilities given to them for their cause.

Wolf-Hawk: The mutated beast with the body of a wolf with the wings of a hawk and talons of an eagle.

Worldquake: A large, great tremor that can cause massive damage to structures and landmasses.

Yaphean: The Northern World. Also known as the Northern sector of Adamah.

KNIGHTS
TY'RON W. C. ROBINSON II
RESISTANCE PROTOCOL
SHATTERED
OMNOUS
OCTAGON
HEAVEN'S CALLED
DARK TITAN UNIVERSE SAGA
WELCOME TO A NEW UNIVERSE

THE HAUNTED CITY SAGA
ENTER A SAGA OF WORLDS WITHIN WORLDS
TY'RON W. C. ROBINSON II
REDEMPTION OF THE LOST
THE HAUNTED CITY
TY'RON W. C. ROBINSON II
THE LEGENDARY WARSLINGER
THE HAUNTED CITY
BATTLE FOR ASTHLAT
A CONFLICT OF THE HAUNTED CITY
TY'RON W. C. ROBINSON II

SYMBOLUM VENATORES
THE GABRIEL KANE COLLECTION
TY'RON W. C. ROBINSON II
A SYMBOLUM VENATORES BOOK
HOD
TYRON W. C. ROBINSON II
SYMBOLUM VENATORES
WAR OF THE TWO KINGDOMS
TY'RON W. C. ROBINSON II
SYMBOLUM VENATORES
"HISTORY IS THEIR PLAYBOOK."

ABOUT THE AUTHOR

Ty'Ron W. C. Robinson II is the author of several works of fiction. Including the *Dark Titan Universe Saga* series (*Dark Titan Knights, The Resistance Protocol, Tales of the Scattered, Tales of the Numinous, Day of Octagon*), *The Haunted City Saga* series, and the *Symbolum Venatores* series.

Also of other books (*Lost in Shadows, The Book of The Elect, etc.*) and One-Shot short stories.

More information pertaining to the author and stories can be found at darktitanentertainment.com.

Twitter: @TyRonRobinsonII

Twitter: @DarkTitan_
Instagram: @darktitanentertainment
Facebook: @DarkTitanEnt
Pinterest: @darktitanentertainment
YouTube: Dark Titan Entertainment